STAR WARS™
PADAWAN

WRITTEN BY

KIERSTEN WHITE

DISNEP • LUCASFILM
PRESS

LOS ANGELES • NEW YORK

Printed in the United States of America

First Edition, July 2022

1 3 5 7 9 10 8 6 4 2

Library of Congress Control Number on file

FAC-004510-22161

ISBN 978-1-368-02349-8

Visit the official *Star Wars* website at: www.starwars.com.

For Kris, who is missed

And for Jen, for making my dreams
come true by inviting me to be a Jedi

CHAPTER

1

The tentacles appeared with no warning, wrapping around Obi-Wan Kenobi's wrist in a deadly barbed grip.

He yanked his hand toward his body. Scalding liquid added to his confusion and pain as he slipped and fell backward onto the hard ground. A bulbously inflating, acid-green-spiked central body writhed, making the tentacles twist tighter. Obi-Wan scrambled for the lightsaber at his waist. He felt the barbs sinking deeper, sensed the poison about to enter his bloodstream.

It couldn't end here. Not like this.

"Help me!" He didn't take his eyes off the creature, trusting that his fellow Padawans would leap to his defense.

"Is that a demon squid?" Prie squealed in her seat across from him, clapping her hands in delight. "Wait, wait, don't hurt it!" She rushed around the dining table and knelt beside Obi-Wan, unconcerned about the hot soup spilled across the floor that was now soaking into her trousers and Obi-Wan's robes.

"Get it off!" Obi-Wan shouted. "Cut it off me!"

Prie scowled at him in disapproval, dark eyebrows drawing low over brown eyes. Her hair was braided away from her face, only her smaller Padawan braid trailing downward. She tucked it behind her ear as she leaned forward.

"It's only a baby. See?" She stroked one hand down the spikes that lined the pulsing main sac of the demon squid's body. It shivered and then, to Obi-Wan's shock and relief, slowly deflated, retracted its barbs, and uncurled from his wrist. Prie lifted it off Obi-Wan's now bright-red and welt-covered skin, cooing at it. This time the tentacle wrapping a wrist did so lovingly.

Obi-Wan stood, covered in the soup that definitely should not have contained a living predator. There was no sign of further threat in the Padawan dining hall, but that didn't mean they were safe. "We should check the kitchens. Someone must have planted this. Maybe an assassin, or—"

The same liquid Obi-Wan was soaked in flew out of Bolla's mouth, streaming down his scaled green chin as he laughed so hard he couldn't contain it. His fingertips were still suctioned to his own bowl of steaming—and decidedly demon-squid-free—supper.

"Ow," Bolla said, trying not to spill his bowl as he wiped under his mouth. "The spices in this soup hurt my skin!"

Obi-Wan's hands clenched into fists. Pain spiked through his raw and throbbing wrist. "Hot soup also hurts when it splashes all over you while a demon squid tries to inject you with poison!"

"But you should have seen your face! When that first tentacle came waving up, and you looked at it like maybe it was part of the meal, debating whether or not to try eating it! Oh, I hadn't even considered you might try to eat it. That went so much better than I had planned."

"*Poison*," Obi-Wan repeated, trying desperately to keep his anger in check.

Bolla had finally managed to set down his bowl, and he waved one long-fingered hand dismissively, his ears still twitching with mirth. "You would have been fine. I have the antidote in my—" he patted his belt where a pouch would normally be, and the white film over his shiny blue eyes blinked once. "Well, I have the antidote somewhere. You really would have been fine."

"I don't feel fine!" Obi-Wan grabbed a cloth napkin from the table. At least they were only in the Padawan dining hall and he hadn't just embarrassed himself in front of—

"There you are," said Qui-Gon Jinn, Jedi Knight and Obi-Wan's master. Obi-Wan couldn't tell whether Qui-Gon sounded amused or irritated to find his apprentice in this state.

Obi-Wan felt his face turning as red as his injured hand.

"You should really be more careful," Prie chided, scowling at Obi-Wan as though any of this had been his fault. "It's only a baby. You could have hurt it."

"But he—What about—" Obi-Wan pointed at Bolla. Now that there was a Jedi Master in the room, Bolla was casually slurping his own soup as though nothing had happened.

Obi-Wan was sixteen years old. A Padawan learner, not a youngling initiate anymore. Still, the urge to tattle on Bolla was nearly overwhelming. If not tattle, at least get a chance to explain why he was covered in soup, holding an injured wrist. To recover some semblance of decorum in front of his master.

"It looks as though you're finished with your meal," Qui-Gon said, lifting an eyebrow. "Or perhaps it's your meal that is finished with you?"

Qui-Gon was definitely laughing on the inside, whether he showed it or not. Obi-Wan wanted to be able to laugh, too, but his heart was still racing, not yet calmed down from the fight. If it could even be called that, since the demon squid in question was apparently so docile when handled correctly that it was now nestled into the space between Prie's shoulder and neck.

She continued to whisper gentle nonsense at it. "Who spawned just right? You did! Who's a good demon squid?"

Obi-Wan didn't know who was a good demon squid, but certainly it wasn't *that* one. Bolla had his bowl tipped up to hide his expression, but Obi-Wan could see his shoulders shaking with barely suppressed laughter.

Anger was a path to the dark side, and Obi-Wan wouldn't take any steps down that path. Much as he wanted to fling Bolla's soup in his face.

Qui-Gon clasped his hands beneath his sleeves. Whether he felt Obi-Wan's turmoil or was simply embarrassed for him, he said nothing about it. "I'm on my way to meditate and thought you might want to join me."

Meditation was the last thing Obi-Wan wanted to do, soaked and still caught somewhere between panic and fury. But given that it was the last thing he wanted to do, it was probably the best thing for him. Many things in the Jedi Order were like that: the less he wanted to do them, the better they were for him.

And he wanted to be better. He wanted to be the best. The best Padawan, the best learner, the best Jedi. He owed it to the Order.

"Could we do saber practice instead?" Obi-Wan asked, hopeful. He hadn't been apprenticed to Qui-Gon for long, but so far his master hadn't moved him beyond the most basic forms. Obi-Wan was good at them. Genuinely good. He was ready to move on, and working out some of this anger and frustration through saber forms would be much easier than trying to meditate. Meditation was always harder than movement, much as that felt like a paradox.

"I'm troubled," Qui-Gon said, not elaborating on what was troubling him. "We'll meditate."

Obi-Wan's stomach, sadly dinner-free thanks to Bolla, sank. Was *he* the source of Qui-Gon's troubles? It seemed like the majority of their training was spent in meditation. The other Padawans were frequently out on missions, serving the Republic, helping the galaxy. Or in Bolla's case, finding creatures to torment Obi-Wan with.

Was it Obi-Wan's fault that he wasn't ready? That Qui-Gon seemed content to remain on Coruscant, meditating? But maybe it wasn't that Qui-Gon was content. Maybe it was that he was troubled by Obi-Wan, worried that his Padawan wasn't actually ready for anything outside the protection of the Temple.

Obi-Wan was trying to be the best Padawan. He was trying so hard. But guessing what would impress and please the gentle, unflappable Master Qui-Gon Jinn was almost impossible. Obi-Wan couldn't pass a test if he didn't even know what he was being tested on.

Not bidding farewell to the others—Prie was absorbed with her new pet, and Bolla was still pretending not to laugh—Obi-Wan followed Qui-Gon out of the Padawan dining hall. They left the lower sections with their vast training rooms and various living areas, then wound their way up toward the gardens Qui-Gon favored. Obi-Wan liked them, as well. Or at least he used to, before they became the location of his most consistent training failures. Now even the fresh scent of a green space triggered a spike of anxiety.

In a quiet corner of the luscious and sprawling gardens, surrounded by vivid orange blossoms and the sound of unseen water, Qui-Gon sat on the floor. His legs were crossed at the ankles, his hands on his knees, his eyes closed, and his breathing instantly even. Measured. Purposeful.

Obi-Wan sat across from him. The rock courtyard of the garden was hard and uncomfortable beneath him. He couldn't decide which ankle should go over the other. Left over right seemed best, but once he started thinking about it, was it really? He switched them. Then switched them back. Three more times. He tried palms down on his knees, and then palms up. Spine straight. Eyes closed. But he was *squeezing* them shut again, not letting them fall gently closed like a "leaf drifting to the ground." Qui-Gon had advised that imagery once. Obi-Wan's leaves were agitated and jittery things, apparently.

Once he had finally gotten as close to comfortable as he could, though, he became even more aware of his own body. His robes, wet in several spots with now cold soup. His wrist had ceased throbbing in time with his heartbeat and burned with a sullen, insistent pain.

That was good, though! He wasn't really meditating if he wasn't working at it. It shouldn't be easy. Should it? It had been easy when he was a tiny initiate. But he hadn't understood it. Not like he did now.

He wanted to ask Master Qui-Gon whether or not

meditation should be challenging, but one crack of an eye revealed Qui-Gon was far, far away. Obi-Wan could even swear there was the slightest hint of air between Qui-Gon and the terrace. He squeezed his eye shut again, lest he be caught cheating.

Meditation. Obi-Wan had to figure it out. He had never been bad at it before his trials, but then again, it had been only one small part of his training. Now, with Qui-Gon, it seemed to be the bulk of it. Obi-Wan couldn't rely on his other skills to compensate. Maybe that was what he hated: meditation laid his weaknesses bare in front of him. There was nothing else to think about, nothing to do but face them. And Obi-Wan was terrified of them.

And then he was terrified of being terrified, because fear was a path to the dark side. Which made his need to figure out meditation even more desperate, which made his heart race, which made his wrist burn even more, which made it impossible to settle into any sort of peace. Any state where he could reach out and connect to the Force was blocked.

He could do this. He had to be able to do this. He reached for the Force, tried to grasp it, and ended up empty-handed time and again. So while his master sat in perfect harmony, Obi-Wan squirmed—miserable, soup-soaked, and utterly devoid of any sort of tranquility. His stomach twisted with the increasing certainty that the source of Qui-Gon's troubles was, in fact, Obi-Wan himself.

He was failing as a Padawan.

CHAPTER

2

Obi-Wan's eyes startled open as Qui-Gon's voice broke the silence.

"Would you like to talk about it?" Qui-Gon asked. His tone was gentle and without judgment, which made Obi-Wan feel even worse. He should be judged! Qui-Gon should be berating him, chiding him, lecturing him.

Obi-Wan's whole body was tense, seized up from trying so hard to be still and avoid attracting Qui-Gon's notice, which apparently hadn't worked. "No! What?" His voice came out an embarrassed squeak. It made him sound younger, and he hated it. He cleared his throat and tried again, trying to sound calm. Trying to sound settled. Trying to sound like he hadn't spent this entire meditation period chasing his own fears around in a circle until he felt completely tied up by them. "Talk about what?"

"I know I'm not what you hoped," Qui-Gon said.

Obi-Wan was fairly certain *he* wasn't what *Qui-Gon* had

hoped for in a Padawan. Was Qui-Gon actually blaming himself for what a terrible student Obi-Wan was turning out to be? Now Obi-Wan felt both scared and guilty. And his wrist still hurt, and his robes felt grimy and stiff, and one of his legs had gone numb from sitting on the stones. If he stood right now, he was fairly certain he would fall over.

He knew he was supposed to try to exist in the present, but he very much wanted to excuse himself from this moment. This whole day, in fact.

"No, Master, I—"

Qui-Gon's comlink beeped. He pulled it free from his belt and answered. "Yes?"

A high, pleasant voice responded. "You wanted me to notify you when he arrived."

"I did. Thank you." Qui-Gon stood, gathering his robes. Obi-Wan stood, too, stumbling and nearly falling thanks to his leg, which still didn't have blood flow restored.

"Where are we going?"

"No," Qui-Gon said, putting a hand on Obi-Wan's shoulder. "Just me. Why don't you get that wrist seen to, and you can change your robes, too."

Obi-Wan's pride stung even more than his wrist. He was half-tempted to follow Qui-Gon and see what was pulling him away, but that would be a betrayal of trust. So instead Obi-Wan trudged to his room. It was small and austere, but a shelf above his bed held a few treasures he had gathered.

A rock from Ilum. A flower Siri had once tucked behind his ear as a joke. A shell Prie had given him that was probably from an unspeakably terrifying creature she adored. The spoon from their initiate days that Bolla had for some reason decided was his favorite, so they all made a game of stealing it. Obi-Wan had won, he supposed, since they were no longer younglings.

He changed out of his dirty clothes, trying and failing not to mentally curse Bolla. Then he washed and wrapped his wrist. All the initiates and Padawan learners had tidy little burn kits, designed to soothe minor burns from lightsaber learning errors. He hadn't used his in so long, but he was glad to have it now. The gel instantly soothed his inflamed skin.

His wrist wasn't so bad, really, but there were marks from the barbs. He was fortunate Prie had been there. Prie's master worked extensively with animals, was known for it across the galaxy. If a planet was having issues with fauna, they requested him. Prie was a great fit as his Padawan. She had an intuitive way with creatures and an endless thirst for knowledge.

All his friends were good fits with their Jedi Masters. Siri's was always taking her out on important, exciting missions. Their friend Jape had a brilliant grasp of astrophysics, which paired him perfectly with his more scholarly Jedi Master. Even Bolla, who had often struggled as an initiate, seemed thrilled with his new duties as a Padawan. He and his master spent much of their time in the Archives, researching. Bolla was never happier than when he had a holocron in his hands.

Everyone else was where they should be. So why had Qui-Gon picked Obi-Wan, when it felt like they couldn't connect on anything?

Obi-Wan was still hungry, but he couldn't bear to go back to the Padawan dining hall and risk seeing Bolla again. Or worse, Siri, who was due back from her latest daring mission at any moment. But if he stayed in his room, odds were someone would come looking for him.

He headed where he always went when he needed to escape. The rarely used formal banquet hall wasn't technically off limits, and he leaned into that technicality. It was one of the few spaces in the Temple where Obi-Wan could go to be truly alone. He had spent so many hours in there, practicing his lightsaber forms when he didn't want to see the other Padawans. He even tried to meditate in there, hoping that if he could get the hang of it alone, he could then impress Qui-Gon with his remarkable progress.

It hadn't happened yet, but that didn't mean Obi-Wan couldn't *make* it happen. If he just worked harder, tried harder, put more effort in, surely he could get it.

He took several sets of stairs upward and then walked down a narrow service hallway that ran perpendicular to the main, soaring hallway. Conversation from that other hall-way startled him, stopping him in his tracks.

"Did you know," someone with a deep, commanding voice said, "that the banquet hall used to be the library? In ancient times, back when the Jedi cared about *true* knowledge."

Obi-Wan frowned. He couldn't place the voice, but someone openly criticizing the Jedi in the halls of their own temple? Who would do that? He wanted to hurry to an opening and see who had spoken, but he also wanted to be able to slip into the banquet hall without being caught. That desire won out. He waited until the sound of steps had passed, and then entered through a side door.

The banquet hall was cavernous, with a brilliantly white arched ceiling. It had all been lovingly carved centuries before. Back when, according to that mystery voice, it had been the Temple library. Obi-Wan could imagine it as a library. Maybe that was why he liked it so much. There was still that hushed sense of promise, that hum of knowledge.

He crossed the empty tiled floor, carefully laid out in mosaics telling the stories of great Jedi long since returned to the Force. Near the far wall, where pillars grew from the tiles to spread like branches and hold the ceiling—and where Obi-Wan could tuck himself to be hidden should someone come in—he lay flat on the floor.

The stars loomed overhead, staring down at the stray

Padawan in silent, stony judgment. Though Obi-Wan Kenobi supposed they weren't capable of any other type of judgment, since the stars in question were carved into the stone. He sighed with longing. What he wouldn't give to be up in those stars! The real ones. Not the ones carved in stone.

But . . . what he wouldn't give to be carved in stone, too. To have his destiny, his path through the Force, already written. Something he could study, reference, cross-check, and follow like his own personal course charted through his own personal stars. Because then he'd know what he was supposed to do and, more important, that he *could* do it. That he wasn't disappointing anyone.

Master Qui-Gon's troubled look flashed in his memory, and he was no longer capable of staying still. His plans to practice meditating deflated, like a calmed demon squid. He stood and paced instead, tracing the pattern of stars with his eyes.

Someone, countless ages before, had taken the time to carve these exact stars onto the wall. Nothing the Jedi did was meaningless. Which made Obi-Wan curious. And not because he was avoiding meditation. Or at least, not *only* because of that.

Why *these* stars? Why here? They couldn't be random. Obi-Wan followed the stars along the wall, looking for something familiar. But before long, his path was blocked by a smaller pillar. It, like several others, had been added during reconstruction to hold up the raised dais where the Council sat during formal events.

It wasn't part of the original room design. There was a narrow gap between the new pillar and the wall, though. And Obi-Wan was quite lithe. (*Lithe* was the word he preferred over the others he was given—skinny, lanky, as stringy as a Wookiee's hair sheddings.)

Letting out all the breath in his lungs, he managed to scrape through. On the other side of the pillar, it was dim. Obi-Wan sneezed. Dim *and* dusty, which was surprising. Nothing in the Temple was dusty. How much time had passed since anyone had even remembered there was space back here, hidden by the dais addition?

Obi-Wan traced the stars that had led him here and then paused, his finger on something new. A planet.

Strange, that whoever had carved this series of stars had added one single planet. He was sure it was a planet, too, ringed by a field of tiny dots, the planet itself perfectly circular instead of pointed like the stars. But what planet was it, and why had it earned a spot on the wall? Were there other planets he had missed?

Even stranger, under the planet two names were carved into the stone: Orla Jareni and Cohmac Vitus. He didn't know either name, and he doubted, based on the relative clumsiness of the letters and inelegance of the placement, that the original artist had put them there. Whoever Orla and Cohmac were, they had also climbed back here and carved their names into the wall of the Temple.

Obi-Wan could barely contain both his outrage—making a literal mark on the Temple!—and his envy—making a literal mark on the Temple. Who had they been?

He went backward, squeezing through the gap once more, feeling the wall scrape his hips beneath his simple Padawan garb. He didn't have many spare robes, so with one set dirty, he had to be careful. Orla and Cohmac. He burned with curiosity about who they were, and why they had carved their names there, beneath that planet. He could find the answers, though.

Obi-Wan hurried toward the Archives. This discovery felt like a mystery. Like something new and exciting. Like an excuse to avoid both the other Padawans and his fears of disappointing Qui-Gon Jinn.

When he arrived, he skirted the edges of the extensive rooms. He didn't want to attract the attention of Jocasta Nu or any of the other librarians. They'd all be more than eager and willing to help him, but he wanted to do this on his own. And he definitely didn't want to see Bolla.

Fortunately, there was no sign of the other Padawan, and all the librarians were occupied with a group of younglings. The younglings watched, rapt, as Jocasta Nu taught them how to navigate the labyrinthine shelves. Obi-Wan envied them their simple awe. Things had been easier back then. She pulled up a holocron that detailed the system where Ilum, the ice planet that held the kyber crystal caves, was located.

It was one of the few planets Obi-Wan had actually been to, thanks to the Gathering where he had harvested his kyber crystal.

His hand drifted to the lightsaber at his side. The Gathering had been beyond difficult. Maybe even worse than the Initiate Trials. The things the caves had shown him, the dread they whispered in his ear . . . He shook himself, a physical motion to try to dislodge the residual fear and worry. He didn't have to hold on to it. After all, he had found his crystal and assembled his saber. He'd passed the test. He had been so proud that day, holding his glowing blue weapon, so sure of his place among the Jedi. So certain of his connection to the Force and his bright future in the galaxy.

Where had that connection gone? Where had that confidence evaporated to? Why, now that he was finally a Padawan, did he feel smaller and more lost than he ever had before?

Orla Jareni. Holding his breath that her name would bring something up, he stood at a table and entered it. And there: More than a little something. She had been a Jedi.

He skimmed the information about her various missions

and assignments and her involvement in the Great Hyperspace Disaster, intrigued by her designation as a Wayseeker.

Did the Jedi Order even have Wayseekers anymore? Obi-Wan didn't think it was allowed. It seemed rooted in defiance of the Council, a Jedi pursuing their own course independent of oversight or assignments. Surely if they still had Wayseekers, Qui-Gon Jinn would be one.

There was more information than he could digest in a single sitting. A quick search of Cohmac was also interesting, but he found himself drifting back to Orla. He felt a connection to her, to this Jedi who had come long before him. He suspected she had carved her name there as a youngling or a Padawan, and wondered if she, too, had struggled. If she had wanted her own destiny carved in stone just like he did.

There was a note in her data marked as a priority. Obi-Wan checked the record and confirmed that no one had pulled up her information in ages. It could have been because of the chaos and upheaval surrounding the Great Hyperspace Disaster, but as far as he could tell, no one had looked at this particular record since it had been made.

He opened the note and found a course charted to a planet. Obi-Wan's heart picked up speed. He manipulated the image, zooming out to see that it was on the most distant reaches of the Outer Rim. The mystery planet didn't even have a number. No official designation, which meant no official record in the Archives. Obi-Wan pulled Orla's charting information, noticing the tricky flight path it would take to navigate to that section of space, and then he read the rest of the data.

Orla Jareni had marked this planet of potential importance and interest, and informed the Council she would be looking into it. But there was no further information, no indication as to whether she had ever made it there and, if so, what she had found.

If an ancient Wayseeker had suspected this planet was important and no one had ever followed up, surely that merited attention. And best of all, it was exactly the type of obscure research and activity that just might lure Master Qui-Gon out of the Temple. He was deeply fascinated by the Jedi of the past and the records they left behind. Or in this case, the lack of records, since Orla Jareni had never followed up.

If Obi-Wan approached this carefully, he might have a story to tell the other Padawans soon. One that didn't involve fighting for his life at the dinner table but rather exploring the galaxy and doing some good for once.

A dark current of fear and worry tugged at him, whispering that the truth of why he wanted to go was much bigger than that. Maybe, going out there and doing something, he might at last feel like he was deserving of his place in the

Jedi Order and worthy of his apprenticeship under such an inscrutable Jedi Knight.

Or maybe, like Orla and Cohmac, he wanted something of himself written on the Temple that had written so much of who he was. Either way, he had to make this work.

When was a beacon not a beacon?

When it was actually a probe, left floating in space, tracking any nearby motion. Hiding in plain sight, hoping to hitch a ride.

All the probes sparkled, little lights on a screen, points of terrible hope and desperate waiting, watching, needing. Pinprick representations of the powerless agony he'd been in for years now.

His financier demanded results, threatened to pull funding, but what did that threat matter? He'd already had everything taken before. Everything that mattered far more than credits ever would.

If he lost his financier, he'd find another way. And a way after that. As many ways as he had to, as long as it took.

Nothing else mattered. There was only what had been left behind, and his way back to it.

He sighed, tweaking the settings on his newest probe, sweeping past endless swathes of empty black space, knowing that somewhere out there was a priceless jewel glowing blue. And somewhere out there, someone knew how to get to it. He was confident that no one who knew how to get there could resist for long.

When they went for it, he'd be ready.

"Out in the stars they gathered," he sang to himself, and let the dream of his future carry him through the darkness.

CHAPTER
3

O bi-Wan paced outside Qui-Gon's chambers, practicing his speech. Qui-Gon had a meeting with the Council this evening, which meant he'd be withdrawn and distant afterward. Obi-Wan might not feel like he knew or understood his master yet, but he was good at learning patterns. As evidenced by his skill with lightsaber forms. This was one of Qui-Gon's most predictable patterns.

So Obi-Wan needed to plead his case *before* the meeting. He didn't like his odds of getting Qui-Gon on his side afterward, when it was far more likely he would decide they needed a week in silent meditation. Qui-Gon would commune with the Force, and Obi-Wan would desperately try and miserably fail to do the same.

Sometimes, Qui-Gon got so deep into his meditation, he barely seemed to be breathing. Meanwhile, the last time Obi-Wan had tried to meditate as long as Qui-Gon did, he had fallen asleep and had a vivid nightmare of being pursued, alone, unarmed, and unable to use the Force, through a cave of horrors intent on eating him.

Qui-Gon's door slid open. "Oh, hello," he said, startled to see Obi-Wan mid-pace, frozen like he had been caught doing something against the Code.

"Master! I have—I discovered—Do you know who Orla Jareni was?" Obi-Wan was definitely bungling this. All his practice, wasted.

But to his surprise, Qui-Gon's distant, troubled gaze became focused. "Orla Jareni? Where did you hear that name?"

Obi-Wan tried to channel the same calm focus Qui-Gon always had. To project confidence, but also peace. To be the opposite of how he was actually feeling. "I was guided to her."

Not a lie, exactly. He would never outright lie to his master. But he was being creative with the truth. He knew how much Qui-Gon liked the more ephemeral qualities of the Force, how much he trusted them to guide him. And while Obi-Wan didn't have the same trust—didn't know that the Force itself trusted *him*, either—he wasn't above playing to Qui-Gon's interests.

"I was meditating"—now Obi-Wan was definitely lying, and Qui-Gon raised a single eyebrow, so Obi-Wan rushed ahead—"in the grand banquet hall."

"Why there?"

"It . . . felt like the right place." It felt like a place to be alone. Which made it the right place for Obi-Wan. "My eye was drawn to old stonework on the walls. Did you know it used to be the library?"

Qui-Gon nodded sagely. Of course he knew. Obi-Wan was only mildly disappointed not to have information his master didn't.

"Well, the carvings on the stone looked like a star chart. I felt compelled to follow the stars." Not a lie. "Behind the new construction for the dais, I found the stars led to a planet. And under the planet were two names carved into the wall. One of which was Orla Jareni. So I looked her up. She marked that planet of interest to the Jedi and left behind a complicated path to reach it. But there was never any follow-up. I don't know whether she ever made it there. Orla the Wayseeker's story ended abruptly, and no one knew about her unnamed planet."

"She was a Wayseeker?" As predicted, Qui-Gon's eyes lit up with curiosity, even hunger. "And we don't know if she ever went there?"

"There was no addition to the records. I don't think anyone ever saw her information on the planet in the first place."

Qui-Gon sat on the simple gray cushion he kept in place of more elaborate seating. He had never added furniture for hosting guests. Obi-Wan always felt like he was somehow intruding, like there really was no place for him in Qui-Gon's life. He knew Siri's master had a table for two in her living quarters where they took most meals together, and Prie's had insisted on a Padawan room right next to his own so they could have easier access to each other when studying together.

"Interesting," Qui-Gon said. "You may have rediscovered information no Jedi has known about for generations. Which makes me think the Force *has* guided you to it."

Making a tremendous effort to keep his emotions under control and not let Qui-Gon see or sense just how triumphant he was feeling, Obi-Wan frowned and nodded. "Interesting," he echoed. "In that case, I know it is not my place as a Padawan to suggest missions, but perhaps we could follow the path the Force led me to find, and see what it is that Orla the Wayseeker sensed was important about this unnamed planet."

Please, Obi-Wan thought, *please please please say yes.*

It was wrong of him to want this, to try to manipulate Qui-Gon into agreeing. Obi-Wan should want only what the Force wanted, should accept and be grateful for whatever path the Force put him on. He should be patient and trust that his master would give him the experiences he needed, when he needed them.

But all Obi-Wan wanted was to be a Jedi Knight, to go out into the galaxy and be an agent of goodness, of order, of the light. He couldn't do any of that stuck in the Temple.

Sure, he could run through the basic lightsaber combat forms in his sleep, and he could use the Force to push and pull and jump. His physical abilities were more than adequate. But he couldn't shake the fear that, spiritually, he didn't have what it took to be a Knight. And that constant fear made him feel both guilty and more afraid. It was a terrible cycle he didn't know how to break out of, one he was certain was holding him back. Both from his connection to the Force and his own potential.

Maybe if he could get out of the Temple, if he could be among the stars, an active Jedi, maybe then he could feel the Force guiding him.

Maybe then he would feel like he deserved to be a Padawan.

Obi-Wan's heart nearly burst with happiness and relief—and a fair squeeze of guilt—when Qui-Gon gave him a proud smile. It wasn't that Qui-Gon was cold or impatient. If anything, he was *too* patient. Obi-Wan shared none of the resolute acceptance that eventually he would achieve what Qui-Gon had. It didn't feel like he could ever get to Jedi Knight from where he was now.

Qui-Gon stood. "Make a flight plan and requisition a ship. A T-5 shuttle should be adequate. And remember . . ." Qui-Gon paused, and a flicker of worry crossed his face. "*Always* remember: sometimes the Force works in very small ways, too."

Obi-Wan wasn't sure what that warning had to do with

anything. Normally he'd obsess over it, but luckily now he had something else to think about. He was going off-planet, on a mission. A mission that he had come up with. He felt like he could do backflips off the four Temple spires, were such a thing not definitely sacrilege and certainly a misuse of the abilities he had through the Force.

Qui-Gon sighed, worry lines pulling his graying brows close together. "I must meet with the Council now."

"Will you tell them about our mission?" Obi-Wan was seized with worry that they needed to get permission, and that Master Yoda, in his infinite wisdom, would immediately know that the Force had nothing to do with Obi-Wan's discovery. Or that one of the other Jedi Masters would tell Qui-Gon that the mystery planet had been explored centuries earlier, and deemed irrelevant. Pointless. Having no importance to the Force and no impact on the galaxy.

Obi-Wan's throat tightened. Either event would prove that Obi-Wan was wrong to want to pursue this. He couldn't say with any certainty that the Force had led him to Orla Jareni and the mystery planet, but his curiosity had, and he was desperate to see it through.

Qui-Gon's frown deepened, and Obi-Wan held his breath. But he was surprised by what Qui-Gon said next. "The Council doesn't need to know everything, much as they might think they already do."

Rather than relief, Obi-Wan felt a prickling of anxiety

at even hearing such rebellious talk. He swallowed the urge to caution his master—even rebuke him. It wasn't Obi-Wan's place to tell Qui-Gon how to engage with the Jedi Council. And he didn't want to do anything to upset Qui-Gon. Nothing could jeopardize this mission out into the galaxy. Obi-Wan *needed* it in a way he could barely explain to himself, much less to his master.

Obi-Wan bowed farewell, then rushed to the hangar. He scheduled the shuttle for the morning and put in a supply request. It was astonishing how many people it took to run the Temple and keep the Jedi functioning. Evidence of how important the Jedi were to the galaxy. Obi-Wan wanted to be deserving of all this effort, too.

As he made his way back to Qui-Gon's chambers, nodding and waving to the various familiar faces, he saw Bolla heading his way. Obi-Wan quickly ducked into a side hall, waiting until the other Padawan had passed. He didn't want to talk to him. With his back pressed to the wall, he heard a squeak.

"Be careful, young Padawan," a man said, in that same deep voice Obi-Wan had heard talking about how the banquet hall had once been the library.

"Sorry, Mast—Count—sir," Bolla said, stumbling awkwardly over how to address whoever he had nearly run into.

Obi-Wan almost wished he hadn't ducked out of the way so he could have seen Bolla embarrass himself. He peered around the corner and caught sight of a tall black-cloaked frame and a head of elegant silver hair disappearing through a doorway.

Whoever he was, that man knew a lot of the Temple's history. Maybe he was a senator. Politicians weren't common sights in the Temple but weren't unheard of. Qui-Gon, unsurprisingly, had no patience for politicians, so Obi-Wan had never engaged with any of them.

Obi-Wan hadn't engaged with much, actually. Sometimes he wondered why Qui-Gon ever took him on as a Padawan. It wasn't required of Jedi Knights. When they did choose an initiate after the Trials, they were always guided by the Force. What had guided Qui-Gon to Obi-Wan? His friends and their masters all made sense together. It seemed to him that he and Qui-Gon had almost nothing in common.

Qui-Gon was a Jedi Knight, and therefore Obi-Wan shouldn't question him, but he didn't ever seem to push Obi-Wan beyond what he had already learned before becoming a Padawan.

Really, the only thing Qui-Gon insisted on was meditation. There were many avenues to becoming a Knight that Obi-Wan was sure involved almost no meditation whatsoever. So why had the Jedi most enamored of meditation picked *him* as Padawan?

At least that was another bright side to this mission: the shuttle didn't have enough room for two to meditate comfortably. And he'd insist that he needed to keep an eye on their charted course, not trusting it to the ship's systems.

Back in his room, Obi-Wan packed quickly. He wondered if he should pack for Qui-Gon, too, but since it hadn't been requested, it seemed too eager for Obi-Wan to take the initiative. Besides, it wasn't like it would take either of them long. Jedi had very little in the way of possessions. His lightsaber, a spare change of clothing. Down to just one for now, thanks to the soup incident. At least he'd finally get to take advantage of some of the pouches on his belt.

With no other preparations to make, Obi-Wan realized that he still hadn't eaten. And, hallway-dodging of Bolla notwithstanding, he didn't need to avoid the Padawan dining hall. He could look forward to seeing his friends with no fear of feeling left out for once. He finally had a mission, and not even Bolla and a hundred demon squids could squeeze this excitement and hope from him.

CHAPTER

4

Obi-Wan gleefully made his way down to the Padawan dining hall. If Padawans weren't busy, they could almost always be found eating. Sure enough, Bolla, Prie, and a few other Padawans he'd known and trained alongside his entire life were gathered around a table. But rather than eating, they were all leaning intently toward Siri Tachi, talking.

Obi-Wan could barely contain his smile as he sat down next to Prie.

"Oh, you're here," Siri said, and her expression re-formed into a worried frown.

"Don't be so excited to see me," Obi-Wan said with a laugh.

"Have you spoken to Master Qui-Gon?" she asked.

"Did he cancel our mission?" All Obi-Wan's hopes would be dashed like blocks of ice they had once snuck up and dropped from the top of the Temple, shattering on the ground so many stories beneath. Lost to the perpetual darkness of the lowest levels of Coruscant.

"What? What mission?"

"We're going on a mission! To look for—But wait, what are *you* talking about?"

Prie squirmed uncomfortably in her seat. There was no sign of her new pet demon squid, to Obi-Wan's relief. "He was fighting with the Council again," she said. "My master told me all about it."

"Again?" Obi-Wan asked. That wasn't good. Both because he didn't want his master fighting with the Council and because it might affect Qui-Gon's mood on their mission.

"I heard he's going to join the ranks of the Lost," Bolla said, antennae twitching.

"He'll do no such thing!" Obi-Wan wished they were in a sparring room where he could do something with the burst of aggression he felt toward Bolla, yet again.

"Hush, Bolla," Siri chided. "Unless you've had a vision, you certainly aren't qualified to speculate about the future of a Jedi Knight."

Bolla scowled. The Rodian and Obi-Wan had never gotten along. As younglings, they trained in separate clans, and it was hard not to feel competitive with each other. Plus, in addition to the soup attack, Bolla was the one who had described Obi-Wan as looking like a straggle of shed Wookiee hair, and Obi-Wan would neither forget nor forgive either offense.

No. A Jedi would release these feelings. It was his duty to release them.

"Don't worry," Bolla said, and Obi-Wan smiled, glad he was working on releasing his resentment. "There will always be a place for you in the kitchens, protecting against assassins there." Bolla's antennae twitched in time with his shoulders as he let out a thin laugh. Obi-Wan vowed never to give up his dislike of the other Padawan.

"They don't post guards in the kitchen," Prie snapped. She continued, her voice kind in the most horrifying way as she tried to be supportive. "If Qui-Gon leaves, you'll simply be assigned to another Jedi Master."

Siri nodded. She and Obi-Wan had been close growing up, and he missed that closeness now. He missed all of them, really. They had been a merry band of brats, as Yaddle had once muttered under her breath during a particularly raucous lesson. "Maybe that wouldn't be so bad," she said. "A master who's a better fit for you."

Was it that obvious he was struggling? Obi-Wan shook his head. "Master Qui-Gon isn't going anywhere. Except on our mission."

"Assuming he doesn't leave with Master Dooku." Bolla dropped the name as casually as a gas canister, turning all the air in the room unbreathable for Obi-Wan.

"Why would he do that?"

"Master Dooku's here. In the Temple. I ran into him earlier. Seems planned, Dooku visiting while his former Padawan is fighting with the Council. Maybe Dooku's here to pick him up."

Obi-Wan suddenly realized who the man he had glimpsed in the hallway was. Not a politician. A count. A count who had been a Jedi and decided not to be one anymore. A count who had trained Obi-Wan's own master, and whom Obi-Wan had never heard Qui-Gon say a bad word about. If anything, Qui-Gon spoke of his old master with respect and admiration.

"He's here often enough," Siri said, folding her arms. "He still meets with the Council on occasion. Just because he's no longer on it—"

"No longer a Jedi," Bolla interjected.

"—doesn't mean he's not welcome here. I wouldn't read anything into it, Obi-Wan."

"I would. Like master, like apprentice," Bolla trilled.

"Master Qui-Gon would never leave the Order." Obi-Wan stood, angry, both because of the slander against his master and because . . . he didn't know for sure that Qui-Gon wouldn't, did he? Qui-Gon was still a mystery to him, and he *did* fight with the Council a lot. And Qui-Gon's master had left, though none of the Padawans truly knew the details. It was Jedi Master business, none of theirs. What if Qui-Gon had similar feelings? Similar reasons?

Bolla repeated himself with a shrug. "Like master, like apprentice."

Obi-Wan hurried from the room, regretting ever coming. Because not only was Qui-Gon Dooku's apprentice, but Obi-Wan was Qui-Gon's. And if Qui-Gon joined the Lost, where would that leave Obi-Wan?

CHAPTER
5

Bolla followed him into the hall, chasing him down. "Listen, Kenobi. I know we've had our differences."

Obi-Wan held up his still red and swollen wrist. "You put a live demon squid in my soup."

Bolla snickered. "It was funny! Come on, you have to admit it was funny."

Obi-Wan had to do no such thing. He would never be able to eat soup again without first checking that it was definitely not alive or tentacled. And he really liked soup, too.

"You need to lighten up," Bolla pressed on. "You're always so serious now. You used to be good for a joke. And competitive, too! Always showing us up in training."

"I did no such thing!"

"You did. But that's beside the point. I heard my master talking, and it was about you, and I think it's information you should have. Especially if it turns out that Qui-Gon is joining his old master."

Obi-Wan gazed down at Bolla, trying for some of the cold, aloof power he had heard in Master Dooku's voice. Was it still "Master" if Dooku had left the Order, though? It felt better to think of him as Master Dooku than as one of the Lost. Less frightening when Obi-Wan thought of Dooku's connection to Qui-Gon. "What's this important information, then?" Obi-Wan snapped.

"Master Qui-Gon Jinn didn't choose you."

"What?"

"He didn't choose you. After your trial."

Obi-Wan felt the planet tilt on its axis. "What are you talking about? Of course he did."

Bolla shook his jewel-green head. "Yoda assigned you to him."

"But . . . that's not how it works. Masters choose their apprentices. When they decide to take on a Padawan, they're guided to the right one. The Force puts us together so we can learn from each other. You know this, same as I do." But even as Obi-Wan tried to deny what Bolla was telling him, something inside him was already seeing its truth.

"That's how it usually happens, yes. But not in your case. Qui-Gon didn't choose you. Yoda made him . . . I mean, *asked* him to take you on."

Obi-Wan didn't know what to do with this information. He and Bolla clashed more often than not, but the Rodian wasn't a liar. It felt like the hallway was spinning around him. The Force hadn't guided Qui-Gon Jinn to take on Obi-Wan as a Padawan. Had he even wanted to, or had Yoda somehow pulled rank as a Council member and made him? No wonder Qui-Gon was always troubled. He hadn't wanted to train Obi-Wan in the first place, and Obi-Wan was struggling so much. A rush of humiliation flooded Obi-Wan as he imagined how frustrating he must be for the Jedi Knight. A problem he had neither asked for nor planned on.

But why assign Obi-Wan to Qui-Gon in the first place? Unless the Council knew Qui-Gon was tempted to leave, like his own master had, and were trying to find new ways to tether him to the Temple until they could win him back over . . .

"Why are you telling me this?" Obi-Wan asked.

"So if things don't work out, you know it's not your fault." Bolla put a long-fingered hand on Obi-Wan's shoulder, as if to be comforting. "I know we haven't always gotten along, but you really are the best of our group. Which is probably *why* we haven't gotten along." Bolla let out that thin laugh. "Don't worry—if Master Qui-Gon joins the Lost, no one will think less of *you*." Bolla left to rejoin the other Padawans, leaving Obi-Wan alone in the dark hall.

Obi-Wan found himself back at Qui-Gon's quarters. He paced outside the door, debating. He wanted to talk to

Qui-Gon, to be reassured. But he couldn't bear the embarrassment. Qui-Gon was always so serene, so wise. Obi-Wan felt like a youngling again, tripping over his own feet, desperate to be taken seriously.

What would he say? Would he burst inside and demand reassurance from a Jedi Knight? Qui-Gon was a generous man, unfailingly kind, but he was also notoriously difficult to get a straight answer from. Even if Obi-Wan directly asked whether Qui-Gon wanted to train him, or if Qui-Gon was tempted to join Dooku in leaving the Order, Qui-Gon would probably answer in some baffling way.

Search your feelings to find your answers, he'd say. Or *What do you think having such questions reveals about your own heart and your connection to the Force?*

Or worse, he'd tell Obi-Wan to meditate on it.

Or worst, Qui-Gon would be packing, and not for their mission. Packing to leave the Temple forever.

No. No, that wouldn't happen. Everything was going to work out the way Obi-Wan wanted it to. He *needed* this mission. It was a chance to go out into the galaxy, to work alongside Qui-Gon Jinn, learn from him, actively use the Force for good on behalf of the Jedi Order. It was what Obi-Wan wanted, what he had always wanted, what he was sometimes afraid he wanted so desperately that *he* was the one blocking the Force from guiding him.

Because Obi-Wan's biggest fear was that maybe, just

maybe, he didn't deserve his place as a Padawan and his destiny wasn't to be a Knight at all. And that by continuing to try to make that his destiny, he was going against the Force itself.

Bolla's revelation was playing into all Obi-Wan's fears with vicious accuracy. He eyed the door once more. The door that separated him from all the answers he needed. The answers he deserved.

The answers he was afraid of getting.

He'd have plenty of time to speak with Qui-Gon on their journey. No reason to bother him now. And if Qui-Gon really was considering leaving the Jedi, then perhaps this mission was what he needed, as well, to remind him of his place in the Order and his duty to the Force.

Assuming there was anything worthwhile at the end of Obi-Wan's flight path, which didn't feel like a safe assumption at all.

CHAPTER

6

Obi-Wan couldn't sleep. He went to the Padawan dining hall in the earliest hours of the morning, hoping to be alone and strangely disappointed when he was. He really did want to hear about Siri's latest mission, or what Prie had discovered about the demon squid. He missed the camaraderie of their days together before the Trials, before becoming Padawans.

He picked at his food. Nothing had tentacles, but it all still stuck in his throat. His stomach hurt with nerves. Even though the mission had been his idea, he couldn't help fearing it was a mistake. That it would ruin everything.

But no. It was a real chance to be out there, using the Force, training for the life he would have as a Jedi Knight.

Hoped he would have.

Needed to have.

Obi-Wan dumped the rest of his breakfast. He wasn't going to be able to keep anything down. He hurried through the still silent hallways of the Temple, up through the various levels, and then to the hangar.

There wasn't much activity so early. The kind-faced Ortolan named Meba Fonox, whom Obi-Wan had spoken to the day before, zipped right over to him on a hovering personal craft, waving her blue trunk. Because her only limbs were legs, she had to do everything with her feet, which necessitated keeping them free to work on ships. Ortolans were known for being incredibly dexterous, employed as everything from mechanics to musicians, surgeons to artists.

"Here you are!" she said. "Everything is ready for you, but we can go over the preflight preparations and make sure you don't have any questions. Have you flown a T-5 shuttle before?"

Obi-Wan nodded. "Once. But only in training. I'll have Master Qui-Gon Jinn with me, though."

Her ear flippers rose and lowered in an Ortolan shrug. "Good enough. And you'll have an astromech, too. They can fly anything."

"A useful quality in a droid."

Meba led him to the shuttle. It was pale gray. Green markings on the large semicircle wings helped pilots and navigators orient themselves, since the wings were built to rotate around the body and changed position depending on what was needed for landing and docking. Right then they were horizontal, but in flight they would be vertical, streamlined around the cockpit and over the engines.

The cockpit itself had more than enough room for the two of them, with seats for pilot and copilot and several seats for passengers. Because it was a transport shuttle, it didn't have any weapons systems. But Obi-Wan couldn't imagine needing those.

"She's a good ship," Meba said, patting the side affectionately with one foot. "Not as roomy as the T-6, but perfect for your needs. You could take her alone into the stars and she'd see you safe wherever you needed to go."

The assigned astromech, domed in green with a black-and-silver body and legs, rolled up to them, beeping cheerily. Obi-Wan was still getting the gist of binary, but from what he could tell, the droid was ready to go. He leaned down to be at eye level—or, he supposed, photoreceptor level.

"Hello, I'm Obi-Wan Kenobi. And you are?"

Meba laughed. "You don't need to be so polite. Droids won't kill you for being brusque."

"Ah, but there's no reason not to be polite."

The droid beeped again, just as cheerily. It was A6-G2.

"Aysix. We can work with that. All right, Aces, let's get you programmed." Obi-Wan crouched and fed a datacard into the droid's dataslot. Several lights flashed in a holding pattern, and then she beeped to let him know the programming was complete. Obi-Wan patted her dome. "I look forward to working with you."

A6-G2 rolled to the loading ramp and up into the ship, where she'd plug into the cockpit. Everything was in place, the preflight checklist squared away, the astromech programmed. All Obi-Wan needed was Qui-Gon.

Meba was called away to do inventory on a supply ship docking nearby. She waved goodbye and wished Obi-Wan a good mission. He waved back, hopeful for the same thing, then watched the doors leading into the hangar and waited.

And waited.

And waited.

A6-G2 beeped patiently from the interior of the ship, letting Obi-Wan know their flight plan was being adjusted based on the new departure window. The *fifth* time A6-G2 adjusted the departure time calculations, Obi-Wan's heart raced, lungs squeezing tighter and tighter so it was hard to breathe.

Qui-Gon wasn't just late. He wasn't coming.

Even if Qui-Gon didn't follow the Order's rules in the strictest sense, Obi-Wan had never known him to be so late for anything. There had to be a reason. He connected to the Temple comms system on the wall and sent an open link to Qui-Gon Jinn's room. If he was inside, he'd answer. Obi-Wan left it open for an achingly long time. Even if Qui-Gon was still somehow asleep, or not feeling well, he'd answer.

He didn't. He wasn't in his room, and he wasn't in the hangar, and he hadn't sent word to Obi-Wan about any changes. The pit in Obi-Wan's stomach kept finding new depths.

Obi-Wan walked as casually as he could to Meba, who was bouncing and humming as she worked on an old Vector, a model that was hardly used anymore. "Excuse me, but do you know if Master Dooku's ship has left?"

"Oh! You're still here. Let's see, the Count?" Meba consulted her datapad. "It looks like his ship left late last night."

All that time Obi-Wan had spent staring at Qui-Gon's door, debating going in and asking for answers. Had the room beyond it been empty already? Would Qui-Gon really leave without telling Obi-Wan? Without so much as a goodbye?

And could Obi-Wan really not sense when his master was gone? Was he so pathetic that not only could Qui-Gon leave him without a second thought but Obi-Wan's senses were too clouded with fear and worry to be able to tell when a room was empty?

Obi-Wan tried to keep his expression calm. It was almost as hard as meditation. "Did Dooku take anyone with him?"

Meba's ears drooped in her version of a puzzled frown. "I don't know. We only keep a log of who's coming in on non-Jedi ships. Not who's going out."

"Right, yes, that makes perfect sense. Thank you!" Obi-Wan's voice was high and tight as he tried to sound unconcerned when he was very much the opposite. He returned to his shuttle, his movements stiff and uncoordinated, like his brain and limbs weren't quite communicating.

He climbed aboard to check and double-check once more that everything was ready for the Jedi who wasn't coming.

What if Qui-Gon really was one of the Lost and Dooku had come to collect his former Padawan? Qui-Gon had been notified when someone arrived the day before. Surely that had been Master Dooku. And then Qui-Gon had argued with the Council. Maybe he had been informing them of his choice.

Obi-Wan genuinely couldn't fathom Qui-Gon doing that. Qui-Gon, for all he disagreed with the Council, still seemed as deeply committed to the Jedi path as anyone Obi-Wan had ever met. He just walked it a little differently. Surely that wouldn't lead him to walk right off, would it?

But if Qui-Gon *was* gone, what would that mean for Obi-Wan? What Jedi would want to take on a Padawan partially trained by someone who had turned his back on the Order? By a Jedi who had rejected the path the Force had put him on. He imagined a future of being passed from Jedi Master to Jedi Master, never finding a place at their sides, never finding himself. Because Siri might be wrong. A different master couldn't be a better fit if the part of the apprenticeship that was broken was Obi-Wan himself.

The twist of fear and dread in his stomach confirmed it. After all, that twist of fear and dread *was* the problem. He was so afraid of failing, so terrified of not being enough, that he couldn't listen to the Force at all these days.

He didn't want to fail. And he knew wanting so much to be a Jedi Knight was wrong, in a way. Obi-Wan should be open to anything the Force called him to do, even if it wasn't with the Order. Almost every Padawan made it through to Knighthood, but there were rare exceptions. What if his fear was the Force telling him he wasn't cut out for this?

The idea of being anything other than a Jedi Knight filled him with quiet, panicked despair. He wanted to help in the galaxy. And he knew—he *knew*—there were many ways to accomplish that. But he wanted *this* way. This was the way that had been prepared for him, the path he had been set on before he could even remember. If he failed, if this path closed to him, what would he be then?

Maybe Qui-Gon wasn't leaving the Order. Maybe if Obi-Wan went to Qui-Gon's rooms, he'd find his master meditating, infuriatingly calm, oblivious to both the comm summons and the complete turmoil of his Padawan. Which would mean that Qui-Gon *chose* not to meet him, chose to ignore Obi-Wan's attempts to reach him, chose to ignore their mission.

And if a Jedi as intuitive as Qui-Gon Jinn didn't feel compelled to do this mission, that meant it really wasn't the Force guiding Obi-Wan. Which Obi-Wan suspected anyway, but this would make it clear that Qui-Gon had only been humoring him. That his master secretly knew what Obi-Wan hadn't accepted yet: Obi-Wan and the Force would never be truly connected, and it was only a matter of time before the Jedi Order realized it and placed him somewhere he actually belonged.

Better perfect that meditation! he could imagine future generations of Padawans saying to each other. *You don't want to end up like Obi-Wan Kenobi, escorted out of the Temple! Sometimes you can see him, crouched in the shadows, watching the doors and hoping for a chance to come back in.* He'd be a cautionary tale, a warning that trying to connect to the Force when the Force didn't want you was an exercise in futility that led only to failure and shame.

Even imagining this made him sweat with panic, which was further proof that he didn't trust the Force. If he truly trusted the Force, then he could accept that there were many ways to be of service to the galaxy.

Obi-Wan groaned in frustration and indecision, tugging on his Padawan braid. What he needed this moment was guidance. Advice. A master.

And yet here he was, alone.

A6-G2 beeped pleasantly, letting Obi-Wan know they were significantly past their adjusted departure time and she would once again adjust their course accordingly.

Before he could talk himself out if it, scarcely believing what he was doing, Obi-Wan moved from the copilot to the pilot seat and buckled in. This shuttle was perfectly capable of being flown solo, as Meba had already so helpfully informed him. Obi-Wan ran through his preflight checklist, made sure A6-G2 had the correct flight plan based on their new departure time, and then put his hand on the ignition.

This was, by far, the most reckless and rebellious thing he had ever done. It could get him pulled in front of the Council for censure. Maybe even something worse. It went against everything he had been taught. But he couldn't deny the absolute need inside himself to see this through. Either to succeed and prove that he deserved his place as a Padawan, that the Force was capable of working through him, or to fail. To fail, and know that he really wasn't cut out to be a Jedi Knight. That Padawan was the end of his journey through the Force.

Either way: his path forward at last was clear. Charted. Determined.

Obi-Wan powered up the shuttle, flew out of the hangar, and let Coruscant grow small behind him. If it was the last time he left the Temple as a Padawan, so be it.

CHAPTER 7

"So be it?" Obi-Wan muttered to himself, tugging on his braid so hard his scalp ached. "*So be it?*" He should never have done this. This was a mistake. Coruscant was a glowing dot behind him, the black void of space open before him. But rather than possibility, that much freedom felt like an ending.

Obi-Wan closed his eyes, trying to get his breathing and heartbeat under control. The way Qui-Gon had taught him. And it worked. Not the breathing exercise but rather thinking of Qui-Gon. It made Obi-Wan just annoyed enough to take the edge off his panic. He opened his eyes and took over flying from A6-G2. But he kept checking all the readings and ship information.

There was something wrong, something off, that he couldn't quite place. It nagged at him. He asked A6-G2 to run a scan, but the droid assured him via the console's translation that everything with the ship was fine. Still, Obi-Wan couldn't shake his nagging unease.

Until he realized with a burst of startled laughter what, exactly, was wrong: this was the first time he had ever been alone. Truly alone.

Sure, he had been separated from his group while finding his kyber crystal, and yes, he meditated alone—or at least tried to. But even then, there had been other people in reach. Someone at the other end of a comm, or behind a door, or across a hall. Someone at the end of his journey, waiting for him.

Now? Obi-Wan was on his own.

A cheery beep reminded him that it wasn't *quite* just him. But close enough. Obi-Wan shook out his shoulders. He was still flying as though an instructor were sitting next to him, critiquing all his choices, offering instruction and correction. With a burst of excitement, Obi-Wan did a completely unnecessary barrel roll, and then a loop just for the sake of it. Nothing could ever ruin flying for him, not when it felt like this!

A6-G2 beeped with alarmed curiosity, sending a burst of messages through the console, asking if they were changing course.

"Sorry, yes, I shouldn't deviate from our flight path. You're right." Still positively giddy with freedom, holding tight to that feeling to stave off the guilt and fear of what his future held, Obi-Wan punched it toward the mystery ahead of him, letting all other mysteries wait.

They had made two hyperspace jumps, both short, requiring careful navigating before a third and final jump. Unfortunately, the complex flight path toward his destination still left enough time for spiraling. Not the fun, flying type of spiraling, but the emotional variety, where Obi-Wan ranged from angry and defiant—*Of course he should be doing this!*—to absolutely mortified and riddled with guilt—*How could he have done this?*

It was actually a tremendous relief when A6-G2 alerted him to a strange signal. He needed something else to focus on. They were in deep space, no planets nearby, nothing livable or even charted on Obi-Wan's records.

"What is it?" he asked.

A6-G2 relayed the coordinates of the signal, which weren't too far out of their flight path. As they got closer, it became clear the signal was a distress beacon broadcasting. A6-G2 couldn't pick up any specifics, only the location of the beacon.

Obi-Wan felt bad for being excited. If someone was in trouble, he shouldn't be thrilled with the idea of being the one to save them. But he couldn't help it. He was finally going to do some good! If he hadn't stolen—borrowed—taken with permission but under slightly false circumstances—this ship, then no one would have picked up the beacon's signal. There was no telling how long it might have broadcast into the void of space, ever hopeful but never answered.

He let his imagination run wild, thinking of what it could be. A ship that had gone off course and lost engine power. An escape pod holding the sole survivor of a terrible accident. A relic of a long-lost civilization, filled with—

At last their target came into view. It was a single beacon, floating in space with nothing around it. There was no wreckage, no debris, not so much as a spare bolt. Just a small orb with transmitter fins, flashing a patient red light.

"What do you think left it?" Obi-Wan asked.

A6-G2 beeped noncommittally. Speculation was not in her programming. After a cursory scan to make sure it wasn't anything nefarious, Obi-Wan cleared A6-G2 to bring it on board. There was no way to get it into the cockpit while flying, but there was a small storage space on the underside of the ship where it could be kept safe until they landed. A6-G2 flew the ship directly over the beacon, then sent out a magnetic grappling hook to snag it and pull it into the storage compartment.

"Is it sending out a message?" Obi-Wan asked. "Anything other than a distress signal?"

A6-G2 indicated that, until she could manually connect with the beacon, there was no further information she could give him.

Obi-Wan sighed, supposing he should be grateful that there was no emergency that desperately required his skilled intervention. That, whatever the distress was, it either no longer existed or didn't exist anywhere nearby. "We'll examine it later. I don't see anything else to do here. Back on course. We're almost to the final hyperspace jump point."

He hoped this wasn't a vision of things to come: a beacon luring him into space, with nothing to show for it. But it was hard not to feel like this eventless sidetrack was portentous.

He was asleep at the controls when a light began flashing. Even behind his closed eyes, dreaming of what he always dreamed, he could feel that flicker, that pull.

That promise.

He startled awake, taking in the information. A movement notification from a probe not on any trade routes, not close to any inhabited planets. The only reason that probe would move was if someone was out there, looking.

He **knew** the others wouldn't stay away. Knew they couldn't. Those monsters who dragged him away from the planet, who threw him down onto a lifeless piece of rock and told him to make a new home. To thrive. As if such a thing were possible, with what they forced him to leave behind. As if they didn't all feel the loss just as deeply as he did.

He'd fled as soon as he could. Found his way out into the galaxy. Shared his story where he needed to in order to lure someone into helping him.

Despite demands for results, he could be patient. He had always been certain that one of his captors would creep back to what they had ripped him away from. To what they had left behind.

Someone had kept the coordinates, kept the pathway back, and now he would find it, too. They might plan to have it all to themselves, but they couldn't keep him trapped, couldn't keep him from getting back what he had lost.

He pulled up the comm system.

"Yes?" came the deep voice of the man on the other end, weary and judging, as if he could possibly care what that man thought.

"Get me a crew and ready the ships. I have a good feeling about this."

"I had better see results."

"You will."

It was a lie, but nothing else mattered. He stared at that blinking light, promising him everything he had longed for these vast, empty, powerless years. Even though he couldn't know for certain that whoever had the probe was taking it to the right place, or that they would activate the final transmission that would guide him, he still somehow knew. He could feel it. At last, at last.

He was going home.

Obi-Wan jolted awake as an impact made the entire ship shudder.

"What was that?" He expected a response from A6-G2, but looking out from the cockpit, his question was immediately answered. The ship had emerged from hyperspace, which was not a cause for concern, other than the fact that they were flying directly into a massive asteroid field. Chunks of floating rock and ice littered his vision. He couldn't see anything past them—or under or over or in any direction. There hadn't been any mention of this in Orla's records. Though he remembered, with a sinking feeling, the carving of the planet had been surrounded by countless small dots. He had assumed they were decorative.

This asteroid field did *not* feel decorative.

"Aces!" He adjusted course as another asteroid made contact with his ship. "A little warning that you were flying us directly into danger would have been welcome. Just for future reference. I feel like we could be communicating better."

The astromech's response made no sense.

"What do you mean your sensors aren't picking up anything? I can *see* them!" There was another jolt, followed by a painful screech of metal that made the entire ship tremble. "And I can feel them!"

A6-G2 simply reiterated that, as far as her sensors were concerned, there were no asteroids. And since her sensors couldn't pick them up, she couldn't guide them through. So much for Meba's assertion that the astromech unit could pilot the ship. Or that being impolite wouldn't lead to death. "Have I done something to offend you?" Obi-Wan asked, but it only confused the droid further, and he couldn't afford a distraction.

His sensors and droid apparently useless, Obi-Wan did a visual check against his own charts. There was no way around this field. Their path was straight through it. If he went back and tried to get around, who knew how far off course it would take them? And with this area uncharted, a deviation from his path could have disastrous—even deadly—results. He didn't want to die alone in space, never having helped anyone.

They were close to their destination. They had to be. After all, someone had very thoughtfully included all these deadly asteroids around the planet on the wall.

"Well, then," Obi-Wan said, laughing nervously. "I'll bet even Siri has never done this. I hope I live to tell her about it." He strangled the controls, gripping them so tightly his knuckles were white, trying to combat the nervous trembling in his whole body. He was shaking so hard that it made all the asteroids around them look like they were shaking, too.

He narrowed his eyes, stilling himself. No. The asteroids actually *were* shaking, somehow moving out of their trajectories, becoming . . . agitated. How did a floating chunk of rock and ice in space become agitated? There was not enough gravity out there, certainly no wind or anything that might allow the asteroids to move from their predetermined orbit.

Obi-Wan swerved and dodged, but the more he moved, the worse the situation got. As rock after rock pelted his ship, Obi-Wan concluded the impossible: the asteroid field was mocking him. Whatever he did, however he maneuvered, it didn't matter. His ship couldn't take much more of this. It was a shuttle, not designed to withstand extensive damage, and without any weapons to fire at oncoming asteroids. Obi-Wan had to turn around or make it through, and fast. But the way things were going, either decision would mean his ship fell apart, or he did. Or both.

He wished, suddenly and fiercely, that unflappable Qui-Gon were with him. Not because Qui-Gon was an excellent pilot but because he could imagine Qui-Gon simply closing his eyes and breathing deeply, telling Obi-Wan to trust the Force.

But how could Obi-Wan do that when he had no idea if this was what the Force wanted him to do in the first place?

Still, the image of Qui-Gon calmly meditating as their ship was broken apart by hundreds of space missiles made Obi-Wan laugh. The laughter released some of the panic in his chest, and he took deep, calming breaths like Qui-Gon had taught him. He did his best to quiet his mind and heart. This was just like a training exercise. Those terrible floating remotes that shot him unless he managed to block their blasts with his lightsaber. He had done that blindfolded. There had been no actual threat of death there, but it wasn't so different.

Obi-Wan decided to keep his eyes open, out of an abundance of caution. But breathing like Qui-Gon and imagining this as another of a series of annoying but helpful training exercises let Obi-Wan calm down enough to focus. He began gliding through the obstacles, twisting and twirling, almost as though he were dancing with them.

And strangely, now that Obi-Wan was calmer, his dance partners seemed less agitated, too. The deadly floating projectiles once again drifted on predictable courses, easy to dodge.

"I don't think this is how asteroid fields are supposed to behave," Obi-Wan mused aloud. "But then again, I'm a

Padawan who stole a ship and is going on a rogue mission without his master, so I can hardly critique behavior now, can I?"

A6-G2 beeped in amused solidarity.

"Oh, that part? The part where I stole this ship? Let's keep that off the official log, shall we?"

His co-conspirator responded by making all the screens go blank before they popped back up again.

"That's my girl."

Obi-Wan didn't know how long it took to get through the field. It had become almost trance-like, the weaving and spinning and twisting. As though he and the field were one, working together, existing in harmony. But as soon as he had the thought, he wondered: Was it the Force? Was he somehow using the Force to control the asteroids? His heart rate picked back up and he reached, trying to feel for certain, trying to grasp the Force so he would *know*—

The field around him erupted into chaos. Obi-Wan yelped, put on a burst of speed, and only just managed to break free as two enormous asteroids smashed into each other where his ship had been mere seconds before.

"That was a little too close for comfort," he muttered, wiping his brow only to be stunned once more by what he was looking at. But this time less in horror and more in awe.

The unknown planet loomed in front of him, a verdant jewel on a vast black-velvet plain. Coruscant was beautiful.

Obi-Wan loved gazing out over the horizon at night, letting his eyes go out of focus so the entire planet looked like a field of glittering stars. But this planet was nothing like Coruscant's endless cityscape. Everything was jeweled colors—the blues vivid, the greens luscious, even the grays streaking through both somehow bold and vibrant. He'd never seen a planet like this before.

Maybe no one had ever seen it, since Orla the Wayseeker. If she had even gotten there at all. Reminding himself that he was on a mission to find out why she had flagged this strange and inaccessible place for further study, Obi-Wan used his ship's systems to run scans. The life-form readings were wildly fluctuating. There was no usable information there, other than that the planet had organic life.

"Let's go see who's home," Obi-Wan said, aiming for the mysterious planet and hoping with all he had that there was something worth seeing there. That someone needed his help, or that he could bring value back to the Temple by finishing Orla's request for further study. That somehow the Force really had guided him to this place, and soon he would have proof.

CHAPTER

9

Fortunately, entry into the atmosphere was easier than getting to the planet had been. Sparse clouds shimmered with a full rainbow spectrum. A6-G2 ran a scan of the environment and found the atmosphere was breathable for Obi-Wan. The temperature was balmy and humid but not dangerous. Pleasant, even. Still sealed in his ship, Obi-Wan felt like he could breathe a little better, with the air so clear he could see to the curvature of the horizon.

He loved Coruscant, the excitement and variety and overwhelming bustle of it all, but this planet was alive in a different way. As he neared the surface, flying close to the ground to look for anything of note, he marveled at the sheer variety of trees and plants. Most were green, but with a lot of deep blues and even some vivid violets thrown in. Lowlands of forest were frequently broken up by jutting peaks of sparkling dark gray, the rocks formed like pillars, hundreds of thousands of them pressed together. He skirted past a roaring waterfall, crystalline and aqua, that fed a pool so clear he could see his ship perfectly reflected . . . giving him a pristine view of all the damage the asteroids had done.

"We'll need to address that," he said, brought back to reality. Poor Meba would be so disappointed in him. Though the hangar tech's disappointment was probably the least of what he would face when he returned to the Temple.

Obi-Wan focused once more. He was here for a reason. He just needed to find what that reason was. He looked closely as they passed over the land but didn't see anything other than rocks and trees and water—until there! On a rocky outcropping jutting up from the ground. Those rounded bumps weren't natural. They were buildings. He changed course and headed straight for them.

A6-G2 brought the ship down next to the edge of the settlement. A handful of homes, all made of stone and what looked like scavenged ship parts, were resting in the center of the outcropping, balanced on top of the rock without disturbing or digging into it. The homes were crudely fashioned, functional without being elaborate, and other than the ship parts, they didn't appear to have any technology at all.

They were also *old*. And as far as Obi-Wan could tell, entirely abandoned.

It wasn't looking promising. But maybe there were clues. Obi-Wan left the ship, but paused halfway down the boarding ramp. Something was . . . wrong.

No. Not quite that. But something was definitely off, even though he couldn't identify what was making him feel that way. He quickly double-checked A6-G2's readings to make sure the air was actually safe for him to breathe. After all, the droid had missed an entire asteroid field. Obi-Wan probably wasn't wise to take her word on everything.

There was definitely a tightness in his chest. Now that he was outside and holding still, he could almost pinpoint a noise. Or not quite a noise. It felt like a humming just beyond the range of his ears. But his own readings confirmed what Aces had reported: the air was perfectly suited to his body's needs.

There were other things that could affect him, though. Magnetic fields, solar discharge, a thousand known and unknown threats that, as a Padawan, he had never encountered. "Are your sensors picking up anything, Aces?"

A6-G2 rolled down the ramp, beeping in the negative.

"In that case, please check the damage to the ship and see if there's anything dire that needs to be fixed. And take a crack at that beacon so we can find out what it was transmitting. And if your sensors do pick up anything unusual, let me know. I'd rather not die here and leave you all alone. You'd be so lonesome without me."

Obi-Wan needed to brush up on his binary, because he thought he detected a faint hint of sarcasm in the astromech's agreement.

Leaving A6-G2 to her work, Obi-Wan approached the

village. The rock underfoot was uneven, the same pillared formation as the other rock formations he had flown past. The rocks themselves were near perfect hexagons, and Obi-Wan marveled at them. How could nature craft something so precise, so geometrically wonderful?

The way the rock pillars soared at the highest part of the outcropping reminded him of the Jedi Temple. Maybe there were rocks like this on other planets and the great architects of the Temple had taken their inspiration from them. Obi-Wan didn't want to think about the Temple, though, and what would be waiting for him when he got back. Or what wouldn't, depending.

"Hello?" he called out, hoping to see a head pop out of one of the vacant, yawning doorways. A rush of overjoyed villagers. Even a rock thrown at him with a demand to leave them alone. Anything, really. But he was greeted only with silence. He peered into the nearest dwelling. It was simple, neat, and stripped clean of anything that indicated someone had ever lived there. All the dwellings were the same. Whoever left hadn't left in a hurry. They'd packed. Or their homes had been cleaned out afterward. Either way, there was nothing to discover, no hint of panic or violence or even, luckily, sickness. No clues as to what had happened.

Obi-Wan stood in the center, deflated. He'd flown over a good portion of the land, and this was the only evidence of settlement he'd seen. If there were a large city somewhere, surely the ship's scan would have picked it up. There were no transmissions, no other ships, nothing. What purpose could he possibly serve by being here when there was clearly no one to help and nothing to discover? The planet was beautiful, yes, but hardly crucial to the Republic. Though the planet appeared capable of sustaining life, it was too far from the Core Worlds and even the more settled parts of the Outer Rim to be a viable settlement option. To say nothing of that asteroid field deterrent. And Obi-Wan didn't have weeks to devote to studying the local flora and fauna.

So if there were no inhabitants and no indication that there was anything valuable on the planet . . . perhaps the reason Orla the Wayseeker had never updated her notation to study it further was because there was absolutely no reason to. Maybe she had come here, shrugged, and left again. Maybe it was only on the wall at the Temple as a test. Maybe Obi-Wan was the most recent in a long line of foolish Padawans to come here and discover *nothing* because he wasn't connected enough to the Force to sense the foolishness of this errand.

Maybe Orla the Wayseeker had a mean sense of humor, or a reputation for teaching curious but struggling Padawans hard lessons. This was what came of not completing his research before jumping into a task.

The planet was just a planet, and Obi-Wan had defied

his master and been disobedient to the entire Jedi Order for *nothing*.

He made his way back and sat, dejected, next to the shuttle. A6-G2 beeped to let him know the minor damage would be repaired within the hour, and then they could be on their way.

Back to Coruscant. Back to the Temple, where Obi-Wan might not even have a home anymore. He tried to imagine the worst possible outcome: arriving at the hangar and being shouted at by Qui-Gon? No. He couldn't imagine Qui-Gon shouting, and it wouldn't be the worst thing. The worst would be enduring Qui-Gon's quiet disappointment as he took Obi-Wan before the Council. Or going back and finding Qui-Gon wasn't there at all, his name already added to the Lost, the Temple Guard ready to arrest Obi-Wan for theft of Temple property and betrayal of the entire Order. He knew they wouldn't do that—it wasn't the Jedi way—but he could still imagine it. In a way it felt more comforting than picturing Yoda's ears falling as he shook his head and muttered, "Worthy, he is not."

But was that really the worst that could happen? Obi-Wan knew in his heart it wasn't. The scenario that made it hard to catch his breath, that felt like a weight on his chest, would be arriving home and discovering that absolutely no one had noticed or cared that he was gone. Having so little importance in the Order, so little presence in the Force, that he was neither missed nor even thought of when absent.

He vowed not to die out here. He hadn't even brought a homing beacon with him, since that was something Qui-Gon would have packed, had he bothered to show up. If anything happened to Obi-Wan, no one would ever know.

The Jedi were his only family, the Temple his only home. They would continue on as they always had, whether he returned or not. After all, Padawan deaths were rare but not unheard of. It wouldn't affect things in any significant way if he was lost to space, or eaten by something, or otherwise failed to reappear.

The Jedi Order would be fine without him. But . . . who was *he* without *them*?

A6-G2 beeped. The ship was safe to fly back, though he'd still have to explain the damage to Meba, assuming he wasn't immediately taken before the Council. But he'd do his best to make sure Meba knew to check A6-G2's programming and see if she maybe needed some updates for detecting little things like an entire section of space teeming with death.

"I guess you can check the beacon on the flight back. No reason to stick around here." Obi-Wan stood with a sigh, brushing off his robes. That off feeling, not like he was dizzy but like he was *about* to be dizzy—Obi-Wan couldn't think of it in a way that made sense—was still there. There was definitely something strange about the planet. But maybe it was just his desperate wish for something to justify his trip. He couldn't even muster the will to explore the forest, teeming with green life, at the base of this rocky outcropping. What was the point?

"All right, Aces. Let's go—" Obi-Wan's tongue tripped over the word *home*. Was it? Would it still be?

A sharp whistle sounded behind him. Obi-Wan sensed movement nearby. He whirled around, lightsaber off but in hand, in case whatever animal he was about to encounter wasn't friendly.

But it wasn't an animal at all.

Standing at the base of the rocks, in the dappled shadows of the trees, was a girl. Her skin was pale violet, dotted with white freckles, and her hair was pure white, as well. She wore clothes both too large and too small, her tunic two tunics fashioned together into one, her boots tied on with strips of cloth. She looked somewhere around his own age, and he found himself smiling in response to the brilliant wide smile she offered him.

"Hello, there," Obi-Wan said, raising a hand in greeting.

The girl raised her hand, too. And then she gestured, and someone snatched Obi-Wan's lightsaber out of his hand, leaping over him with an impossibly high twist and flip to land side by side with the girl. The thief passed the girl the lightsaber and disappeared into the trees.

10

Obi-Wan stared down at his empty hand. The hand that had been holding his lightsaber. *His* lightsaber, his sacred Jedi weapon, powered by the kyber crystal he had struggled to earn, hand-assembled under the genuine risk that it might explode and kill him. His lightsaber, which was now in the hands of a mysterious girl in the forest.

Perhaps this planet was not such a dead end, after all.

"That's mine, and I'll be taking it back," Obi-Wan called.

The girl ran into the forest, her laughter trailing behind her.

"Blast," Obi-Wan muttered. A lightsaber should be an extension of a Jedi, and his extension was extending much too far beyond his reach. "Stay here," he shouted to A6-G2 as he raced after the girl. He leaped off the rocks, using the Force to enhance his jump, too worried to even feel the thrill of flying through the air. As he landed in the trees, nearly on top of the girl, the temperature dropped several degrees, the shade near total. This stretch of forest floor was carpeted in bold blue moss and the occasional bright blue sprout of plants that looked like drink pitchers. They waved gently in the breeze, furling and unfurling delicate antenna-like leaves.

All the leaves curled in immediately as the girl switched directions, racing through the trees and away from Obi-Wan. He reached with the Force to pull his lightsaber back. Almost as though she sensed it, she switched directions once more, then leaped into the air impossibly high, clearing an outcropping of rocks without struggle.

Unless she was some previously unknown species—though Obi-Wan thought she looked Mikkian—that type of leap was impossible. Impossible, that was, without using the Force. But what was a Force-sensitive girl doing on this empty planet? And why was she running away from him? And how was she so annoyingly fast?

"I just want to talk!" Obi-Wan shouted, still chasing her, nearly caught up after his own rather impressive leap. "And retrieve my personal property!"

He lunged, almost touching her shoulder. With another laugh, she pushed off the trunk of a tree, flipping up above the canopy. Who *was* this girl?

The trees beneath her groaned, their silvery trunks shivering. And then they began to sway dangerously, as though there were a monstrous storm blowing through. But there was only a sweet-scented light breeze. The movement made it easy for Obi-Wan to follow her trail from the ground. He could see where she was, but she couldn't see him. He raced through the trunks, dodging and twisting, not unlike he had in the asteroid field, although luckily these trees stayed rooted in the ground. Obi-Wan leaped over the pitcher plants, both to avoid damaging them and also to be careful about coming in contact with any unfamiliar local flora. The delicate leaves seemed to reach out for him, fluttering as though waving hello.

The plants on this planet were strange indeed, and Obi-Wan wondered if they had some sort of sentience. Or maybe they were connected to the girl. They certainly seemed to react to her. Either way, he would have to catch her to get the answers he wanted. Not to mention his precious property.

Up ahead, he saw a clearing large enough that the girl, no matter how good she was, wouldn't be able to leap over it. Watching her progress based on the tree agitation, he timed it and gave one last furious burst of speed. Just as she flew free of the treetops, he jumped into the clearing, tackling her to the ground. His lightsaber rolled free and he grabbed it. Relief washed over him to have it back in his hand.

He popped onto his feet and turned to face the girl. "I don't believe we've been introduced." He was winded but keeping a much firmer grip on his weapon as he looked over his shoulder for her thief friend. "I'm Obi-Wan Kenobi, and you are . . . ?"

She stood, still smiling. Up this close, he could see that she didn't have hair so much as a dozen waving tendrils extending from her head. Definitely Mikkian, so not known for extreme strength or jumping abilities. She *had* been using the Force. Hadn't she?

He *also* saw what he had been too focused on her to sense, as half a dozen other beings appeared from the trees, surrounding him. Including the one who had stolen his lightsaber to begin with, who was wearing a hooded cloak that hid their features.

Obi-Wan sighed. "And you are not alone." The others appeared to be more or less the same age as him, all dressed in the same bizarre, haphazard fashion as his thieves. They were a mix of species, some he recognized and some he didn't. And they all eyed him with a combination of wild curiosity and tense wariness.

"Welcome to Lenahra," the girl said. "We—" Her head tendrils stilled, and she turned to her left. Obi-Wan looked that way, but all he saw were the trees they had come through.

A boy—taller than both Obi-Wan and the girl but the same species as her, skin green tinged with shadows of blue—nodded. "I feel it, too. Back to camp!" he called. Half the group was already moving, as though Obi-Wan no longer mattered to them. What was alarming them?

Obi-Wan felt it before he heard it: a trembling of the ground beneath them. Like frenzied footsteps coming toward them. Very *large* footsteps.

"You have to move fast," the girl said, running forward and taking his hand to tug him along. "You can't stay in one place. Otherwise it figures out where you are."

"What's *it*?" Obi-Wan demanded, running alongside her. Judging by the speed of everyone around them, whatever was coming was not something they wanted to meet. Which made Obi-Wan certain he didn't want to meet it, either.

"Lenahra, silly."

"The planet figures out where you are?" Obi-Wan asked, aghast.

"Jump!" The girl pushed off a rock, leaping high over a hole that suddenly dropped out under them, the ground falling away as though someone had tugged on it from beneath. Obi-Wan barely had time to get enough footing to propel himself through the air after her. The other teens around them sailed easily over the gap.

Unless gravity worked differently on Lenahra, and Obi-Wan was fairly certain it didn't, every single one of these feral-looking forest teens was jumping farther, higher, and faster than was possible without Force assistance.

"Are you all Jedi?" he gasped after landing and rolling on the other side of the ravine.

The girl looked at him, her head tendrils rising and moving as though affected by the same wind Obi-Wan couldn't feel in the trees. "What's a Jedi?" she asked. "Mind the gobbler." She pointed calmly past him.

Obi-Wan turned to find himself face to gaping maw with a creature that seemed to be made entirely of teeth.

CHAPTER

11

Obi-Wan *did* mind the gobbler. He minded it very much. He jumped and rolled as fast and as far away from those teeth as possible. To both his relief and confusion, it didn't follow him, chasing after a pair of teens who were farther away, instead.

"We should help them!" he said, but the girl tugged on his hand once more.

"They'll be fine. Keep moving. An avalanche is coming."

"Avalanche? But there's no mountain here, so—"

Once again the ground rumbled, but this time it was clear there was more than a single creature coming. Obi-Wan glanced behind them to see a flood of what could only be described as living rocks. The rocks gleamed and glittered in the sun, opalescent and beautiful and approaching very, very rapidly.

Obi-Wan ran. He leaped over surprise canyons and gorges, dodged swipes of tree branches, changed direction constantly to confuse their pursuers and keep up with the girl. Meanwhile, the land around them passed in a blur of menace and threat. How could such a beautiful place be so hostile? It wasn't just the animals. The trees, the rocks, even the ground itself seemed to conspire against them.

"Up ahead!" the girl shouted, pointing. A huge outcropping of rock, old and weathered and cracked, loomed over the surrounding forest like a ship that had run aground. As they got closer, Obi-Wan realized that was exactly what it was—a great behemoth of a ship, jutting up from the land. It had blended well enough with the landscape that he hadn't noticed it from the air.

The girl whistled sharply, and several metal cables snaked down. She grabbed one, then held out her hand. Obi-Wan took it, and they were cranked upward, the motion jerky and filled with worryingly fast starts and sudden stops. The others materialized around them, grabbing their own cables and speeding away from the ground. The rocks chasing them slammed into the side of the ship, then stilled. They unrolled, revealing many-legged, big-eyed, surprisingly furry little creatures beneath the rock-shell exteriors. With noises like a grumbling stomach, the animals ambled away.

"Why were they trying to get us?" Obi-Wan asked.

The girl shrugged. "Lenahra," she said, as though that were a complete sentence and required no further explanation.

They arrived at their destination: a platform extending from the side of the ship at a precarious angle. It opened to an interior space. Obi-Wan followed the girl's lead as she jumped off the cable and walked inside the ship. To his surprise, the people controlling the cables and waiting to greet them were several younglings, smaller than the gang from the forest. They stared at him, wide-eyed and scared.

"You brought something back from the trees?" one tiny pink Twi'lek demanded, backing away warily, never taking her eyes off Obi-Wan.

"Relax," the thief said, patting the head of the nearest youngling, an Iktotchi so young his side horns had barely grown past his chin. "He's not from here. He's from off-world."

The little Iktotchi scoffed. "There's no such thing as off-world."

"I assure you there is," Obi-Wan said.

"Sky trash," the male counterpart to Obi-Wan's thief grumbled. "Like when you're done with your supper and you toss the rest over the side of the ship. That's what the sky did with him. Tossed him down onto Lenahra to be eaten by scavengers. We saved him, though."

"Ouch!" Obi-Wan slapped his hand over the side of his head where the little Iktotchi had tugged hard on his Padawan braid.

"What is that? What does it do?" he asked.

"Do?"

"Yeah, does it hear? Or sense things, like my ears or Audj and Casul's tendrils? It can't keep you warm. It's too small."

"No, it doesn't do any of those things. It's symbolic."

"What does that mean?" the little Twi'lek asked, frowning.

"It means . . . it shows my status? Among my people?"

The grabby youngling wrinkled his nose. "I don't like it."

"Thank you for your unsolicited opinion," Obi-Wan said, unsure how to respond. But then again, he didn't know how to respond to anything here.

It was an odd scene. The floor slanted to a mildly alarming degree. Anything that wasn't bolted down had long since rolled or slid to the far wall, which was lined with hammocks. Obi-Wan wanted to shoo the little younglings away so he could speak to the girl he had followed here. He turned around as the final three teens leaped into the room, sailing across the floor to land right in front of Obi-Wan.

"Who *are* you?" Obi-Wan asked, watching in amazement.

"Who are *you*?" said a pale hairless girl with skin cracked like parched desert ground, sidling to get far away from him without ever showing her back. She hit the far wall and stepped behind a hammock as though it offered cover. "We thought you were one of them, coming back. But you're not."

"Who's 'them'?" Obi-Wan asked.

"I'm Audj Seedol," the thief said, reaching into a container and pulling out a spiky bright-magenta piece of fruit. She tipped her chin toward the green version of herself. "That's my brother, Casul." He grunted in acknowledgment, busy examining the winches that moved the cables up and down, trying to see where they were catching. Audj continued down the line of teens. "Nesguin," she said, and an older Iktotchi, his skin a mix of pinks and browns and his horns down to his shoulders, raised a hand. "Mem." She pointed to the girl glaring at him from her hammock cover. "Shush." A Nautolan not unlike the Jedi Kit Fisto, but with a sickly cast to her pale green skin, regarded him impassively with her huge black eyes before she slipped under the water in a large barrel. "And Zae-Brii." Zae-Brii had leathery skin, a long, thin mouth, and yellow eyes that blinked thoughtfully at Obi-Wan. "They're the one who saw you fly over," Audj added. "We're debating whether that means they have dibs on your ship if you die."

"If I'd had the dibs, I would have left you to be eaten by the gobbler," Casul said with an indifferent shrug.

"But he's the first new person we've seen in . . ." Nesguin's voice trailed off, and he frowned. "How long has it been?"

Audj spoke hurriedly, changing the subject. "So if you agree, Zae-Brii gets your ship if you die."

"I would very much like to avoid that scenario," Obi-Wan said. "Is this *your* ship?"

Audj shrugged. "Yes. Though *ship* is a generous term."

"More like shipwreck," Zae-Brii said. Then, with a blurring twist of their face, Obi-Wan was staring at himself. "Haven't had a new face to try on in a long time. I forget how weird it feels." They twisted Obi-Wan's features, making exaggerated expressions. Obi-Wan really didn't think his face was capable of some of the things the changeling was making it do, but then again, the Temple didn't have a lot of mirrors. Perhaps he looked this bizarre all the time and no one had bothered telling him.

That couldn't be true, though. Bolla would definitely have told him.

The changeling touched a hand to the top of their head and then went back to their own form, which was something of a relief. Obi-Wan didn't want to look at himself anymore. It was terribly unnerving. Zae-Brii's eyes narrowed thoughtfully. "Why do you have so much hair on top and none elsewhere? It makes no sense."

"When did you crash here?" Obi-Wan asked, ignoring the question about his hair and also lack thereof.

Casul was passing out fruit to the children. "Not our parents, not their parents, but their parents."

"Four generations? You've been here this whole time? But where are the adults?"

Casul threw a piece of fruit to him with more strength than was strictly necessary. Obi-Wan nearly dropped it in surprise, his palms stinging. Was Casul using the Force? Surely, he had to be.

"They left us," Casul said, as casually as Obi-Wan might have informed someone Qui-Gon was meditating.

"They *left* you?" Obi-Wan demanded, aghast. "Is that who you thought I was, coming back?"

Audj laughed. "You should see your face right now. Zae-Brii, show him his face."

Zae-Brii obliged, and Obi-Wan didn't appreciate it. "I do *not* look that shocked. And my mouth was almost certainly closed, not hanging slack-jawed like that."

"If you say so." Zae-Brii went back to their own face with a dismissive blink.

Mem peered over the edge of her hammock, watching Obi-Wan's every movement as though afraid he was going to attack at any moment. Given what he had experienced in just a little time on this planet, anticipating attack was probably a reasonable default mode.

"Anyway, it doesn't matter that they're gone," Audj said. "We're doing fine on our own. We've been on our own for so long. Until you! Where did you come from? We never had stories about others coming from the sky. Only our people."

"I'm from . . . far away," Obi-Wan answered, distracted as he watched the younglings finish eating and then begin an elaborate game of keep-away with the last piece of fruit. Was he imagining things, or did they all seem to be more coordinated than normal, leaping and twisting and flipping through the air in ways he had seen only among Temple younglings?

"Good," Casul said, coaching them. "Now, go faster." The younglings obliged with giggles.

"How can you do that?" Obi-Wan demanded. "Who trained you?" Surely it was the Force. He could think of no other explanation.

Casul cut a sharp look at him. "*We* trained them. And we trained ourselves, too. It's the only way to survive."

Obi-Wan's head was spinning. "I don't understand how it's possible." How was this entire group of younglings and teens so adept in the Force? Was there a connection to Orla Jareni? But what would that connection be? If she'd made it here, it would have been decades before their people crashed.

Maybe their ship had been filled with Force adepts on their way to the Temple. Or maybe Orla had established some sort of Jedi outpost that had since fallen, leaving only these few young people behind. But if that were true, why wouldn't Orla's archive record note something so important? And why didn't Audj even know what a Jedi was?

And why, with so many Force users around him, could Obi-Wan not sense them the way he could sense Master Qui-Gon or the other Padawans? And *what* was that terrible low humming just outside his hearing that he could feel in his teeth?

It was apparent that his trip here had not been futile, after all. But whatever he had thought he might find, this was not it. And he had no idea what to do now that he had found it.

———

"Does he ever stop talking?" The tiny Twi'lek, Amyt, yawned as she brushed her friend's fur. He was one of two nearly identical younglings named Jarper and Tumber, both with button noses, long ears trailing down their backs, and full-body mottled brown-and-gray fur.

"And you're certain you've never heard of Orla? Or Jedi?" Obi-Wan paced. "When exactly did your people arrive here?"

"Our ancestors were on a settlement ship," Zae-Brii said with a long-suffering roll of their eyes. "It crashed here, and we settled. Orla and Jedi aren't in any of our songs or stories."

So what was the connection? How were they using the Force? And why wasn't anyone here in charge and capable of answering his questions? "But where exactly did the adults go?"

"They *left*," Audj said, and this time her voice had an edge like gritted teeth. She flashed her eyes at Obi-Wan in warning, then nodded toward the younglings. "But it's fine, because we're happy, and safe, and we take care of each other."

"Right. Of course." Obi-Wan grimaced apologetically at her. Not good to upset the younglings. And Audj was right. They all looked fine. Healthy and happy. They had clearly done the best they could with what they had to work with, all wearing a mismatched assortment of old clothes, but everyone was clean and no one appeared to be starving.

"Why do you live in the ship instead of at the old village?"

"The ship is the safest place for us. Lenahra has tried taking it apart and swallowing it, but it's too old and did too much damage to the ground when it crashed. Every once in a while we get a good shake, but the ship's big enough to withstand it. And gobblers, avalanches, and the others can't get up here."

"The *others*? There are more?"

Audj laughed. "There are always more. For example, there's a beautiful pool that's a short, pleasant walk through killer trees from here. Shush, Trill, and Whistle"—Audj pointed to the barrels that held the older Nautolan and the two little ones, whose names were not actually Shush, Trill, and Whistle, but rather those *sounds*—"would love nothing more than to be able to live there so they wouldn't have to spend most of the day sitting in the tubs we use to collect rainwater. But if you set so much as a foot in those pools . . ." Audj clapped her hands together in a terrible imitation of something Obi-Wan did not want to meet. "You wouldn't have a foot anymore. And we like having our feet."

Shush nodded solemnly, her large pure-black eyes fixed on Obi-Wan.

"I have a breather in my ship," Obi-Wan offered. "It can be calibrated to gills. That might help, or at least make daily life more comfortable." Kit Fisto didn't use one, but he was also remarkably strong. Obi-Wan didn't know much about Nautolan younglings, since they were all raised underwater. Maybe they needed to stay submerged until they developed enough to go between water and dry land.

"Really?" Audj's face warmed, her violet skin going pinkish with happiness. "That would be wonderful."

Obi-Wan resumed pacing. "It's a temporary fix, of course. I'm trying to figure out how to get you to safety. I don't have room for all of you on my ship, and no way to send word back to Coruscant. It's not exactly an easy trip back and forth, what with that asteroid field. I suppose I could take you in shifts to the nearest—"

"Take us?" Casul asked.

"Yes. Get you off this terrible planet." That had to be why he was here. To save them, and to take them back to the Temple so the Council could assess their abilities.

"Who says we want to leave?" Casul stood, looming over Obi-Wan and glaring down at him. "We're the ones who *stayed*. Our families died so we could."

"Wait—died?" Obi-Wan shook his head in surprise. "You said the adults all left!"

"The other ones did. Our parents stayed, kept us here. We're not going anywhere. But you can leave any time you want, sky trash." He pointed at the gaping hole leading out.

"But—" Obi-Wan hadn't been expecting that. He wanted to ask more about what had happened to their parents, but it hardly seemed like the right moment.

It was odd, too, that none of them had asked more about where he came from. He would have thought they'd be curious. But Audj, especially, seemed to interrupt any inquiry along those lines, redirecting it. Perhaps he had violated some cultural taboo by even mentioning life off-planet. Casul, at least, seemed very intense about their place here. Which was no wonder, given the trauma they had been through, being abandoned by their people and then losing their parents, too.

He'd thought they would want his help—be grateful for it, even. Look to him as a leader, a rescuer. The way he hoped to be as a Jedi Knight. And even though a sixteen-year-old Padawan was far more mature than average, having trained his whole life, they didn't know that. They looked at him and saw someone the same age as themselves. Of course they wouldn't view him as an authority, or someone who could save them.

And if they were the only people here and had no need of his help, then maybe the Force hadn't led him here. It really had been all him. Trying too hard, once again. Only this time, his trying broke the rules. No one here needed—or wanted—him, and no one back at the Temple would after this, either.

But this couldn't be it. There had to be something else. There *was* still the mystery of how everyone here could use the Force, and why Orla had marked this planet. Surely that was worth sticking around to investigate. Surely the Force could have guided him here for that.

Obi-Wan knew he was stalling. That he should go back, inform the Council of what he had done, and let them deal with him as they saw fit. But if this was to be his only chance to do good in the galaxy before losing his place at Qui-Gon Jinn's side and facing whatever unknown future awaited him afterward, then he was going to see it through.

To whatever end. He wasn't ready yet to give up the hope, however slim, that there was something here for him to accomplish. That he could still be of some use to the Jedi, or the young ones here. Or to anyone, anywhere.

It had been such a long time since Obi-Wan was around new people. Obviously he met Jedi he hadn't known before, but not that often. Besides which, they were always Jedi, so he knew how to act around them and what to expect.

This was something totally different. There were six younglings. Amyt, the Twi'lek girl; Gremac, the Iktotchi who glared at Obi-Wan's braid with startling animosity; Jarper and Tumber, who barely seemed to need the Force to jump absurd distances; and then the two aquatic younglings, Trill and Whistle, currently sitting together in a barrel filled with water, with only their eyes peering out.

Shush caught him staring. "Our younglings aren't meant to be out of the water," she said. "Their lungs don't develop as fast as their gills, and their skin and eyes are too sensitive to light. They're meant to be deep beneath the waves until they're older."

"But you grow out of it?"

Shush's smile was tight, her eyes steady on the little ones. "I can handle the pain. I don't ask them to."

"There's no way for you to live in the water? I saw so much of it flying in. Surely there's some pool somewhere that's safe enough."

Shush shook her head. "This is the best life we can give them."

"But—it's not. Even if no one else wants to leave, I could take you three. There are so many places in the galaxy where you could live. I know a Jedi who is—"

"No," Shush said, cutting him off. "We have to stay together. It would break my heart to leave my family." She looked at the others, making it clear that it wasn't just Trill and Whistle she considered family. "Besides, how do we know anywhere is better than here?"

"Because I've been other places, and—"

"And you came here." Shush's black eyes were filmed over with her first set of translucent eyelids, but she still looked sad and a little scared. "The Power protects us."

Before Obi-Wan could ask her who or what the Power was, she retreated to the barrels and slipped into hers next to the two younglings.

Trill and Whistle watched as the rest of the younglings chased each other around the living floor of the ship, occasionally joined by the older Lenahrans. Obi-Wan didn't have a better name for them than that. It was the only thing that unified them: living together on this planet that didn't want them.

Aside from Audj, Casul, Zae-Brii, and Shush, there was the older Iktotchi named Nesguin and Mem, white and silent as a bleached rock, who still tracked Obi-Wan everywhere he went.

Amyt stomped one pink foot, glaring at Audj. "Why didn't you take me when you went out? I could have helped bring back the sky trash, and picked fruit, too."

"The sky trash has a name. And you're not old enough to go out with us yet," Audj answered, busy mending a shirt.

"I am, too! I can jump as high as you!"

"It doesn't matter how high you can jump. When you're as tall as I am, then you'll get to go out with us. Until then, you have to keep practicing so you're ready. Maybe you'll take over for me."

The little Twi'lek girl scowled. "I don't want your job. Your job is boring. I want to be like Casul. He does exciting things and teaches us how to use the Power and doesn't ever have to take care of the younglings." She glanced derisively at her fellow younglings, most of whom were her size.

Casul smirked, in the corner. "It's true, Audj. You're pretty boring."

"Oh, am I?" Audj flicked her wrist, throwing a particularly mushy piece of bright-orange fruit against the side of Casul's face.

Casul wiped the pulp away, then licked the juice off his hand. "They're old enough to go for runs. It would be good for them."

"Not until we're sure they can keep themselves safe." Audj's sharp tone brooked no argument. Casul shrugged apologetically at little Amyt, who skulked off into the corner.

Even though no one here had parents, it was clear they were a family. It made Obi-Wan miss the closeness of his own youngling initiate clan.

No wonder he felt a little lost, and more than a little alone. After they had passed their trials, they separated, assigned to different Jedi. He had lost his clan, his Padawan friends were all busy, and the most important bond he had was supposed to be with a Jedi who couldn't even bother to show up when he promised he would. A Jedi who had never wanted to train him in the first place.

"Lids are going on soon!" Zae-Brii shouted. Obi-Wan had no idea what that meant. Zae-Brii chased various younglings around, helping them wash faces and brush teeth. Gremac grumbled extensively about having to polish his horns.

"You don't want to get horn rot, do you?" Zae-Brii chided.

"That's not real!" he shouted.

"Oh, it absolutely is. Your horns will rot, and rockmites will burrow in and set up a nest. Isn't that right, Obi-Wan?"

Obi-Wan blinked in surprise. "Oh, yes. It's a hopeless

situation for a warrior like yourself, once rockmites settle in. All you are then is living quarters, and they're terrible tenants. Always making too much noise and keeping you up at night, never cleaning up after themselves. Not to mention the noise of them chewing, chewing, chewing away on your horns."

Gremac's eyes went wide, and he grabbed the coarse-bristled brush from Zae-Brii, getting to work. Even Nesguin looked mildly alarmed, snatching the brush from Gremac as soon as he was done.

Zae-Brii winked at Obi-Wan. He smiled back. It was a strange living arrangement, certainly. Chaotic, but not unhealthy. Obi-Wan wanted to keep talking to Audj and the others to figure out how they could use the Force, but according to them they had no idea what he was talking about. Besides which, they were busy getting the younglings ready for sleep. It was a little baffling and almost insulting how little impact Obi-Wan's presence had on their routine.

"Sing us the song!" Trill said, in the barrel she shared with Whistle.

"Only when everyone's where they're supposed to be," Audj said, her voice firm.

"We're always where we're supposed to be," Whistle grumbled, dipping her face below the water.

"I know you are." Audj reached in and patted her head, stroking one of the long tentacle-like tendrils that went down to Whistle's shoulders. "You're wonderful examples." The rest of the younglings scrambled to get into their hammocks, and then Audj began to sing. Her voice was soft but carried well through the echoing space, tucking in all around them.

> *"Out in the stars they gathered,*
> *Hoping with joy and delight.*
> *Out in the stars they gathered,*
> *Flying straight through the night.*
> *Then from the sky they fell,*
> *Down to a planet so green.*
> *Then from the sky they fell,*
> *Down to a planet—"*

All the younglings shouted, "So mean!" in unison, giggling. Audj continued.

> *"All they had was each other*
> *To hold against death and fear.*
> *All they had was each other.*
> *They held to what was most dear.*
> *Our family and the Power,*
> *Our friends and our ship and our home.*
> *Our family and the Power,*
> *And always it is our own."*

Mem and Zae-Brii went to the hammocks, touching each youngling on the forehead. "Don't forget," they murmured. "This is ours."

"What does that mean?" Obi-Wan whispered to Casul.

Casul shrugged. "It's what our parents sang to us, what they told us every night. So now we tell it to the younglings."

Obi-Wan wondered about their history, about the isolated culture that had developed here. How strange it was that they were so proud and protective of a planet that seemed actively miserable, how uncurious they were about what lay beyond it. It was clear that Audj and the others were still busy with their night preparations, so Obi-Wan settled on the floor for his own nighttime routine. He put his palms on his knees, closed his eyes, took a deep breath, and—

"What are you doing?" Audj asked.

Obi-Wan cracked an eye open. "I was going to meditate." He did it every night before bed, even though he hated it and it never helped.

"Is that how you sleep?" asked Jarper—or Tumber; Obi-Wan really couldn't tell—one long ear drooping over the edge of the hammock.

"No, it's not sleeping. It's—well, it's a way for me to connect with the Force. In theory. I don't have much luck with it lately."

Audj frowned, sitting across from him, one knee up and

the other leg splayed straight out. "The Force is the Power, right? That's why you could keep up with us instead of being eaten in the forest."

"Yes, that's—Wait, if you didn't know I could keep up with you, why did you lure me into the trees? I could have died, for all you knew!"

Audj gave him a sheepish grin. "Well, if you couldn't have kept up, you were going to die anyway. And I wanted to know what that was." She gestured to his lightsaber. "And what you were. We were curious. Maybe a little scared, too. We haven't met anyone new, well, ever. We're used to things trying to kill us, so once we saw you weren't someone coming back, we had to be sure you weren't another trick of Lenahra. A new way to try and catch us off guard and smash us to pieces."

"I suppose that's fair." Obi-Wan couldn't possibly understand the way they had grown up. No wonder Mem still seemed terrified of him. And maybe that was why they hadn't asked about where he came from. They still didn't entirely trust that he wasn't going to hurt them.

Audj frowned, gesturing at his seated position. "But why would you need to connect with the Power? What does that even mean? You just *use* it."

"I wish it were that simple for me." It certainly seemed to be that simple for the other Padawans. "I try to connect with it so that I can listen, and be guided to what I should be doing."

"It talks to you?" Her eyes widened dubiously, and she shared a concerned glance with her brother. Her voice got lower, more careful and deliberate. "What does it say?"

Obi-Wan laughed. "It doesn't *say* anything. It's not like that. If I can clear my mind and reach out to the Force, then I can get feelings. Impressions. I can sense things."

"Oh, so like our tendrils." Audj gestured to her head tendrils, which Zae-Brii was carefully wrapping in a soft cloth for the night. Obi-Wan assumed they were sensitive and wouldn't be comfortable against the rough material of their hammocks.

"No. Well, maybe? What do your tendrils sense?"

"Movement. Heat. Things like that."

"Not exactly like that, no. All your kind have those."

Casul's gaze darkened. "We wouldn't know."

"Right. Sorry. I left my family at a young age, too, but I had people to teach me."

"Don't need them. We taught ourselves." Casul cuffed Audj affectionately on the shoulder, then nodded good night to Zae-Brii and retired to a large hammock in the corner. Zae-Brii sat next to Audj, and Audj leaned her head on their shoulder.

"So your Force is like the Power, plus my head tendrils, but also not." Audj's expression was dubious. She was humoring him, he could tell.

"The Force is more than just *physically* sensing things. It can help you sense moods, calm emotions, connect with—well, almost anything." Obi-Wan was struggling to explain. He knew the Jedi explanations by heart, but those were memorization. Rote learning. Personally, he still felt like he didn't truly *understand* the Force. Sure, he could push and pull, jump, and sense threats with the best of them. But when it came to the other aspects of the Force—communing with it, not using it as an extension of himself, like a lightsaber to be wielded, but getting to the point where *he* was an extension of the Force—well, maybe that was why Qui-Gon didn't bother with him. Why Qui-Gon apparently hadn't even wanted him in the first place.

Obi-Wan scowled, drawing his knees up. Who was he kidding? He couldn't explain the Force to anyone, because he couldn't figure out what it was to him in the first place.

"The Power exists for us," Audj said, patting his knee. "It helps us survive. It doesn't do anything else."

"It can, though. It should." If Obi-Wan really was destined to be a Jedi Knight, if he really did have a place in the Force, shouldn't it be easy to connect to it? Shouldn't he understand it completely, and effortlessly?

"Where did you get it?" Zae-Brii asked. "You weren't anywhere near the cave."

"Where did I get what?"

"The Power. The Force, or whatever you call it."

Obi-Wan didn't understand the question. "I've always had it. That's why I went to the Jedi Temple."

"So that's like your cave? Is it hard to get the Power from it? Does the Temple try to eat you?"

Obi-Wan laughed, imagining it. "Sometimes I do feel like I've been swallowed whole by it. And it can be difficult, yes. Not everyone makes it through. What is this cave, though? And what you do mean, you *get* the Power? Is there some sort of ceremony?" They were speaking of the Force in a strangely transactional way, and he was afraid there was something he didn't understand. "We go through trials to progress as Jedi. Is that what you're talking about?"

"The cave is—" Zae-Brii started, but Audj stood, cutting them off.

"You should get your ship tomorrow. No telling what Lenahra will do to it, if it's even still there."

"You want me to leave?" Obi-Wan was surprised to find that this stung. Obviously they didn't need him, but at least they could pretend to be interested in the first new person they'd ever met. Was *everyone* in the galaxy ambivalent about him?

And he really did want to try to find a way to help. Even if it was just figuring out a better living situation for Shush, Whistle, and Trill. He could manage that.

Audj looked surprised. "No. I mean you should bring your ship here, where the planet can't eat it. I thought we made it clear when we let you come up: you're welcome. Sounds to me like you didn't have it any better at your temple than we do. And we can always use the extra help. We don't even have to train you." Audj grinned slyly. "Though I would like to race one of these days. See which one of us is best at using the Power."

Obi-Wan laughed. "We're not supposed to be competitive. Everyone uses the Force as best suits their abilities."

"Well, I'm guessing my abilities out-ability your abilities, so." Audj held out a hand to help Zae-Brii up. "Until the morning, Obi-Wan." She and Zae-Brii unhooked glowing seedpods from the walls and put them into containers, then covered them with lids. Suddenly their expression made a lot more sense. "Lids on" meant lights out.

"Where's Amyt?" Jarper—or Tumber—asked. "She's not in her hammock."

"Don't be a gobbler," Tumber snapped. "Keep your mouth closed."

Zae-Brii frowned, grabbing a light pod and rushing to an empty hammock. "She's not here. Everyone, look for Amyt."

Casul rolled out of his hammock with a groan. "I'm going to hold her upside down until her face is purple," he grumbled. But soon their grumbles and annoyance turned to fear and worry. Obi-Wan helped them search the accessible areas of the ship, but there was no sign of the little girl. He walked to the edge and, sure enough, one of the cables was extended.

"Over here," he called, pointing.

"She went down by herself." Zae-Brii's face shimmered reflexively into a copy of Amyt's face, expression horrified. "She'll be dead within the hour."

"Go eat!" Audj shouted.

"This hardly seems the time for a meal," Obi-Wan said, grabbing hold of the cable.

"We'll have to move the harvest up," Casul cautioned, opening a new box. The contents glowed with a soft blue light, similar to their luminescent seedpods. Why were they stopping to eat?

"It doesn't matter!" Audj answered.

Obi-Wan didn't need to wait. He wasn't hungry, and even if he was, that wouldn't take priority over a missing youngling. He grabbed the cable and used the Force to steady himself as he zipped down it and landed on the ground far beneath. He was almost immediately joined by Audj, Casul, Zae-Brii, Nesguin, and Mem.

His stomach roiled, head spinning. He took a staggering step away from them and the ship. That sense of wrongness had picked up, thrumming through him, setting every nerve on edge. "Can you feel that?" he asked.

Audj ripped the cloth away from her head tendrils. "Do you sense her?"

Obi-Wan shook his head, trying to ignore whatever was trying to overwhelm him. The youngling was out there somewhere, alone on this hostile planet, and he would have to use everything he had to find her in time. It was the biggest test he had ever faced, the most important thing he had ever done. Because it was no longer about becoming a Padawan, or finding his kyber crystal. It was about saving a life.

He didn't know if he was ready, but it didn't matter.

"Split up," he said, and raced into the darkness alone.

CHAPTER

13

With every footstep Obi-Wan expected the ground to swallow him, a tree to swing down and smash him, or teeth to claim him. But the forest was quiet, the night warm and soft. Above him, the dome of the sky was glittering indigo, an infinite starry pattern broken only by the occasional breathtaking flash of an asteroid hitting the atmosphere and burning away. The farther he got from the others, the better he felt. In fact, he felt . . . good. Awake and alert and alive in a way he couldn't quite explain. Either the night wasn't as dark as it seemed, or there was something odd about Lenahra—well, something *else* odd about it— because Obi-Wan felt like he could see every branch, every leaf, every plant. The pitcher plants were luminescent, but the sense of what was around him was more than that. Like the forest itself was written on his mind in perfect detail.

Movement drew his attention. He slowed and crept toward it. A gobbler raised its head from where it had been nuzzling a pitcher plant. Obi-Wan lit his lightsaber, waiting. The gobbler, illuminated in the dual blue glow from the saber and the pitcher plant, tilted its head and closed its mouth. Its eyes, when not blocked by its gaping maw, were large and round and reflected the light of the saber back at Obi-Wan. It crouched low, its powerful thick tail swinging back and forth. Obi-Wan braced for attack.

And then he burst out in surprised laughter. Instead of lunging, the gobbler had rolled onto its back, wiggling six stubby legs with large padded feet in the air. Its long black tongue lolled out the side of its enormous toothy mouth, also reflecting Obi-Wan's saber light. Obi-Wan lowered his weapon and saw the gobbler's tongue was still glowing, coated with something from the plant that gave off a soft blue light.

All those teeth were far less threatening when coupled with that silly long tongue. Now that Obi-Wan wasn't braced for attack, he realized he didn't sense any threat from the gobbler. He deactivated his saber and hooked it onto his belt, then put one tentative hand on the gobbler's exposed belly. It kicked three legs in the air, twitching them, and made a low rumbling sound that was all satisfaction and no anger.

"Why were you so vicious before?" Obi-Wan crouched next to the creature and idly scratched its smooth scaled belly while looking around the forest. "Maybe that was a different gobbler."

From his lower vantage point, Obi-Wan noticed that the inside of the pitcher plant was filled with liquid that was the source of its subtle glow. He didn't know whether the plant produced the liquid, or if it merely gathered there. The gobbler must have been drinking it. Perhaps it had a chemical quality that made gobblers, well, *silly*, for lack of a better word.

There was a shout from somewhere in the night—not of alarm or discovery, just communicating position—and the gobbler tensed, flipping back onto its feet and growling softly in that direction.

Obi-Wan had an idea. Many creatures were sensitive to the Force. He knew it academically, and Prie had confirmed it on her missions with her animal-adept Jedi Master. It was his turn to move from knowing something as a concept to simply *knowing* it. Obi-Wan rested a hand on the gobbler's head. He pictured the little Twi'lek in his mind, trying to form a complete image of her, and then he pushed it toward the gobbler. Not a physical push, but a mental and emotional one. Or at least, he hoped he did. He had never tried to do this before, had no idea if he was even capable of it. If only *his* master had given him experiences other than constant meditation.

To Obi-Wan's surprise, the gobbler immediately turned around, looking another direction and growling softly. Obi-Wan followed its gaze. In the distance, he sensed the trees shivering with agitation. Like they had when Audj was in them.

"Thank you, friend." He scratched the gobbler once under its broad flat chin and then ran in the direction it had shown him.

It took longer than he expected to get there, which meant he couldn't possibly have *seen* the movement of the trees. He had simply known where it was. But there was no time to explore why, or question it. Amyt was clinging desperately to one of the smooth silvery trunks as its branches swung wildly to try to knock her off. And surrounding the base of the tree, roiling with menace, was an entire avalanche of the rock creatures.

"Well, that's not good," Obi-Wan said with a sigh. He reached for his lightsaber but paused. The gobbler hadn't harmed him. And these little rock creatures surely couldn't overwhelm him before he could get away from them. Luring them to another part of the forest would give the others time to reach Amyt and get her to safety.

Time to be bait. "Hey!" he shouted. "Over here!"

The avalanche of creatures didn't so much as move in his direction. "Look at my ankles, all smooth and unbroken! Wouldn't you like to smash some bones?" Either his ankles were remarkably unappealing, which he tried not to let hurt his feelings, or the creatures genuinely didn't care about him.

He took several steps toward them. No reaction. Preparing to be swarmed, he stepped right into the middle of them. They parted for his feet, as though they knew where he was going to step before he did it. But other than that, they didn't react to him at all, their focus entirely on the tree and Amyt.

"Curious," Obi-Wan said. This planet made no sense. How could anyone ever live here, not knowing whether it was going to attack or simply ignore them? It was a wonder any of them had survived. A testament to Audj's leadership, he supposed.

He jumped onto the tree, grasping it above the terrified youngling. "What a surprise, running into you out here," he said, smiling at her to let her know it was going to be okay. "Perhaps you shouldn't go off alone at night. Or ever."

She nodded, eyes big and scared. "I wanted to help. I was going to harvest alone."

"That sounds like a group activity to me. Come on. Let's get you home." Obi-Wan gestured and she climbed onto his back, hanging like a pack with her arms around his neck.

Obi-Wan jumped down from the tree—and barely dodged a vicious swipe from a branch. "Pardon me, friends," he said, stepping down into the avalanche. But rather than parting for him, they rolled against his legs with bruising force, nearly knocking him over. "Hey, now!" he shouted. "I thought my ankles weren't worth your time!"

The little rock creatures unfurled, eyes like slits, teeth bared. They began popping up, climbing onto each other with blurring speed. Building up height and momentum . . . to strike him. Obi-Wan decided he was, in fact, very fond of his ankles and their intact bones. All his intact bones, really. He ran, headed for his gobbler friend, hopeful that he might find help there. But as he got near, he heard and felt six legs racing toward him and thought better of it.

"I think perhaps my welcome has worn off, little Amyt." Sure enough, the gobbler pounded through the trees, teeth-first. Obi-Wan leaped across a new sinkhole. He shouted over his shoulder at the gobbler. "You're sending me very mixed messages! We had a connection!"

"Over here!" Audj shouted from somewhere in the night.

"I have her!" Obi-Wan yelled back. "I'm heading for the ship. With a lot of company." The avalanche behind him was picking up speed, rolling around the gobbler's pounding legs. Maybe this was why he hadn't been chosen by Prie's master. Obi-Wan had *definitely* not understood or connected with that creature. How could he have been so wrong about it?

He looked over his shoulder, trying to gauge how close he was to death. It was a mistake. Not because of what was behind him, but because of what he wasn't seeing in front of him. He skidded to a halt as a treacherously steep, narrow canyon gaped ahead. He was certain he had come from this direction. When had a canyon happened?

"Hold on!" someone next to him roared. Casul grabbed him by the waist and threw him over the slot canyon. Obi-Wan landed on the other side, the youngling still cling-ing to his back.

"I could have managed on my own," he said.

"Sure," said Casul, landing beside him with a laugh. As they ran through the night, the others converged on them. Together, they dodged trees and sped ahead of the veritable army of creatures behind them.

Casul whooped with joy as he leaped over a tree crash-ing to the ground in front of them. Even though Obi-Wan was still more than a little worried they were all going to die, he couldn't deny it was thrilling. He had only ever used his Force skills in practice. Using them to jump and dodge and leap, reacting only to the need to survive and the rush of moving without time to question or second-guess every decision? Obi-Wan let out his own whoop of joy, a sound he hadn't even known he was capable of making.

At last they reached the ship, grabbing cables and fly-ing into the air as the creatures slammed against the metal beneath them in a clatter of rocks and a clashing of teeth.

"Not tonight, Lenahra!" Audj shouted. The others yelled in agreement, and even Obi-Wan found himself shouting defiance, the sheer giddy relief of having won the only feel-ing in his heart.

Once they set foot in the ship, Audj grabbed Amyt from Obi-Wan. She squeezed the little one in a hug, whispering both admonishments and comfort in her cone-shaped ears.

But to Obi-Wan's surprise, everyone else gathered around him, hugging him and patting his shoulders. Casul even grabbed him around the waist and twirled him around, laughing.

"To Obi-Wan!" he shouted. "The most powerful sky trash on Lenahra!"

Even though he was far from home and not where he should be, at that moment Obi-Wan couldn't help feeling like he was exactly where he *wanted* to be.

The next morning, Audj, Zae-Brii, Casul, Nesguin, and Mem were preparing to do a food run. Most of the fruit could be harvested only during the day and rotted quickly once picked. Shush couldn't be in the sun for long, so she usually stayed back to watch the younglings. Obi-Wan was trying to disentangle Amyt from his back. She had apparently decided he was her preferred form of transportation.

His comlink beeped, surprising him. "Aces!" he answered, relieved that the droid and his ship still seemed to be in one piece. And feeling slightly guilty that, with all the excitement of the previous night, he hadn't gone back for her yet. "Can you fly the ship to me?"

A6-G2 responded in the negative. She added much more information, but he wasn't fluent enough to catch the details. He'd have to go to the ship and retrieve it himself. "Hold there," he said. "I'll come to you."

He finally managed to peel Amyt off his back, setting her in a high hammock where it would take her a moment to get down. "I can't join you getting food," he said to Audj and the others. They looked genuinely disappointed, but not worried. Which meant they *wanted* him there but didn't need him. He wasn't sure how to feel about that.

Casul clapped him on the shoulder. Obi-Wan suspected his shoulders would soon be black and blue if Casul kept approving of him. "We've done plenty of food runs without you. Go get your ship."

Obi-Wan reached for a cable, then—knowing such an unnecessary use of the Force would be considered excessive, even distasteful, at the Temple—he jumped straight off the ship, savoring the freedom of falling while knowing he would catch himself at the bottom. He hit the ground running, ready to dodge trees, avoid sudden sinkholes, and wrestle with gobblers.

None of which was necessary. After a few minutes he stopped running, eyeing the silver trunks around him. Glittery magenta leaves grew closest to the ground, turning blue and then green toward the top of the canopy. Nothing moved, nothing attacked, nothing looked or felt like a threat.

He couldn't figure out Lenahra. He had thought maybe it was dangerous during the day and docile at night, but that had changed as soon as he had Amyt on his back. Maybe it reacted only to certain stimuli, which he hadn't yet fig- ured out? Perhaps it didn't like groups, but individuals were acceptable.

But then why had Amyt merited aggression? Because she had climbed a tree? The trees clearly didn't like that.

Obi-Wan stepped aside to let a flow of avalanche crea- tures roll cheerily past. Several unrolled and looked at him curiously before getting back into formation. Now that he wasn't running for his life, he noticed a lot of other animals. Jeweled creatures with webbed wings connected to their feet glided from tree to tree, their long snouts covered in pollen. The giant pitcher plants did not, in fact, have stems com- ing up out of them but rather were occupied by single-eyed worms coated in shimmering blue. And the forest floor was alive with skittering, barely glimpsed things.

Obi-Wan climbed one of the big rock outcroppings to get his bearings. Behind him was the Lenahran's home base ship, once again appearing deceptively like a rock formation at this distance. And not too far ahead was the settlement where he had left his own ship. He wondered what Qui-Gon would make of all this. What he would be doing differently. Would he want to study the Lenahrans? Figure out how they could use the Force? Would he have come up with a clever way to get them all off the planet, since Lenahra was so intent on killing them?

But *should* Obi-Wan try to get them off? They seemed to

be doing fine on their own, and they clearly loved each other and didn't mind living here, trials and all. A lot of planets were inhospitable in many ways, and their inhabitants had to adjust to survive there. So Lenahra wasn't that different.

You're rationalizing, he heard Qui-Gon say in his mind. *It's fine to negotiate with others over something important, but when you begin negotiating with your own conscience, you are trying to justify what you want, rather than listening to what the Force wants.*

Obi-Wan kicked a rock.

It popped open with an enraged squeak. "I'm so sorry!" he shouted as the little creature ambled away, squeaking complaints.

What if the Jedi were wrong, though? What if they were all just fooling themselves that the Force was guiding them, listening and deciding for themselves what it was saying based on what they wanted to do anyway? What if there really was just power, and how you used it?

No. That line of thinking reeked of the dark side. And while there was definitely something off here, something strange that Obi-Wan couldn't deny, he had seen Audj and the others. They cared for each other. They put others' safety above their own. They didn't seem to move through their world with hate or greed or fear. Well, probably with some fear. It was a scary world when it wanted to be.

Luckily, Obi-Wan arrived at the old settlement before he could think about it any further. He didn't want to think about things. He wanted to feel the way he had the night before, racing through the darkness, leaping and jumping and twisting, all action and no thought. It had been so much easier.

"Hello!" he called out, and was greeted with cheerful but slightly admonishing chirps from A6-G2.

"I should have contacted you sooner. That was careless of me. I've been rather distracted." Patting the droid on her green head, he crouched in front of her. "Have you had any problems? Any attacks? The ground opening to swallow you whole?"

The droid twisted her dome back and forth in the negative.

"That's good at least. I would have felt very bad indeed if you had been eaten. And I imagine you would have given some poor creature terrible indigestion. Come on. We'll go to the other ship, and you can tell me everything you've been up to."

Obi-Wan climbed aboard, followed by A6-G2. The empty copilot seat seemed to offer silent judgment, and he resisted the urge to justify his murky decisions to an absent Qui-Gon. "Besides," Obi-Wan muttered, "you're the one who didn't bother showing up."

But absent Qui-Gon was right. Obi-Wan needed to make a plan of action. He had saved Amyt, yes, but that hardly justified his trip here. This afternoon he would focus on finding a safer way for Shush, Whistle, and Trill to exist. Or try to convince them to leave. Though even his short time on Lenahra had made him more sympathetic to why they would stay. There was something intoxicating about the planet.

Or maybe just about the free young people here.

Obi-Wan flew over the trees, noticing they were more agitated in some places. He wondered if that was where his friends were foraging. Wanting to use his time well, he flew low, sweeping wide to do a survey of the land now that he knew it better and wasn't preoccupied with finding a settlement. To the west, a great sparkling sea crashed against the gray rock pillars. Tumbling waterfalls spilled down, half the water blown back up by the powerful coastal wind. More of the gliding creatures were there, swooping in and out of the water, grabbing playfully at each other.

Turning back inland, Obi-Wan passed a whole gang of gobblers. They rolled and wrestled, playing with their young. That day, at least, they looked like they were in a good mood. What strange, changeable creatures. A few klicks east of the ship there was another huge gash in the ground where part of the ship must have broken off upon entry. The trees around it were dead, blackened and charred.

Obi-Wan flew directly over it, trying to get a better view. Something changed, like slamming into cold water. His chest tightened, his heart raced. He struggled to breathe.

Something radiated upward; Obi-Wan could almost see a shimmer in the air.

"Do your sensors pick anything up?" he asked A6-G2, steering away from that place with relief. "Radiation? Toxic gas? Anything?"

The droid sent atmospheric readouts to the control panel. There was nothing unusual about the area. Obi-Wan stared over at the blackened scar, more puzzled than ever. Surely with how big the settlement ship was, it must have been twice as large for a broken piece to cause that much damage. But he saw no signs of the rest of the ship.

Obi-Wan turned and headed for the base camp once more. He would have to explore.

Or would he? He was acting like a Padawan, still trying to gather information, to find something to present to his master to prove he had done a good job.

Scowling, Obi-Wan landed on top of the Lenahrans' ship. He resolved to stop thinking about the Code and the ways he was or wasn't following it. To stop thinking about Qui-Gon and what he would be doing in this situation. This was Obi-Wan's mystery, and he would solve it as he saw fit.

Which, right now, meant hanging out with his new friends and trying to figure out how they could create a pool on top of the ship.

"How close are you on cracking that beacon?" Obi-Wan asked, helping Aces along the uneven top of the crashed ship where he'd landed his shuttle. At several points Obi-Wan had to carry the heavy droid, grunting and regretting not bringing a model with booster capabilities.

A6-G2 beeped noncommittally, then added more information, which Obi-Wan didn't understand but suspected was admonishment for leaving her behind, expecting her to take initiative and work without commands or any idea when she would receive them.

He would have to learn binary. Or not. It was kind of nice, not really knowing what she was saying. Which fit in with the entire theme of this planetary sojourn. No one knew anything.

Obi-Wan usually liked knowing things. He liked having answers. He even liked having rules, now that he thought about it. They gave him something to follow—and something to push against. Without rules and checklists and expectations, he didn't know whether he was making the right choices.

But what good did all his Jedi diplomacy and history training do him out here, where sometimes the planet tried to kill you and sometimes it didn't, and where a bunch of teens and younglings could train themselves to physically use the Force nearly as well as he could?

When Obi-Wan got down to the main living area, the younglings all gasped in shock. Then, like the avalanches of the forest floor, they swarmed the droid. Amyt was the bravest, patting A6-G2's head and peering right into her main photoreceptor. Jarper and Tumber squeaked and screamed, jumping away every time Aces moved, then giggling and scooting close again.

Mem appeared to be even more suspicious than ever, actually hiding from Obi-Wan, though her stark white skin made it difficult for her to blend in against the dark gray of the ship.

"You made it," Casul said, sounding surprised. "Did you have to fight very many things?"

Obi-Wan shook his head. "No, I—"

"That's a relief. You're probably not a good fighter."

"I am!" Obi-Wan cleared his throat, trying to tamp down his defensiveness. "I am perfectly adept. But I've been trained to always negotiate before jumping into a fight."

"What's negotiate?" Audj asked. "Is that a type of fighting?"

"No. It's a way to avoid fighting. You talk through your differences and try to reach a conclusion that is acceptable to all the parties involved."

Casul snorted, taking a bite of a piece of fruit. "Try to negotiate with a gobbler's teeth, let me know how that goes."

One of the younglings screamed. They all turned, alarmed, but it was a scream of delight as A6-G2 popped out one of her mechanical arms to show it off.

"They've never seen working tech," Zae-Brii said, dumping an armful of the spiky fruit they survived on into the box at the center of the room. It came in a variety of colors and flavors, from nutty to sweet to surprisingly salty. And it never had surprise demon squids inside, so that was definitely something in its favor.

"Have *you* ever seen working tech?" Obi-Wan asked.

Zae-Brii shrugged. "I watched as the last ship was launched. It was loud. It hurt my ears, even from where we were hiding."

"You were hiding? Why?"

Casul added his haul to the box. "Because our families didn't want to go, and the other families wanted to make us."

That was new information. Obi-Wan hadn't known there was a conflict involved. "How many of you stayed?"

Casul looked around the room at the dozen citizens of Lenahra. "Thirty-eight."

"That many have died?" Obi-Wan was aghast. He really did need to find a way to get them off Lenahra. He would have to convince them, somehow.

"Everyone dies," Casul said dismissively.

"Yes, but not everyone is eaten by wild creatures, or murdered by trees!"

"That's not how most of them died." Casul turned his back on Obi-Wan, effectively ending the conversation.

How did most of them die, then?

Audj climbed back in, the last of the foraging group to return. She dumped a bag of fruit into the box, then casually bandaged a deep gouge on one arm.

Obi-Wan looked in the container. Did they really eat only this? The fruit wasn't terrible, but it was stringy and fibrous. Too much longer here and he'd even be willing to risk tentacles to get some variety. With so many different species living at the Temple, there was always something unusual to try. "Have you ever had anything to eat besides this fruit?"

"It's food," Mem said, scowling at him from behind the container. She always kept something between them.

"Yes, I know, but there are other types of food. Varieties. Textures and flavors and spices and a million ways to prepare them all."

Mem frowned. "Seems excessive."

"We used to eat the pitcher plants," Nesguin said. "But it was too much work for too little reward."

"They were hard to eat?" Obi-Wan asked.

"No, why would they be hard to eat? They're just plants."

Obi-Wan tilted his head. "Then why was it so much work for so little reward?"

Nesguin shrugged. "We had to eat a lot of them for the same effect. Hey, do you have any with you?"

"Pitcher plants?" Obi-Wan was having a difficult time following this conversation.

"No. Why would I want to eat those? I told you, they aren't worth it. I'd like to try some of your food. Something new."

"We have what we need," Audj said. "We have what they wanted us to have."

Nesguin deflated, nodding his horned head. "You're right."

"You can still try it," Obi-Wan said, not understanding why Audj wouldn't want him to. "First things first, though." Obi-Wan handed his breather to Shush. "I've adjusted it for gills, but if the settings don't feel right, let me know. I'm sorry I only have one."

Shush slipped it over her mouth, two extensions attaching to her neck. Her huge black eyes filmed over with the translucent membrane that covered them. She made a small keening noise, and Obi-Wan was terrified he had done something wrong. But then Shush threw her arms around him.

"I can breathe," she said, shaking with emotion. "Every moment out of the water hurts, but now—" She rushed to

Trill and Whistle's barrel and let them take turns with it. Obi-Wan watched, deeply regretful that he didn't have two more. How hard, how sad it was, that they had to stay out of the planet's bodies of water. Lenahra was hostile to all of them, but Shush, Trill, and Whistle paid the steepest price.

Audj sniffled, but when Obi-Wan looked at her, she quickly ducked her head, checking on the amount of fruit in the box.

"So that's your harvest finished then," Obi-Wan said, wanting to give Audj something else to focus on. He'd talk to her later about other possible solutions.

Audj shook her head. "Oh, this isn't the harvest. This is food."

"Then what's the harvest?"

Audj shared a meaningful look with Zae-Brii and Casul. "Should we bring him?"

"He'll be useful," Zae-Brii said, and Obi-Wan expanded with pride at their esteem.

"He probably won't die." Casul neatly deflated all Obi-Wan's newfound pride.

Zae-Brii shifted into Obi-Wan's face and stuck a tongue out at him. He laughed. "Thank you for your votes of confidence."

"But seriously," Zae-Brii added, "please try not to die."

"I promise to do my best."

"Good enough," Audj said. "We'll go tomorrow. We

need a good sleep before, since we didn't get one last night." She tugged one of Amyt's lekku playfully. "No midnight adventures, okay?"

Amyt nodded solemnly. "I know how important the harvest is."

"Good girl."

Obi-Wan watched as the younglings continued clamoring around his astromech. He wasn't aware that it was a quality ever programmed into droids, but A6-G2 was apparently fond of an audience. When it looked like the younglings were losing interest, she began replaying old holovids. They were boring technical instructions on how to repair various ships, but the younglings were captivated. They kept trying to grab whoever was talking, then screaming and dissolving into giggling fits when their hands and claws passed right through.

"You're thinking they should be with their families," Audj said, her voice soft. Obi-Wan looked at her in surprise. It was clear Audj felt both responsibility and guilt for everyone's circumstances. Perhaps Obi-Wan showing up and offering Shush and the two aquatic younglings something that could help them—that Audj never could have provided— had made Audj's guilt worse.

"No," Obi-Wan said. "That's not how I was raised, either. Though I suppose most people would think they should at least have *some* adult supervision."

Audj shrugged. "We're what they have, and we do the best we can. It's what our families wanted for us, the legacy they left us. We have to trust them."

"I think you're doing a good job." After all, Obi-Wan had been raised in a pristine, beautiful historic temple among the best and brightest in the galaxy, and he didn't know that he'd ever felt as happy and free as these younglings being raised in a derelict ship, running in circles around his droid.

"Keep-away!" Casul shouted. He tugged Obi-Wan's lightsaber free from his belt and flung it through the air toward Zae-Brii. They snatched it and threw it to Mem, who scowled at it like it might bite her, before tossing it to Nesguin. Obi-Wan, not threatened this time since he knew who was trying to steal his weapon, laughed and used the Force to pull it back into his own hands.

"I think that's cheating," Casul said, frowning. "How do you do that?"

"I'm surprised you can't." Obi-Wan had seen them jump and run in ways that could be explained only by the Force. Perhaps he could teach them to use it more fully, too.

Audj fixed a stern look on the others. "What did I say about resting? We have to save it for tomorrow."

"Right. Best preserve our energy," Obi-Wan said.

"No, just the Power," Audj corrected. "Come on," she said, taking Zae-Brii's hand. "Amyt, since you want more responsibility and you're getting big enough to have it, you're in charge of lids-on tonight. I expect everyone in their hammocks or barrels faster than an avalanche."

Amyt nodded solemnly, then turned on the other younglings. "You heard her! I'm in charge! And if I hear so much as one complaint, I'll toss you over the edge and feed you to the gobblers!"

Trying not to laugh at the tiny, fierce dictator they were leaving behind, Obi-Wan followed the others up a ladder to the hatch that led to the top of the ship.

He took them on a tour of his shuttle—Nesguin seemed curious about everything, but Audj and Casul were deeply uninterested. Mem, naturally, hid outside the shuttle, watching them from a distance.

Obi-Wan pulled out a couple of packets of travel rations and passed them to Nesguin. "You can try these, if you want. You have to add water. And they're better heated, but—"

Nesguin, darting one guilty look toward Audj, who was waving at Mem from the cockpit, ripped open the top of the shiny silver packet and licked the contents. They expanded in his mouth as soon as they hit his saliva, and his eyes went wide.

"What's happening?" he cried, the food spilling from his mouth.

"I'm so sorry, I—"

"This is delicious!" Nesguin continued his horrifying

eating technique, and Obi-Wan turned away so he wouldn't laugh and hurt Nesguin's feelings.

"Would anyone else like to try?" Obi-Wan offered.

"It's disrespectful," Casul said, his tone dark.

"Oh no, I don't mind. I have plenty for—"

"It's disrespectful to our heritage. We have everything here we need. We have what our families sacrificed to give us. We don't need anything else." Casul stalked out to the portion of the ship top with the most horizontal surface. There were several mats and blankets piled there.

Audj put a hand on Obi-Wan's arm. "You'll get used to him," she said, her tone comforting. "But he's right. We have everything we need. You don't have to give us anything."

The others followed Casul, so Obi-Wan did, too. They lay in a circle, staring up at the stars. Because of the shimmering atmosphere, the stars glowed in a rainbow of colors, twinkling violet and blue and green and gold.

It was hard to see stars on Coruscant unless he was using the observatory, which initiates and even Padawans had to have special permission for. Obi-Wan felt like he was drinking them in. It was easy to feel small looking up at the galaxy like this. But here, tucked in among people he hoped were now friends, he felt small in a comforting way. No one else was looking up and feeling anxiety or stress, wondering what they should be doing, what way they were failing the Order, or the Force. How they might be derailing their own destinies.

He didn't owe that galaxy anything, did he?

Did he?

Zae-Brii whispered something in Audj's ear, and they leaned close to each other, giggling and talking in tones too low for Obi-Wan to hear. Mem and Nesguin were doing something similar. Obi-Wan was hit with a sudden pang of longing. Not for any of them specifically, but for that intimacy with *anyone*, generally. To clasp fingers, sneak off into the dark, have the weight of secrets and affection and—

Connection. Attachment.

His stomach hurt with a pang of guilt. Two days away from the Temple, and already he was imagining what it might be like to abandon all the tenets of Jedi life. But was what this group had really so different from what the Padawans shared? They had all lived together, trained together, become like a family.

Maybe that was what he was missing. Separated from his friends, watching the other Padawans grow into the Jedi they would be, stuck with ambivalent and possibly even lost Qui-Gon, Obi-Wan felt *alone*. And he shouldn't. He should feel buoyed by the Force, connected to everything, determined to find his future as a Jedi Knight.

So why didn't he feel that way?

The Lenahrans didn't have the rules he did, the structure. They were free and wild and half-feral sometimes, but they also loved and took care of each other with the same fierce determination Obi-Wan had planned to take care of the whole galaxy. And sure, they didn't have any of the nuance of the Jedi, using only the most basic physical aspects of the Force, but they could be trained to use more. *He* could train them.

Then again, why bother? What was he going to do, make them meditate? Talk them through connecting spiritually when he couldn't manage it himself with any significant results? Then they could all feel bogged down with doubts and fears of failure, like he did. What a gift he would be giving them.

He was a fool to pretend he was still here because he could do anything to help them, or to help the Order. To lie to himself that the Force had a purpose for him on the planet.

He was here because he genuinely didn't know where else to be.

Zae-Brii settled next to Obi-Wan again, turning to look at him. "You seem conflicted," they said softly.

"Can you sense that?" Obi-Wan propped himself up on an elbow, excited. "You can feel my emotional state? So you *are* using the Force in more than just—"

Zae-Brii held up a hand, laughing. "No, not like that. Learning to imitate faces also teaches you how to read them."

"Ah." Obi-Wan lay back down with a sigh. "Well, you're not wrong. I am conflicted. I just—I don't know how to *know* I'm on the right path. My whole life, I've been taught about the Force and how to use it. I've only ever had one goal. And I've studied and learned and memorized everything I needed to do to get there. But watching you all, it looks like none of that matters."

"It looks like that, sure. But we both know looks can be deceiving." Zae-Brii flashed through a variety of faces to prove their point. "So don't tell me what it *looks* like. Tell me what it feels like."

Obi-Wan turned his head, looking at all the Lenahrans around him. Having fun. Laughing and talking and tossing a piece of fruit around the platform. Part of him wished he could let go. Give up on becoming a Jedi Knight. Have what they had here.

But . . . it still felt *wrong*. Not Zae-Brii and their friends around him, necessarily. He didn't think any of them were bad. The opposite, really. But he couldn't shake that undercurrent pulling at him, tugging his emotions from the happiness and ease he wanted to feel, leaving him floundering in deep unease.

Maybe he shouldn't trust his feelings, after all. Maybe *that* was his problem. He had been trying to feel the way the Force wanted him to feel for so many years, he didn't know how to have his own feelings. For all his focus on letting go of the past and being fully present, he had anchored everything he was on a singular future:

Jedi Knight.

Anything that wasn't rigidly aimed toward that would make him uncomfortable, wouldn't it? Maybe it was his own guilt he'd been feeling this whole time on the planet. His fear that he had permanently removed himself from the only path he'd ever walked.

"I wish I could," Obi-Wan said with a sigh. Qui-Gon was always telling him to trust his feelings, but so many of his feelings were rooted in fear. How could he trust them, when they led to the dark side?

"How long will you stay?" Zae-Brii asked.

"I've still got some things to figure out," Obi-Wan answered.

"The mystery of how we use your fancy Force?" Zae-Brii's tone was gently teasing.

"That, yes. And how to help Shush, Whistle, and Trill. I know we can figure out something better for them." But also, and he didn't say this aloud, because that felt too scary, too treacherous . . . he needed to figure out whether he wanted to go back at all.

The others would accept him here, would let him stay. He'd have a home on Lenahra. Maybe that was what Orla had been seeking, too. Maybe that was why she had never updated her record. Maybe she ran here, too, and never left. Because going back to Coruscant would be an act of faith— faith that he could face whatever was waiting for him at the Temple, even if it meant no longer having a future as a Jedi

Knight. If it had ever truly been his future at all. Going back would mean trusting that the Force would put him where he *needed* to be, regardless of where he *wanted* to be.

But what if the Force didn't need him at all, and it was only arrogance that made him assume it ever had? Maybe being here was all the evidence he needed that there was no destiny for him, no place for him in the Order or the galaxy.

Maybe the Force had led him here. Maybe it hadn't. Either option meant he was in exactly the right place for now. The only thing that was wrong here was his own stubborn, arrogant insistence that the Force tell him who he should be and how to be it.

"I don't know," he said. "How long I'll stay. And I don't know when I'll know." Obi-Wan hated not knowing things, but he tried to settle into the uncertainty. Tried to exist in it, in the present, the way Qui-Gon always wanted him to.

"Well, at least stay through tomorrow to help us with the harvest, please." Zae-Brii sounded uneasy for the first time. "It's getting harder and harder, and I worry that Audj takes too much on. If I lost her . . ." Their voice trailed off.

"I'll help. Whatever you need me to do."

He meant it. His stomach still hurt, and the sense of wrongness was stubbornly resisting his determination to ignore it, but he wasn't going anywhere.

A little later, an indignant beeping from the hatch down

into the main living quarters of the Lenahran ship summoned Obi-Wan from a game of catch.

He ran over and helped haul up A6-G2. Apparently, she didn't relish babysitting duty quite as much as he'd thought. But that wasn't why she had demanded his attention. One of her mechanical arms held out the beacon. She had connected to it at last and scanned the information.

He took the beacon and climbed into the shuttle to read the display of her report. But other than a huge burst of transmission at the moment Aces managed to communicate with the beacon, there was nothing. No message he could decipher, no information about who had left it, who needed help. It was simply old tech, left behind in space.

Which made him suspect he might know whom the beacon had belonged to, after all. Obi-Wan left the shuttle and held the beacon next to the old wrecked ship, trying to see if the materials were comparable. It was impossible to tell without tools for sophisticated analysis. Maybe the beacon had been sent out when the settlement ship first went into distress, before it found its way into the asteroid field and its fate was sealed on Lenahra. There wasn't anyone left alive who could say.

The beacon had sent its desperate plea into space, but there was no one on the other side, no one waiting. "I know how you feel," Obi-Wan said, sympathizing with an inert hunk of metal.

*T*he others grumbled, clunking around the ship with nothing to do. They demanded answers. Questioned whether he knew what he was doing. Their financier's representative insinuated he would send negative reports, even threatened to take over the ship. But all that was required was patience. What were a few hours, a few days floating in the cold void of space?

They were as close as he could get without the last puzzle piece. He had suffered so much for so long. He could bear this last wait.

Perhaps it was foolish to believe as strongly as he did, but he didn't care. No one would keep him from what belonged to him. What he had been forced to leave behind. How had they let that happen? How had they dragged him, screaming, to their ship, knowing what they were doing? What they were forsaking?

He haunted the controls, staring at the screens. Thinking about the planet. What was there. What had changed. What would never change. With silent, obsessive determination, he stared and willed the last piece to come to him.

And then, at last, there it was in a burst of numbers. "I found you," he whispered, tears in his eyes. "I'm coming."

The morning dawned, bright and clear and warm. The sky shimmered with opalescent welcome above them. Obi-Wan had never opened his eyes to something so beautiful. He stretched, sitting up from where he had fallen asleep on top of the ship with a few of the others. It was strange that he could sleep so well outside of the environment he was used to.

He nearly settled in for his morning attempt at meditation before catching himself. No one was watching. No one was expecting him to meditate. He didn't like doing it and didn't get anything out of it. So why did he still feel like he *should* do it? He needed to stop doing things simply because he felt like he would get in trouble or somehow be letting someone down if he didn't.

He pushed away the impulse to meditate, ignored the nagging *wrong* feeling that still hadn't diminished. It was only there because he was doing things outside his routine, outside the only life he had ever known. He would get more comfortable with this, eventually.

Would he?

Had he already decided not to go back?

Would he really live out the rest of his life on Lenahra, running wild with his new friends? Would that be enough for him? *Could* it be? If the other Padawans were right and Qui-Gon had left the Jedi Order, who was to stop Obi-Wan from doing the same? At least he'd be doing it before he spent his whole life there.

But . . . he couldn't imagine a future without the other Jedi. A future where the Force was reduced to something he used when he needed it, no longer something he structured his life around.

"You look worried," Casul said. "The harvest?"

"Thinking about my future," Obi-Wan said with a sigh. "Which I'm not supposed to do. I'm supposed to stay grounded in the present, connected to the living Force, not being weighed down by the past or worried about what the future might bring."

Casul laughed. "How's that working out for you?"

"Not well," Obi-Wan admitted. "The more I try not to worry about the future, the more it feels like a gobbler lurking up in the trees, waiting to devour me."

"Oh, that's not right." Casul patted him comfortingly on the shoulder. "Gobblers grab you from beneath, not above."

"Thank you. Very reassuring."

"Stay here and we'll teach you how to worry only about what's immediately in front of you. There's more than enough here to keep your fears occupied. And very little future to worry about, anyway."

"What do you mean by that?" Obi-Wan asked, but Casul had already hopped down the hatch. Did he really think so little of Obi-Wan's abilities, that Obi-Wan would die sooner rather than later on Lenahra?

Obi-Wan peered over the edge of the ship at the waiting forest. The trees shivered under the morning light, leaves unfurling to greet the sun. They almost seemed to glow. From up here, they were pristine. Beautiful. Decidedly nonthreatening.

"Today's the day." Audj sounded grimly determined. Obi-Wan turned to face her. She was already dressed, wearing layers of old clothes, her boots tied tightly around her calves with strips of what might have once been a shirt. "Do what you need to in order to prepare, but know, in the end, only the Power will keep you safe. And that's why we do this."

"How do you handle it? Being the leader here?" Obi-Wan was genuinely curious. He couldn't imagine having as much responsibility as she did without anyone to guide him, to tell him the rules. To make the final decisions. Maybe that's why the Lenahrans were all so capable, why they could use the Force. They didn't have anyone telling them they couldn't.

"Aren't you the leader where you're from?"

Obi-Wan shook his head. "I am most definitely not."

"Well, what are the good leaders like there?"

Obi-Wan thought of Master Yoda. The way he taught by prompting them to find their own answers, never giving them information when they could gain experience for themselves. "They see the best in people, and help them get there."

A flicker of doubt crossed Audj's face. "Here, a leader does the best she can to keep everyone alive. And that's it." She stalked off to check on everyone else.

Audj led by sheer charisma and skill, not because she had any innate authority, like the Council. Though Obi-Wan supposed the Council hadn't always been the Council. At some point in the past—the far, far distant past, because they were *old*—they had been Padawans, too. Had they struggled? Had they questioned their connection to the Force, their place in the galaxy? Or had they always known exactly who they were and how to act, and that was why they were on the Council?

"Your sister is impressive," Obi-Wan observed as Casul rejoined him.

"She and Zae-Brii are in love and have been forever," Casul cautioned.

"Oh, I know!" Obi-Wan smiled at the warning, touched that Casul didn't want Obi-Wan getting his hopes up. "I can't form attachments like that, anyway." Couldn't he, though, if he didn't go back? Was that something he would even want? It had always been so forbidden, even thinking about it was like holding his hand right next to a lightsaber blade. He knew some of his friends had dabbled in physical relationships—suspected Siri would have been open to it, had he ever wanted to—but it had always seemed like an obstacle, not a temptation.

"And besides," Obi-Wan said, rushing to change the subject for himself more than anyone, "I would never want to be in a relationship with a leader. Too close to politicians or royalty. I'm sure if I ever fell in love, it would be with someone calm. Peaceful. Easy to get along with."

"So you want someone who doesn't challenge you."

Obi-Wan laughed, then shrugged. "I don't know what I want, if we're being honest."

Casul mirrored his shrug. "Not many choices around here. I don't think love is in my future, either, and I'm fine with that. As long as I have the Power to keep my family safe, that's enough for me. Though I *will* admit I've been curious about kissing and why Audj and Zae-Brii enjoy it so much. So if you're ever curious, too, let me know."

Obi-Wan blushed. "I will. Let you know, I mean. Not that I will do that, right now, with you. Or anyone." Would he ever get to a point where kissing someone felt like anything less than a betrayal of himself and the Jedi? And if he did get to that point, who would he want to kiss? The Lenahrans were confident and charismatic, which was attractive. But he couldn't imagine just . . . kissing any of them.

Maybe he didn't want to be *with* any of them but rather to be more like each of them.

Or maybe he wanted to kiss all of them. Not Mem, though, because he had a feeling that would upset her very much.

He wasn't going to kiss any of them, regardless. Everything on Lenahra seemed simple and felt impossibly complicated, and that would doubtless make it all worse.

"When can we start this harvest?" Obi-Wan shouted, wanting the simplicity of movement, the live-or-die immediacy of ranging out into the forest. It was all easier when the only path forward was pure survival.

Audj answered. "We leave now. The hike will take us half the day. And you'll all have to ration your Power."

"You mean not overextend ourselves and get too tired?" Even though they spoke Basic like Obi-Wan did, there were some weird phrases and words that made it clear they had been isolated a very long time.

Audj waved. "Just don't use up your Power. We had better get moving."

"What if we took my shuttle?" Obi-Wan offered. "If it's half a day's walk, we could make it in a fraction of the time."

"Is it safe?" Audj eyed the craft warily.

"It's certainly safer than the forest. I promise not to go too fast or too high." None of them had ever been in a working ship, and he didn't want to frighten them. But maybe he did want to impress them a little. He took flight for granted, and it was nice to view it as potentially wondrous. "And Aces will be with us. She's great at flying."

The droid beeped in the affirmative. The beacon was lying, abandoned, on top of the Lenahran ship, so A6-G2 had nothing to do except entertain the younglings. She rolled eagerly to the boarding ramp.

"But what if something happens and your ship gets destroyed?" Nesguin asked.

Obi-Wan felt a spike of fear at the thought. And then a hint of confused longing. The decision would be made for him in that case, and he wouldn't have to choose. He'd be stuck. He'd felt stuck at the Temple, too, which was why he was here at all. Stuck there or stuck here. It felt about the same, except here people actually needed him.

Was he being reckless with his ship? Or was he self-sabotaging so he didn't have to make up his mind? No. He was simply choosing the best course of action to help these fellow young people who had no one else to help them. As a Padawan, it was his duty to extend that help.

He still thought of himself as a Padawan, he realized. No matter what he might be considering, it was his identity.

Obi-Wan gestured to the cockpit. "If things get dangerous, Aces can pilot the ship back here without me." He hadn't considered the astromech in all this. If Obi-Wan did stay here, eventually her battery would die, which made him feel guilty. She'd be gone, and he'd lose his last connection to his old life and the Republic. It was a sobering thought.

There was a training exercise he'd done once, with Qui-Gon. The sparring room had been set up with obstacles. Little droids were firing at him from all directions. Then, to Obi-Wan's surprise, the pillar he had climbed atop to get a better vantage point had begun to split apart. He didn't know which side was a better option—which side was the right choice to get through the rest of the obstacles. And while he debated, the rift widened, and he fell hard to the floor.

"Sometimes," Qui-Gon had said, smiling gently down at Obi-Wan as the Padawan rubbed his bruised backside, "any choice is safer than not making one at all."

Obi-Wan was still straddling that ever-widening void, not sure where to plant his feet.

Audj eyed the shuttle warily, but apparently approved of the plan. "Good. And we'll be fine on the way home after the harvest if you have to send the ship back."

Everyone nodded in agreement, flexing their fingers and bouncing on the soles of their feet in anticipation.

Shush stayed behind to mind the younglings, who were all waving goodbye from a safe distance. In the cockpit, Obi-Wan took his seat while the others nervously hovered around him. Except Mem, who was crouching next to the door, looking like she was ready to bolt. Where she thought she could bolt to in a moving shuttle, Obi-Wan didn't know.

He eased the T-5 into the air, trying to make the ascent as smooth as possible. The others gasped, holding on to anything they could reach.

"Which direction?" he asked. Audj pointed—hitting him in the head as she did so, since she was gripping the back of his seat so hard her usually violet knuckles were as white as her freckles. He followed her directions.

"It's so beautiful," Zae-Brii said, pressing one hand against the cockpit window and staring down. "I had no idea." Rather than happy, they sounded deeply sad about the view. The others refused to look, huddling in the center of the cockpit. Obi-Wan didn't press them, and he opted to avoid any fancy maneuvers that might scare them. As it was, Nesguin looked like he was on the verge of losing his breakfast, which Obi-Wan had no desire to deal with.

On foot, this would have taken hours, but even flying as slowly as possible, within a few minutes Obi-Wan didn't need directions anymore. It was obvious where they were going.

"I have a bad feeling about this," Obi-Wan muttered, staring into the burned black gash scarred deep into the ground.

CHAPTER
17

The horribly scarred gash in the ground stretched beneath a giant outcropping of rock. The outcropping was made of the same geometric pillars that appeared everywhere on the planet. But as Obi-Wan flew around the rocks looking for a landing place, he realized this particular formation had a feature the others didn't: high up, near the top, there was a *doorway*.

"Is that a building?" Obi-Wan asked, incredulous. The doorway was perfectly carved in an already existing rock formation, making evidence of habitation visible only upon close examination.

"We don't go in there," Audj said curtly.

"Why not?" Obi-Wan asked.

"We just don't."

Obi-Wan felt drawn to it. He had promised himself he'd explore mysteries here, and a door in the middle of a giant rock formation? Mysterious. "It's the best place to set down," Obi-Wan said. It was only partly an excuse. He really didn't want to leave the ship in the trees, having seen how active they could be when they wanted. And there was no way he was putting the ship in the middle of that terrible gash. He still remembered how it had made him feel when he flew over it the first time. There was something repellent about it, and despite his indecision about his future, he wasn't going to be reckless with his shuttle.

The doorway into the rock was on a platform overlooking the gash, just large enough for the T-5. Obi-Wan eased to a landing there, powering down. "How are things looking, Aces?" he asked as everyone scrambled out of the cockpit and down the ramp.

The astromech cheerily beeped and sent information over the display that the scans were all clear.

"Aces says we're in the clear," Obi-Wan said, joining the others on the platform.

"Aces isn't very smart, is she?" Casul pointed at the horizon.

Obi-Wan followed his gesture. Behind them, a massive storm was building, racing across the sky. Lightning traced through the red-tinged clouds. It almost looked like it was pointing right at them.

"You can't see that storm on your readings?" Obi-Wan asked his droid as she rolled down the ramp.

A6-G2's negative answer sounded far less cheerful than normal. Surly, even.

"I'll have to check you out when we get back." Obi-Wan had no particular skills with technology or droids, but surely there was something wrong with A6-G2 that she wasn't picking up a major atmospheric disturbance. Or maybe it was the shuttle's systems that were faulty. Either way, it was inconvenient at best and deeply worrying at worst to have failing technology this far removed from help.

That would be the norm for him, if he stayed. That, and only fruit to eat, forever. Did it make him spoiled if the idea of no technology and no food variety was perhaps more horrifying than the idea of leaving behind everything else he'd ever known? Or at least equal to. It was definitely easier to think about things like technology, food, and new clothing, as opposed to abandoning the only life and future he'd ever wanted.

"Come on," Obi-Wan said, stepping toward the doorway in the stone, once again opting for action over reflection. Action was simpler. "There must be a way down through the doorway. Otherwise, how would they get up to this platform?"

"No," Audj said, shaking her head.

"We don't go in there," Zae-Brii agreed. Everyone was hanging back, as far from the entrance as they could get without falling off the platform.

"Is it dangerous?"

"We don't know. It's one of the rules they gave us."

"Who?"

"Our parents," Casul said.

Obi-Wan understood following rules simply because they existed. He didn't want to be disrespectful of their traditions. But he had no such rule, and the pull of that doorway would not be denied. There had to be answers in there about Lenahra. Much as his friends might be content to live in the present, Obi-Wan wanted to know more about the past. Maybe it would help him decide his future.

And it wasn't against his own beliefs. He was supposed to let go of the past, yes, but also learn from it. That was why the Jedi had such extensive archives, after all.

Obi-Wan peered over the edge of the landing. It was a long way to the ground. "I can fly you down?"

Mem shook her head, somehow even paler than her chalky white skin normally was. "No! No more flying. We can jump."

Audj didn't agree. "We can't afford to use the Power like that right now. We'll have to climb."

"I'm quite confident there will be a way down inside," Obi-Wan said.

Audj bit her lip, clearly torn. "You go ahead. We'll meet you at the bottom."

Unable to push it further without being rude, Obi-Wan nodded. "Be careful." He turned his back on his friends and entered the arched doorway. Maybe at one point there had been a door, but now there was only the opening, welcoming him inside.

There was no light, the walls solid rock. Only a few steps left him in near-total darkness. He unhooked his saber and turned it on, letting the pale blue glow of his blade guide him.

He was tensed for attack or any threats. Surely this place was off limits for a reason, and for something on this planet to be off limits, it had to be toothy-annihilation levels of bad. But as far as he could tell, this smoothly carved passageway was the *least* dangerous place on Lenahra. There were no creatures, no trees, nothing to eat him or try to break him.

He came to a large opening, what he assumed was the hollowed center of the rock formation. This didn't feel the same as the rudimentary buildings in the old settlement. If the Lenahran settlers had had the ability to hollow out entire mountain-sized rock formations, surely they would have had more complex homes. Obi-Wan followed the wall, trying to get an idea of how large the room was, or discover any passages that led away from it. But his eyes caught on what his lightsaber revealed.

Carved along the wall were giant murals, not unlike those at the Jedi Temple and as old, if not older. In here, protected from the elements, they would age slowly. How much time must have passed to leave them so crumbling and worn?

"So the settlement ship wasn't the first sentient life

here," Obi-Wan mused. "What happened to the original inhabitants?"

There were some markings, letters so ancient and primitive he couldn't read them. But the pictures told enough of a story. There was a craft of some sort, falling from the stars and landing here. Crashing, actually. He traced his fingers along the gash in the wall. It matched the mark he had seen outside—though it seemed smaller, proportionately.

Then there were several murals of working, of life. The old settlers were slender, three-legged, their heads angular and towering. They danced in the trees and rode gobblers, alongside many depictions of the trees and the pitcher plants. The art was serene, peaceful. Beautiful.

Then the art got bolder. The figures in it were larger, even more angular. They stood atop the rocks, holding their hands toward the sky with orbs above them like small suns, or crowns. It was hard to say.

The gash appeared in the art again, but with small figures all around it, instruments in their hands. It looked like they were digging, or maybe planting something. The large figures became even larger, grander, holding their hands up with tracing bolts coming from them.

And then, abruptly, there were no more carvings at all. Until—

Obi-Wan hurried forward. On the last section of wall, scratched in without the care or artistry of the earlier works, was a final mural. At first Obi-Wan couldn't make sense of it. And then he realized whoever had made it wasn't just scratching chaos onto the wall.

It was bodies. The lines of them, the same tall angular shapes, but now all prone, lifeless, broken. Piled up next to the gash in the ground. One figure stood alone, bowed, broken, holding out a pitcher plant toward the scar in the planet's skin.

And that was it. The end.

"That can't be good," Obi-Wan muttered. Whatever this civilization had been, wherever they had come from, everything had ended in catastrophe and mass death. And it must have happened a very, very long time before, because other than this hidden temple—Obi-Wan could think of no other word for it—there was no sign that anyone had been on Lenahra before Audj's people.

Obi-Wan stepped closer to the art. There was a dark hole next to it, the exact size of a lightsaber blade. He shined his own blade closer. There were burn marks around the hole. It had been made, and made deliberately. Reaching inside with two tentative fingers, Obi-Wan felt something cold and metallic. He pulled out what looked like a datachip—though one far bulkier and older than any he had ever seen.

Orla the Wayseeker! It had to have been her. She had made it here, after all. He tucked the datachip into one of his pouches, hoping there was some way for A6-G2 to access it. He couldn't help the rush of elation. He'd found evidence left by a Jedi long before. But it was also laced with a surprising amount of dread. What would he find on it? Would it help him make up his mind about his future?

Did he want it to?

Obi-Wan did a last scan of the room, looking for any other information or evidence, but he found nothing and didn't want to keep his friends waiting outside where it wasn't safe. He hurried away from the last terrible mural and found another passageway. This one went down in a gentle spiraling slope, but came up short at a dead end. Had the rocks closed around it? Or had this tunnel always led to nowhere? Obi-Wan could go back up to the platform and climb down like the others, but he found he desperately wanted out of the oppressive darkness.

It wasn't a temple, as he had begun thinking of it at the top. It was a tomb, holding the history of an entire species.

Obi-Wan put his hand against the rock. It wasn't solid, after all. He could sense the cracks where a door leading out had been sealed shut. But the sealing was clumsy, a simple mortar. It didn't seem as old as everything else, either. He wondered if Audj's people had been the ones to close it.

Pushing out, he used the Force and dislodged the door so he could squeeze through. Blinking against the light, he stepped out to see the door was directly above the terrible gash in the ground. Even though he was no longer in the dark, Obi-Wan hesitated before powering down his light-saber. If anything, being out of the temple-tomb only strengthened his fear and worry.

Audj and the others dropped down right next to him, done with their climb.

"Is that a stick made of light?" Casul asked, pointing at the saber hilt now hanging from Obi-Wan's belt. "What does it do? How does it work? Can I try it?"

"It's a weapon," Obi-Wan said. "It's complicated, and no. Not right now. Maybe later."

Audj regarded Obi-Wan with a wary expression. "What did you find?"

"History. Did you know the planet was inhabited before your people?"

"They left, too?" she asked.

Obi-Wan shook his head. "No. But they're gone. And I don't think it was pleasant or peaceful."

Audj's face betrayed a shadow of fear, then went hard with determination. "Well, we're still here. And if we want to *stay* here, it's time for the harvest."

She stepped to the edge of the terrible black gash and jumped in. Obi-Wan looked over. The platform they had landed on far above had hidden this detail: the gash ended in a terrible pitch-black hole down into nothing. A hole that had just swallowed Audj.

"I—" Obi-Wan started.

"You have a bad feeling about this?" Casul asked.

"No. Feelings, plural. Many bad feelings." If Qui-Gon were here, he'd tell Obi-Wan to listen to them. To trust them. To explore them.

Casul shrugged. "Ignore them."

Then he pushed Obi-Wan in.

O bi-Wan fell into the dark. But he wasn't alone. Casul was falling beside him, and below him he heard Audj hit the bottom. He barely caught his descent in time, landing in a hard crouch. The ground beneath him was brittle and unyielding. He stared up at where they had come from, the distant hole of sky above them the only light. It was several degrees cooler down here.

"What could you possibly need to harvest from this hole?" Obi-Wan paused to brush off his robes. They didn't have any dirt on them; he just needed a moment to gather himself after the panic of being pushed in. That breathless, tight-chested squeeze wasn't fading, though. Maybe because the panic was *external*, not internal. The low hum of wrongness he had felt since landing on the planet was no longer low, but buzzing and agitated, swirling all around him. It was like the sensation he had gotten flying over the gash the first time. Only instead of breathing in the vapors of it, he was fully submerged.

It felt like he was under attack. He kept looking over his shoulder, waiting to see the darkness take form. But would the darkness devour him, or would it take him over?

"This way." Audj hurried deeper into the hole. The others landed behind Obi-Wan, blocking his way out. The ancient ship must have caused the original opening when it crashed here, but something else had widened it. Ahead, the rocks showed deliberate marks where they had been blasted and carved away. The passageway was gaping and deep, no hint as to what it led to. He had seen this in the murals. The crash, and then what he had thought was farming. It hadn't been farming at all. It had been gouging out this tunnel.

He knew how those murals ended, and he didn't want to experience it himself. Obi-Wan was frozen. No part of him wanted to go a single step farther, but he also knew he couldn't abandon his friends and make them do it alone. Whatever they were harvesting, they needed it in order to survive. He couldn't imagine anyone willingly coming here otherwise.

He took a centering breath, trying to stay tuned to the moment and not let the sense of wrongness around them cloud his mind or distract him. He could function in the midst of paralyzing fear; he had proved it in his trials. It was time to prove it again. Not to the Council, but to himself.

Audj led the way, followed closely by Zae-Brii and Casul. Obi-Wan let Mem and Nesguin go ahead, choosing to bring up the rear. That way he could keep whipping around and looking over his shoulder as much as he wanted to.

Some of the others stumbled on the uneven rock-littered floor, though Audj was quiet and sure-footed in the lead. Obi-Wan was tempted to light his saber—he wanted the comfort of it in his hands, as well—but it wouldn't provide illumination for the whole group, which seemed selfish.

Soon it wasn't necessary. There was a slight glow up ahead. The temperature, too, was getting warmer, not colder. But they hadn't ascended at all.

"What—" Obi-Wan started, but Audj hissed to cut him off and make him be quiet. He supposed his answer would come soon enough. They had picked up speed now that it was brighter and brighter, the blue glow ahead of them not limited like that of his lightsaber, but coming from something much bigger.

When they at last broke free of the tunnel, Obi-Wan stopped in shock. They were in a cavern, walls wide and ceiling soaring overhead, those same hexagonal pillars hanging down and coming up all around to create this pocket of nothingness beneath the ground.

That was wrong, though. It wasn't a pocket of nothingness. In the center of the cavern, beneath a tremendous network of delicate pale roots, was the source of the light. It glowed radiant blue, pulsing softly as though with breath or heartbeat, so that the light itself seemed to be alive.

It reminded him of Ilum in a way, but only in that it was a cave that inspired awe and fear. Ilum was frigid and crystalline, whereas this cave was warm and living. Still, there was a sense of wonder. Of having stepped into a place bigger and older and more sacred than Obi-Wan could understand.

He moved reverently across the cavern floor until he could see what was making the light. A pool of brilliant azure was bubbling up from somewhere deep beneath them. Several dozen meters long and wide, the spring took up the entire center of the cavern. But the water—if it was water—was hardly placid. It churned and shifted, and as it did, orbs of light the size of his palm floated to the surface. Snaking extensions of the roots overhead wrapped the orbs, gently enveloping them. The fibrous roots glowed with traces of orb light that went up and up until they disappeared into the web of roots along the cavern ceiling. Light being pulled up and through, not to a single destination, but to countless ones.

The nourished roots glowed the same color as those strange pitcher plants. And the leaves on the trees. And now that Obi-Wan thought about it, the startling blue of the gobblers' eyes, the shimmering iridescence of the little rock creatures' outer shells, the coating on the symbiotic worms' exteriors, on and on through all the creatures he had seen here.

Was this pool the source of all that, then? He was awed,

and glad he hadn't given in to fear and stayed outside. This was incredible. No wonder the others felt it was worth the risk to visit. What was this place? How had they found it?

But he had a bigger question as Audj and the others unfolded the bags they had each brought: what were they about to harvest?

"Audj, wait," Obi-Wan whispered. He needed to tell them about his feeling, about how this place was sacred but also that something here was very, very wrong. Because his awe hadn't displaced that warning feeling. They shouldn't be here. But the others didn't use the Force like he did, so they couldn't feel it the way he did. He needed to warn them, to guide them back out so they could talk.

Audj's eyes flashed a warning as she put a finger to her lips. Obi-Wan gestured back the way they had come. She shook her head, held up a hand, and then closed it into a fist. "Now!"

All the others darted forward, plunging their hands into the water and scooping out as many of the orbs as they could, then shoving them into their bags.

That was when the screaming started.

CHAPTER
19

Obi-Wan smashed his hands over his ears, but he could still hear the screaming. He could *feel* it, like needles in his entire body.

"Stop!" he shouted. "Something's wrong!"

But the others didn't listen, didn't pause. They continued scooping out as many of the glowing orbs as they could, shoving them into their bags.

"Come help us!" Casul glared over his shoulder at Obi-Wan. "We all need to carry as much as we can."

Obi-Wan could barely think straight. It was a wonder he was still standing. How were any of them functioning? And how could they not feel that whatever was happening was *bad*?

"Is that enough?" Zae-Brii closed their bulging pack.

"Throw me your bag!" Audj demanded, sealing her own and holding out her hands for Obi-Wan's.

He took a step away. The cave around them was rumbling,

trembling, and he finally had enough of his senses back to understand that the scream wasn't a voice so much as a sensation. Whatever his friends had done, it had hurt . . . the cave? The water? The roots? The *planet*? Obi-Wan had no idea. But it was hurting, and Obi-Wan was hurting, too.

"Put it back," he said.

"You said you'd help with the harvest. This is the harvest." Audj's face was hard, her glare cutting. "What's wrong with you?"

"But—"

"Forget him." Casul's bag was full. He grabbed one last orb and popped it into his mouth, tossing one to each of the others. They all swallowed them, tipping their heads back, eyes closed. A shiver went through them and—*there*, the Power, what Obi-Wan had thought was the Force. It had never been the Force at all. The Force wasn't something that could be consumed, could be stolen. But whatever strange magic this planet had could be taken and used.

This close, seeing it all happen, Obi-Wan could finally sense it. And he knew where that *wrong* sensation had been coming from this whole time. He had been so distracted, so convinced that his friends were the ones who needed help and protection, he had never figured out the truth: *they were what was wrong on Lenahra.*

The ground trembled. "It knows we're here!" Zae-Brii said. "Let's go!"

The group raced out of the cave, full packs strapped on. Obi-Wan followed, because what else could he do? The scarred and blackened rock around them groaned. This entrance truly was a scar on the land, a wound carved straight into the planet. Maybe that was why it couldn't close itself, why, even though in other places the rocks and the ground shifted regularly, this place remained gaping and vulnerable. Just like the planet couldn't swallow the Lenahrans' ship because of the damage it did when crashing.

"Incoming!" Audj shouted from the lead. The ground rumbled with a familiar sensation. All the teens jumped, leaping over the avalanche of creatures rolling toward them, sailing farther and faster than Obi-Wan had ever seen them do. He followed suit, trying not to step on any of the creatures or smash his head against the roof of the passageway.

"Gobblers won't be far behind," Casul warned. "Get out your light stick, Obi-Wan."

"*No.*" Obi-Wan wouldn't hurt any of these animals, not unless he absolutely had to. Not when he was beginning to suspect that the animals were only aggressive because they were protecting something harmed. Something stolen. "Make for the ship."

He'd take the others through the temple-tomb, whether they wanted to go or not. He needed another look at those carvings, which were suddenly making terrible sense.

"About that," Audj said as they burst free of the tunnel

and into the long gash in the ground that led to it. The air was charged around them, the sky roiling with green-and-red-tinged clouds. A bolt of lightning struck the ground where Audj had been moments before, and she barely rolled free. Nothing would survive this storm, especially not a ship.

Obi-Wan pulled out his communicator. "Aces! Get out of here!"

Though the connection was crackling and disrupted, the droid made it clear that she had already done so, as he had instructed.

That was good, at least. But also bad, because now they had a long journey back to their home base, and an entire planet trying to kill them before they got there. Something—something was about to—

Obi-Wan tackled Casul, knocking him out of the way of a deadly strike of lightning. The ground smoked and sparked where Casul had been standing, the air so acrid and dry it hurt Obi-Wan's nose to breathe.

Audj held out her hands to help them both up. "Don't worry!" she shouted, trying to be heard over the screeching wind and deafening thunder. "It can't sustain the storms for very long!"

"How long is not very long?" Obi-Wan demanded. All it took was one bolt to hit its target and end a life. Even though he was furious with his friends for failing to tell him what, exactly, they had been up to, he also didn't want to watch any of them die.

Death was a part of the Jedi path. A few years before, when he was just a youngling initiate, a Padawan had been killed. She was collateral damage in a senseless attack. Youth was no guarantee of safety, not among the Jedi. Padawans weren't full Jedi, but they were fully engaged in the Jedi's duties, which meant they were just as likely to fall—if not *more* likely, due to inexperience.

In all his longing to get out into the galaxy and do some good, Obi-Wan had never fully thought through how fragile his own life was, how quickly and easily his path could be cut short. He was very much thinking about it now.

What would Qui-Gon Jinn do if he were here? Obi-Wan closed his eyes. Qui-Gon was maddening and puzzling, but Obi-Wan could almost hear his voice. *Exist in the present*, Qui-Gon had said many times, trying to ground Obi-Wan when it was clear Obi-Wan couldn't settle into meditation. *Move through the present as the Force moves through you, connecting you to everything. You are one small part of an infinite whole. Find peace and purpose in that.*

Obi-Wan certainly couldn't meditate right now, and he doubted there was much peace to be found. He could, however, follow the advice to move through this moment like the Force, connected to everything around him. He opened his eyes and reached out, trying to sense specifics in the chaotic turmoil around them.

"Gobblers on the right!" He leaped onto the lip of the gash. The others followed him just as a herd of gobblers careened down teeth-first from the other side. "Follow me and do exactly as I do!"

Obi-Wan ran along the top of the gash. Columns of rock, uninjured by the centuries-old wound, crashed and twisted around them, trying to knock them off. An avalanche of creatures had zeroed in on them, coming down a hill with terrible speed. The gobblers had nearly caught up, too, faster on six feet than any of them on two.

As one of the massive rock columns pushed up, trying to smash them, Obi-Wan got an idea.

He held up a fist and waited as the others caught up. "On three!" He felt another lightning strike coiling like a Garollian ghost viper to kill them from above. The gobblers were almost there, and the first blows of the avalanche crashed into his ankles, but he couldn't be bothered to react. He had to focus.

"Now!" He jumped into the air as one of the rock columns trembled and then shot forward. He pushed off it, using the rock's momentum to launch himself upward, free from gobbler teeth and avalanche crush. The others around him shouted in relieved exhilaration as they soared free, lightning obliterating the path behind them.

They hit the forest running. Obi-Wan dodged branches and leaped over ravenous mouths of sinkholes opening beneath them.

"Split up!" Audj commanded. "That way it can't focus

on any one of us. And if we don't all make it back, at least part of the harvest will."

Obi-Wan dropped to the ground to avoid a branch so swift and vicious it would have taken his head off. "No. We're all making it back."

"You're not in charge," Casul said, shoving him. "You didn't even help."

Anger flared in Obi-Wan's heart and he pushed Casul back. "Because what you were doing is wrong."

"Survive now, argue later," Zae-Brii urged. But they didn't follow Audj's advice, either, sticking close to her instead of breaking off on their own.

"I'll get you all back alive," Obi-Wan promised. "And then we're going to have a talk."

"Can't wait." Casul glowered, but he followed Obi-Wan as the Padawan led them through the trees, sensing the path of least resistance. Though he could feel many things—too many things—trying to converge on them, he was fast and the group with him was somehow even faster. They jumped and dodged with such speed that they didn't really need to sense things before they happened. They could react fast enough to save themselves.

Which was good, because Obi-Wan certainly couldn't have saved them all. He jumped free of a gobbler's lunge, landing on its back and pushing off from there into the trees. They swayed, trying to knock him down, but the others were already up there, too. They leaped from tree to tree, avoiding being swallowed by either the ground beneath them or the waiting gobblers.

Fortunately, the storm wasn't fast enough to keep up. It raged in angry impotence behind them. Not having lightning to contend with made things a little easier.

"Almost there!" Audj shouted, pointing to the jutting home ship not too far in the distance. "We'll make it."

Obi-Wan agreed. He was going to fulfill his promise of getting them all back safely.

Or not, he thought as a branch wrapped around his ankle, snatching him from the air and slamming him to the ground in the middle of a slavering circle of gobblers.

There was the sound of screaming from the comms, and then silence.

"That was the second ship," one of the crew said, accusation in his tone and tears in his eyes. "We're the only one left. You could have mentioned the asteroid field. None of those crews signed on to die for you." There was a pause, and the next question came out in more awed fear than criticism. "How are they moving like this?"

He didn't answer, because he didn't need to. He hadn't mentioned the asteroid field because it didn't matter. It had allowed them out when he didn't want to leave. And now it would let him in, welcome him home. He piloted the ship with absolute calm. Nothing was going to keep him from Lenahra. He knew it. The asteroid field agreed. Where it had claimed the other two ships with violent fervor, it parted for him.

It recognized his right to enter.

"I don't like this," the crew member said, staring warily out at the asteroids behaving like no other asteroids could or would.

He laughed, then, unable to hold it back. "I don't care what you like."

The crew member eased away, retreating back into the ship. He was glad. He wanted to be alone, wanted to savor his triumph years in the making. He watched as Lenahra grew bigger and bigger before him. His planet.

When they had dragged him away, screaming and fighting, he had looked for his brother. Had hoped that, together, they could be strong enough to stay. His captors didn't even listen when he begged, when he told them they were leaving his brother, leaving children. He couldn't make them stop.

But now no one could stop him. He was back at last, and he would be strong enough by himself, forever.

CHAPTER
20

Obi-Wan stood in the center of a ring of very angry, very sharp, very large teeth.

His hands twitched toward his lightsaber. But looking around, he noticed half these gobblers weren't even fully grown. And besides, he had interacted with one before. He even thought he recognized his friend from the forest, familiar stripes going down its scaled side. He didn't want to kill any of them.

"I think," Obi-Wan said, holding his hands out wide, "that we can negotiate a treaty. I'd much rather negotiate than fight, wouldn't you?"

The gobblers growled in unison. While Obi-Wan wasn't fluent in gobbler, he didn't take it as a particularly positive sign. But they hadn't attacked him yet, which was hopeful. He kept his hands extended, trying to send out soothing emotions. He hadn't mastered those particular Force skills yet—they weren't the most common among Jedi, many forgoing developing them entirely—but if Obi-Wan could use the Force to calm the animals, then maybe—

"Hey! You horrible toothy beasts!"

"Bring your rancid breath over here!"

"Look what I have!"

"Wouldn't you like someone who actually tastes good? Not that dusty sky trash."

The voices came from everywhere, confusing the gobblers, who began spinning in circles, trying to find a target. Obi-Wan took this as his cue to end negotiations. He jumped over them, landing hard on the ground outside the circle of teeth, and ran. Soon he was joined by the others.

"You came back for me," he said, panting and nearly at the edge of his endurance. He trained a lot in the Temple, but oddly none of the training exercises had focused on trying to survive while running long distances when an entire planet was conspiring to end you. He supposed some things had to be experienced in person.

Audj sent out a sharp whistle, and the cables dropped down the sides of the behemoth ship. "We don't like to lose people. Not when we have a say."

"Besides," Mem muttered, "you're so spindly. Wouldn't want the gobblers to choke on you. Terrible way to die, even for them."

"Thank you." Obi-Wan's tone was as dry as his mouth after that much exertion and stress. "That means a lot. To the gobblers, I'm sure. It means rather less to me."

Casul climbed next to him. "You really were trying to negotiate! Why didn't you fight them? You could have cut through them easily."

"I don't think they deserve to be killed," Obi-Wan said, reaching the top. He checked his communicator and made sure A6-G2 and the shuttle were back safely, then turned to Audj as she helped the others in.

"You owe me some answers." Obi-Wan tried to keep his anger in check. It was difficult, though, with the memory of that screaming in his ears. The feeling of intense wrongness was still strong and clear now that he could pinpoint the source.

"What do you mean?" she asked.

"You lied to me."

Audj looked genuinely confused. "When?"

"This whole time! You let me think the Force and your *Power* were the same thing, but they're not. Not at all."

"I didn't let you think that. *You* were the one who told *me* they were the same!"

Obi-Wan shook his head. "If I had known how you were getting it, I would have known what was wrong."

"We told you about the harvest."

"But not what it really is!"

"What is it?" She held out her hands. "Please, outsider who knows nothing about Lenahra or us or what we have to do to survive here. By all means, tell me what the harvest is!"

Obi-Wan deflated. He tugged on his braid, trying to

focus, to re-center himself. "Will you please explain the full history of your people? What really happened to them? It will help me figure out what, exactly, is going on here." He had his theories—theories that were quickly being strengthened by the energy he felt pulsing off the glowing orbs the others carried. But he needed more information.

Audj glanced at the younglings, who were crowding around, also asking to hear about the harvest. She shot a look at Zae-Brii, and they nodded toward the ceiling hatch. Obi-Wan followed the two of them up onto the top of the ship. He waved at A6-G2, glad the droid and the shuttle were both in one piece.

Audj settled onto a mat, with Zae-Brii pacing behind her. "I don't know what else you need to hear," she said. "We told you our history."

"In the center of that rock formation, the one you won't go in, there were stories," Obi-Wan said. "Stories of the people who came here before, long ago. They found that cavern, like you did. They took it, like you are. And they all died."

Audj's head tendrils shivered as she looked away from him, out over Lenahra. "Oh. I didn't know about them. It's a hard battle to fight, living here. But one our parents believed in. When our people's ship first crashed, it wasn't too bad. They quickly learned they couldn't hunt—that ended terribly. Fortunately, the fruit here is enough to sustain most life. Then someone had the idea to try the glowing forest plants, the ones that look like big cups."

"In my experience, one should never eat something that glows," Obi-Wan said with a lift of an eyebrow.

Audj glared at him. "They liked it. And it made them stronger, faster, able to jump just a little farther, a little higher. So they ate more. And more. The gobblers got aggressive, began patrolling the forest. It was harder and harder to get any food, much less the food they most wanted. Things went like that for a long time. Stealing as many of the plants as they could, dealing with the gobblers. We were on the verge of starvation. I don't remember much. We were pretty young."

Zae-Brii nodded. "Amyt was only a baby. I helped her mother."

"Then someone found the ancient wreck, and what was under it."

"My family," Zae-Brii said, staring sadly over the landscape. "Five went in. Two came out. But they brought the Power with them. The answer to all our problems. They didn't have to scavenge the pitcher plants anymore. The orbs were far more potent, their impact immediate and incredible. Nothing could stop our people from feeding themselves once they had the orbs."

Audj nodded. "That was when the planet fully turned against us. But we were stronger than we had ever been. We had been given a gift, a way to survive."

"Not everyone agreed." Zae-Brii finally sat, their face flickering through a variety of other faces, as though they were remembering. How many people had they lost? How many faces lived on in Zae-Brii's memory alone? "They didn't like the cost of the orbs. They had been working on a ship, cobbled together from pieces of this one. There was a vote. They decided it was time to leave Lenahra."

"Our families disagreed. There was no guarantee their ship could make it off-planet and to another habitable world. And this was—is—our home. If we left, we also left the Power." Audj's expression went soft and filled with wonder. "They didn't want that. Neither do we. You understand what it is to feel it, what it is to have it."

Obi-Wan nodded. The Force and their Power weren't quite the same thing—he didn't think, at least—but they were close enough that he really did understand. More than they knew. His entire life had been about the Force. Learning it. Using it.

"Imagine giving it up," Zae-Brii said. "Imagine being cut off from it, forever."

In all his agonized indecision, he hadn't considered that. Because even if he wasn't a Jedi, he would still be connected to the Force. But . . . it might change. If Force adepts weren't identified and trained young, their connection was haphazard, chaotic. Dangerous even, at times. And in a lot of them it faded, becoming a hum in the background of their lives. Not vital or active.

He didn't want that. Whatever else he might question, he knew the Force was a part of him, and much as it tormented and frustrated him, much as he struggled to connect with it, the idea of reaching for it and having it just be . . . gone? That was too terrible to imagine. Worse by far than the idea of not ever becoming a Jedi Knight.

Audj continued. "Our families hid. The ones who left dragged everyone they could find along with them, insisting they were saving them, doing the right thing. But they didn't find us. We didn't join the others, the ones who flung themselves into the sky, into the stars, into the cold emptiness of the unknown, because they were scared of what they knew."

"Rightfully so," Obi-Wan countered.

Audj's face got fierce again. "This is my home. These are my people. This is the life our parents gave us."

"What happened to them? Your parents, I mean. Were they killed getting the orbs?"

"We don't live long," Zae-Brii said. "You know."

"No, I don't. What does that mean?" Obi-Wan demanded.

Audj huffed dismissively. "As you get older and you have to consume more, your body breaks down. It happens to everyone."

He couldn't believe what he was hearing. Their parents hadn't been killed. They hadn't even died of old age—they never made it that far. "It does not happen to everyone! Believe me. I don't have much experience with all your species, but I do know that Nautolans, for example, have long life spans. So do Iktotchi. An early death is not a natural one."

"How long?" Zae-Brii asked, their face almost hungry. They glanced guiltily toward Audj but continued. "Because I remember—I think I remember . . ." Their appearance shifted to that of an old woman, gray hair braided in a crown over a face covered in fine wrinkles.

"Decades. Longer even, for many. Some live well over a hundred years. But, barring sickness or accident, most live until they are old. Not just grown—well past then. Long enough to see children, grandchildren, even great-grandchildren."

Zae-Brii looked as though Obi-Wan had wounded them. Audj's eyes went distant and unfocused, and she put a hand over her stomach, like it pained her.

"No," she whispered. "We live enough. We live *enough*." Audj stood, swiping her hand through the air as though cutting off the conversation. "This is what our parents wanted for us. What they *chose* for us. We're honoring them by using the Power to protect ourselves."

"But it's not yours to use," Obi-Wan said. He could feel the orbs in the room beneath them, the pulses of stolen life. "It belongs to the planet. I don't know how to explain it. I don't know that anyone *could* fully explain it. But I think this whole planet is connected, symbiotic even, and that those things, your so-called Power, are a physical manifestation of its life. You aren't using the Power like Jedi use the Force. You're stealing it. You're consuming it. You're hurting Lenahra and everything on it."

"You can't know that," Audj snapped.

"Before I helped you, everything here was ambivalent toward me. Friendly, even. Because I wasn't stealing from the planet, or harming it. It only ever tried to attack me when I was with one of you."

"But we're part of Lenahra," Zae-Brii said, tears in their eyes quickly blinked away. "We've sacrificed so much to be here, to live here."

"What if you stopped using the Power?" Obi-Wan suggested. "Left it alone. You said your people lived here for two or three generations without it. The planet didn't change and become more hostile—the people changed, taking more. First the pitcher plants, and then the Power."

Audj shook her head. "The planet changed. All we did was adapt. You don't understand."

"I think I do."

"No, you don't! You have your Force already. Why should you get to use your power, but we can't?"

"It's—well, it's different." Obi-Wan struggled to find the explanations. How could he have been raised in the Jedi Temple and not be able to tell them why the way they were consuming this Force-like power was wrong, but the way he was using the Force was right?

He could give detailed lectures on the light versus the dark, the different abilities the Force could offer a Jedi who was trained and prepared and capable, the history of the Jedi. But the more nebulous aspects of the Force, the reasons why it worked the way it did, why some people could forge stronger, deeper connections with it than others—well, who was he to lecture?

It was his struggle with his connection to the Force, his fears about his future within the Jedi Order, that had spurred him out here in the first place. He hadn't run toward a mystery. He had run away from his struggles. He could admit that now. He had been so afraid that he wasn't cut out to be a Padawan, that he didn't deserve his place in the Temple, that he wouldn't be enough and he would fail. He was struggling with the loss of the life he had known, the friendships he'd made, the confidence and surety he'd enjoyed as a youngling. So he ran and ended up here, where they were willing to die to stay connected to power in the only way they could.

Obi-Wan tugged harder on his braid, the symbol of his status as a Padawan. It felt heavy that day. "I don't know how to tell you what the Force is. But that power? It belongs to the planet. You're taking it, and giving nothing back. There's no balance in what you're doing. Without balance, there's chaos. And violence. And death."

"So you're allowed to use the Power, to have it with you

all the time, and since we've figured out how to do it, too, we're bad?" Audj's face darkened so the white spots nearly glowed in contrast. "You're jealous. That's what it is. You're not special here. We can all do what you can, and you want us to stop so you can be the only one with power."

"I assure you, that's not it. Though not everyone can use the Force, where I grew up, in the Temple, I'm hardly special. But I *can* sense things you can't, just like you can sense things with your tendrils that my own eyes and ears don't. Trust me that, whatever this planet is, you've pushed it out of balance. I know what you're doing is wrong because I can feel it. And if you could feel what I feel, you'd know it was wrong, too."

"I think *you're* what's wrong," Audj snarled, turning her back on him and heading for the hatch to the ship. "We didn't ask you to come here, and we don't need you. We don't need anyone. Our parents gave us everything we need."

Obi-Wan stood to follow her, but Zae-Brii put out a hand. "Let her go." Their voice was soft and sad. "She's worked hard all these years to keep everyone safe. She had to grow up fast, and take on too much. You're asking her to give up the path our parents died to stay on, and the only way she knows to protect us."

"But it *doesn't* keep you safe. It's going to kill you all eventually, one way or another, and I don't—" Obi-Wan knew that death was simply returning to the Force, but still. He didn't want that for them. Not yet. "I don't know how I can help you if you continue this way."

"We haven't asked you for help. Besides, how can we risk stopping? You think if we gave up using the Power, Lenahra would suddenly become friendly? It would welcome us with open jaws and gaping sinkholes." Zae-Brii patted him on the shoulder, their expression sad but resigned. "Even if, eventually, things returned to this balance you've spoken of, how would we know when it was safe? We can't take that chance. It's an impossible problem. For *us*. But you can go. Any time you want. You're not locked into our life-and-death struggle. I don't mean this to be cruel, but why would anyone here listen to you?" With that, Zae-Brii followed Audj down into the ship.

Obi-Wan was left alone, wondering if Zae-Brii was right. He really didn't know their history. He wasn't one of them. And who was he to give them guidance and advice? He wasn't a Jedi Master, or even a Jedi Knight. All he had were a bunch of old murals plus his own feelings that everything was wrong here. Could he trust his feelings, when those feelings—hurt, resentment, and a deep and terrible fear of loss—were exactly what had led him to this place?

Maybe he brought it all with him. Maybe he was the thing that was the most out of balance on Lenahra.

He had answers now, but they led only to more confusion, to more questions. If he were at the Temple, he'd turn to Master Qui-Gon or another Jedi for help. Or he'd research in the Archives. Actually, knowing Qui-Gon, that would be his advice: Do more research. Seek the answers for himself. Obi-Wan resisted the urge to roll his eyes. Sometimes he just wanted to be given the answers.

He didn't have the Archives here. But he did have an ancient record of the planet. Those murals were the only saved history other than the stories Audj and Zae-Brii had shared. Stories their parents had given them, stories that told only what they wanted.

Obi-Wan slapped his forehead. He had more than the murals! In their rush to get back, Obi-Wan had forgotten all about his discovery.

"Aces!" he said, running up the ramp. A6-G2 blinked a light at him from where she was plugged into the ship, charging. "Can you read this?" He held out the ancient datachip.

A6-G2 extended a mechanical arm and tried to plug it in to one of her dataports. It didn't fit. She beeped in frustration, then tried a different end. Still no luck. A rapid series of responses in binary was translated when Obi-Wan looked at the control panel screen.

"Do what you can," he said, reading A6-G2's doubtful offerings of different ways she could try to access the information on the chip, even if she couldn't fit it into any of her ports or the shuttle's systems. "And thank you."

A6-G2 got to work. With nothing to do but wait, Obi-Wan climbed down through the hatch into the main living area of the Lenahran ship. The looks he got from the others as he walked up to them were far from warm, but he ignored the judgment.

"You need to see the history of this planet," Obi-Wan said. "In the place where you never go. There's a reason those who came before you didn't want you to know." Obi-Wan suspected they were the ones who had sealed that door, then made the entire place forbidden. Knowing the past meant learning from it, and it was clear the Lenahrans—at least the ones who had stayed behind—did not want those who came after to learn anything that would contradict what they were doing.

Maybe by showing his friends the fate of the first civilization here, Obi-Wan could convince them that continuing to survive as they were would lead to nothing except destruction and death. Maybe he could help them figure out a new way to live. Either on Lenahra or off it. "You need to learn about the past."

"I thought you Jedi weren't supposed to live in the past," Casul grumbled.

"Live there, no. But learn from it? Always."

"It's pointless," Audj said, her tone flat and brooking no argument.

"It's not," Zae-Brii said, quietly but forcefully.

"What?" Audj turned to them in shock.

"We tell the stories of our family, of our people, every night," Zae-Brii said. "Those are our *only* stories. So those are the only lives we can imagine, the only world we can create. Obi-Wan wants to show us someone else's lives, someone else's stories. We can at least look. Learn. Maybe talk about options." Zae-Brii's face flickered into the old woman's. It was only for a brief moment, but it was clear they hadn't stopped thinking about how much life there could still be ahead of them. Ahead of all of them.

"I would like to know, too," Shush said quietly in her barrel.

Obi-Wan wanted to jump in to support Zae-Brii and Shush, but the tension in the room was thick. He thought it best he let their people, their family make this argument. It hurt, a little, that he wasn't one of their own. Still, he understood that when Zae-Brii had asked why they would listen to *him*, it wasn't a condemnation of Obi-Wan. It was recognition of the fact that this push had to come from within.

"We don't need to talk about options," Audj said, but she sounded less sure. And then, unfortunately, she pivoted to anger like a door sliding shut. "He can't come in here and tell us how to live, when he hasn't been here living with us!"

"But I have!" Zae-Brii's face shimmered, and it turned into Audj's face over and over, whether intentional or a reflection of what Zae-Brii couldn't stop thinking about. "I've watched you! You're using more and more of the Power every time. How long before you start to fade? How long before you die? We all watched our parents waste, leaving us here alone. They said they wanted to stay to protect us, to keep us where we could have the Power. But—but they ended up leaving us, just like the others, all the same."

Audj opened her mouth to argue, but Zae-Brii cut her off. "If what he said is true, if we're all supposed to live longer, I want that. If we can find a way for Shush, Trill, and Whistle to be able to stay in water, to be free of those absurd barrels, I want that. If we can figure out something— anything—*any* other way to survive here, then I want that. For all of us."

"They're right," Casul said. He was sitting on the floor, looking out the opening above. At that angle, it was only sky, clear once more. Clear and full of promise, or empty and depthless, depending. "I didn't remember until Zae-Brii showed us that face, but people used to live longer. So much longer. We're taking more of the Power every time. And every time, the harvest gets harder."

A few of the others mumbled assent. Shush had one arm out, around Trill and Whistle where they peered out of their barrel. "I know our parents chose this for us. But we're old enough to make our own choices now."

"All I'm asking is that you look, and then we talk."

Obi-Wan extended a hand to Casul. "Will you come with me and learn? Please?"

Casul stood and pushed past Obi-Wan without taking his hand. But then he called over his shoulder, "Well? Let's get this over with."

Audj shook her head. "I don't like it. It's forbidden."

"Everyone who forbade us is dead." Zae-Brii sounded tired. "I don't want to join them."

Audj threw her hands in the air. "Fine. We'll betray our parents, who gave up everything for us. We'll go and look at those blasted rocks. But we're taking the shuttle. I won't waste any of the Power on this."

"Of course." Obi-Wan didn't want them to have to fight their way there and back, either. It wouldn't make a good case for giving up their stolen abilities.

Audj assigned Shush to watch the younglings once again as she was climbing the ladder. Shush looked upset. Of all the Lenahrans, she had the most motivation to change how they lived.

"I'll tell you everything," Mem promised, then scurried up the ladder so she wouldn't be behind Obi-Wan.

Obi-Wan stopped at Shush's barrel. "I'll make a record for you. Aces can bring back images."

Shush lowered her voice so the younglings playing nearby couldn't hear. "Even if they don't decide to—If they want to—Obi-Wan, I've been thinking. Ever since we spoke.

I wanted to be loyal, but what am I being loyal to? I don't want this life anymore. I don't want it for me, or for Trill and Whistle. We can't live out our whole lives trapped here. No matter what our parents sacrificed, *this* can't be what they hoped for. And if it is, then they were wrong and selfish and only wanted to stay powerful. I won't make the same decision for the little ones in my care. Not now that I have options." She glanced down at Whistle and Trill, once more beneath the surface of the water. "Please don't tell Audj. It will break her heart."

"I won't." Obi-Wan clasped Shush's extended hand. "And I promise, I'll help you. Whatever you decide."

Obi-Wan climbed up the ladder and got settled into the pilot's seat to fly once more to that terrible tomb of a structure. He didn't know how the others would feel after seeing what he had seen. He hoped it would be enough.

CHAPTER
21

"Those pictures could mean a lot of things," Casul grumbled as they emerged from the darkness and back into the light, stopping on the platform that overlooked the terrible gash in the ground. At least Obi-Wan couldn't see the hole that led down into Lenahra's heart from here.

"How many things do you think a pile of bodies can mean?" Obi-Wan asked, aghast but also genuinely curious. Aces trundled along behind him, having provided light and also recorded the murals so they could play them for everyone else back at home base.

"They could have gotten sick."

Obi-Wan answered as gently as he could. "You mean . . . wasted away and died too young?"

"No," Casul snapped. "That's not what I mean. Or there could have been a fire. Or something else."

"They were peaceful." Zae-Brii stared out over the land.

"In the beginning. They lived here in harmony. And then they got bigger—in their own minds, in their own egos. And they took, and didn't stop taking. So the planet stopped them."

"Obviously there was someone left, to carve the last images!"

Zae-Brii's features flickered angrily. "Do you want to be that person, Casul? The lone witness? Because I don't."

"We don't know anything for certain," Audj cautioned. "We should go back and talk, give everyone the same information."

Keeping Nesguin between herself and Obi-Wan, Mem said, "I think—" But she stopped mid-sentence, staring at the sky with a frown. "That's a weird storm."

Obi-Wan followed her gaze. "That's no storm." Something had broken through the atmosphere, leaving a trail of dark gray smoke billowing behind it as it slashed across the sky right toward them. "That's a ship. A large one."

"More Jedi?" Mem looked at Obi-Wan accusingly. "Did you tell them to come here?"

"I have no way of communicating with them." A huge oversight on his part, obviously. And so far away from Coruscant, they wouldn't be able to track his shuttle. He didn't think so, at least. He narrowed his eyes, looking closer at the atmospheric invader. The craft was nearly black, whether in color or from damage. It was massive, blocky and bulky, more like the tremendous construction equipment Obi-Wan had seen on Coruscant than a sleek Jedi transport. And it was getting closer. Very, very fast.

"That's not a Jedi ship," he said.

"Is it crashing?" Zae-Brii asked.

Audj grabbed Zae-Brii's hand. "It's changing direction. Heading right for us. We need to run!"

"Look, there." Obi-Wan pointed where thrusters were burning to slow the descent. Its flight was awkward and ungraceful, but the ship managed to decrease speed enough that it was no longer in danger of smashing into the ground. It lurched heavily toward them, staggering through the sky, and then at last set down with a metallic groan in the center of the great gash . . . right next to the entrance to the passageway down into the planet.

"That can't be a coincidence," Obi-Wan muttered. Of all the places on the entire planet the ship could land, it had aimed for the harvesting spot.

"What do we do?" Mem asked, clearly terrified. She had barely gotten used to Obi-Wan, and now there was a whole new ship to deal with. He felt sorry for her, and also puzzled. What were the odds that no ships had landed on Lenahra in generations, and then there were two in rapid succession?

"Come on," Casul said. "Someone has to greet them. Maybe we'll get lucky and it'll be filled with dozens of annoying Jedi like Obi-Wan, here to tell us how to live our lives and what we can and can't do on our own planet."

"It isn't *our* planet," Zae-Brii said sadly. "Any more than this is my face." They shifted so Casul was looking at himself. "I took it, but that doesn't mean it belongs to me."

"You know I hate it when you look like my brother," Audj said, a shudder going through her from toes to tendrils as she released Zae-Brii's hand.

Casul groaned in exasperation. "Can we go see who's in the ship? We've been alone for so long, and suddenly visitors are raining from the skies. I'd like to know who it is this time."

"I agree," Obi-Wan said, and Casul's head tendrils lifted in surprise. "Whatever this ship is, I don't like it. And I have a feeling it's going to make your lives much more complicated."

"Sky trash always does." But Casul put an arm around Obi-Wan's shoulders to soften his sentiment. "Come on. We can discuss power and safety and how to fight the world that's been trying to eat us our whole lives later. First, let's meet our new friends."

"Aces, stay here." Obi-Wan watched as A6-G2 trundled back up the ramp. "Hopefully their sensors are as fried as yours and they didn't see us. I want you close. But if there's a threat, go back to home base."

The droid beeped in the affirmative, letting Obi-Wan

know she had no problem leaving him. It was less comforting than she probably intended.

Even though it still made the others skittish, Obi-Wan insisted on taking the easy way down through the temple-tomb passages. They exited near where the ship had landed. Up close, it looked even worse. There was carbon scoring on nearly every surface, with sparks and smoke and even a few open flames where the damage from asteroids was too heavy. The whole thing sizzled and groaned and popped, like roasted chando peppers taken from the stove and still too hot to eat. Though Obi-Wan didn't find anything about this ship appetizing.

He had been right, too, about it being different from a Jedi ship. Judging by how many hatches there were, all currently closed, this was a construction-type vehicle, one with far more utility than simple transport or even combat. There was a hiss and a release of steam as a walkway in front of them lowered.

Obi-Wan put one hand on his saber hilt. "Be careful," he warned. "We have no idea who they are or what they want, so engage with caution."

"Steal something and run into trees," Mem suggested. "That helped us with you."

"Good plan," Obi-Wan said, trying not to laugh. "But perhaps we try to speak with them first."

A figure appeared and stepped down the ramp. He was

tall, broad-shouldered, powerful-looking but with a battered air about him, much like the ship. He was also blue with tinges of red, especially on his head tendrils.

"Uncle!" Audj and Casul cried at the same time.

CHAPTER

22

"'*Uncle*'?" Obi-Wan repeated, turning to Zae-Brii, who looked as shocked as he felt. Then Zae-Brii and the others ran forward, too, desperate hunger on their faces.

"Uncle Loegrib!" Audj flung herself at the man.

He put his arms around her, a puzzled expression on his face as his head tendrils moved toward her and Casul, who had joined the hug. "You aren't—You can't be—Are you Ampher and Chemi's tiny children?"

"Yes!" Audj said, pulling back and staring up at him with wonder, like she couldn't believe what she was seeing.

"How are you still alive?" He noticed the others gathered eagerly, trying to see past him into the ship. His head tendrils drooped. "No one else on the crew is from Lenahra."

Zae-Brii's shoulders fell as they nodded, their brief spark of hope smothered. Mem and Nesguin, too, wilted.

Obi-Wan had envied them their freedom, had thought

they relished it. But he saw now that they really were *young*, and they had been alone for so long. He'd never been alone. The entire Temple was filled with mentors, teachers, helpers. There had been one time as a youngling when he had gotten sick. He still remembered the comfort of the Temple nurses, gently caring for him and bossing the droids around. It had felt nice to have nothing to do but get better, and to have capable, patient, caring adults there to make sure it happened.

He felt a little shame, watching. Knowing that he hadn't necessarily taken his life in the Temple for granted, but he definitely hadn't fully appreciated it.

Loegrib looked past them to Obi-Wan, still standing on the periphery. His head tendrils rose in a way Obi-Wan thought looked like a wild creature's hackles rising in alarm or warning. But he didn't know Mikkian body language well enough to accurately interpret their physical reactions.

"You're not from here," Loegrib said with an easy smile that contradicted his wary tendrils.

"My name is Obi-Wan Kenobi."

"Judging by that braid and the weapon at your waist, you're a Jedi youngling."

Obi-Wan lifted an eyebrow, surprised that Loegrib would know about the Jedi. Then again, he had been off-planet for years. He also tried not to be annoyed that Loegrib had called him a youngling when they were nearly the same height. "I'm a Padawan learner."

Loegrib grew more alert as he scanned the surrounding area. "Where's your master?"

"I'm here alone." Obi-Wan tried not to flinch with shame as he said it. If Loegrib knew a Padawan was always with a master, then he knew that Obi-Wan was breaking rules. That or Obi-Wan had been rejected. And really, it might be a case of both if Qui-Gon had left the Temple and the Order.

The others bombarded Loegrib with a flurry of questions, impatient and hungry for news. "Where have you been?" "Where are the other families?" "Why did you come back?"

"Well, little ones"—Loegrib smiled, looking around at the not-so-little Lenahrans—"I never wanted to leave in the first place. I've been trying to get back this whole time." His eyes flitted toward the dark entrance to the harvest tunnel, as though drawn there by gravity. "Which was not an easy task. There were no charts to this region, no map that contained Lenahra."

Obi-Wan had only managed to chart a course thanks to the Jedi Archives and Orla the Wayseeker. But he supposed Loegrib didn't have access to any of those. No one but a Jedi would, and even then, no Jedi had known where to look until Obi-Wan chanced on the old carvings and reopened Orla's notes.

"Why couldn't you come back the way you left?" Nesguin asked.

Loegrib's skin flushed a darker color. "The cowards who dragged me away destroyed the ship's records once we got far enough into space. They didn't want anyone to be able to return, not even knowing full well they hadn't managed to capture everyone. They were more than content to leave you all here. But really, you were the lucky ones!"

Obi-Wan thought of his friends, watching their parents die, fighting to survive ever since. Poor Shush, Trill, and Whistle unable to breathe freely. Audj having to step up and take charge when she was barely past being a youngling. *Lucky* was not how he would describe them.

Loegrib gestured toward the sky. "For the last few years, I've been sweeping this whole vast section of space. Leaving beacons wherever I could, hoping eventually one of them would be found, and whoever found it might have a way back here."

"The beacon was yours?" Obi-Wan couldn't believe it. How many had Loegrib scattered across space? It hadn't even been that close to Lenahra. If Obi-Wan hadn't brought it here and then had A6-G2 crack the code, Loegrib would have never found his way. It wasn't a coincidence that two ships arrived at this lost planet in such a short time, after all.

"And you brought it here." Loegrib frowned. "How did you make it through the asteroid field? You must have an incredibly fast, agile ship. We barely made it through alive in this beast." He patted one of the ramp supports. "And the other two ships didn't make it at all."

"Two ships were lost?" Obi-Wan gasped. "I'm sorry."

Loegrib shrugged. "We knew it wouldn't be easy. And we only needed one to get through, so we succeeded."

"I would imagine the souls on board the other two ships don't feel that way."

Loegrib laughed, the sound bright in contrast to the charred and ruined environment around them. "Grim thing, aren't you? But you must be a skillful young Padawan, that you were drawn here and then activated the beacon to bring what these young ones needed: me."

"I—That's not exactly what—Well, you see, I—" Obi-Wan felt himself blushing. He couldn't admit that he had come here as an act of rebellion against the Order. He had let Qui-Gon believe it was the Force that guided him to the discovery, but really Obi-Wan was afraid he might have been rebelling against the Force as much as he was against the Order. Because while he knew his place in the Order and understood it, his relationship with the Force had become fraught and tainted by fear.

"Well, your mission is accomplished and you've done the Jedi Order proud. You reunited a family. Now that I'm here, you younglings aren't on your own. You have nothing to worry about. Look at the state of your clothing!" Loegrib laughed again. "Let's get you in some new things. Hey!" he shouted behind him. "Bring out some clothes, and some rations."

"Can we go on your ship?" Nesguin gazed eagerly at it. "It's so big. Obi-Wan's ship is small."

Obi-Wan resisted the impulse to defend the honor of his shuttle, which was a very nice ship. Much nicer than this monstrous hunk of metal.

"I'll give you a tour later. It was a rough ride here, and I don't want to go back in until I have to. It's so good to be outside, to be home." Loegrib clapped Nesguin on the shoulder, leading all of them away from the boarding ramp.

As Audj passed Obi-Wan, she squeezed him in a quick hug. "You were right that change needed to happen, and here it is. Thanks to you. You brought family back to us." She beamed at him, then hurried to Loegrib and the others.

Obi-Wan wasn't sure whether or not to follow. No one gestured for him to, or seemed to notice he wasn't standing with them. This reunion was possible because of him, but it wasn't *for* him.

There was still something off, something wrong, but then again, this entire planet felt that way all the time thanks to the harvests. And maybe—maybe Loegrib was right and Obi-Wan had been drawn here by something other than desperation. Maybe the Force *had* led Obi-Wan here, to reunite a family. To bring a protector back, and take the burden away from Audj.

Or maybe it was all a happy coincidence with nothing to do with the Force, and the reason why Obi-Wan felt so lost was because his part in this story was done. They didn't need or want him to stay, and he wasn't wanted or needed anywhere else, either.

CHAPTER
23

Obi-Wan kept watch, worried about a gobbler attack, or an avalanche, or a lightning storm. Anything that would require him to leap into action, to help the others.

Lenahra had never been so quiet. Obi-Wan took it personally.

He hung back near the ship, his feelings as bruised as if he had personally fended off an avalanche with nothing but his emotions. A Besalisk man, tan tinged with green, came out holding uniforms in each of his four arms, all of which ended in enormous, powerful-looking hands.

"Oh! Didn't see you there." The pouch under his jaw wobbled as he talked, and his wide-set yellow eyes narrowed. One tremendous hand scratched the topmost raised crest on his head. "Didn't expect to see *anyone* on the planet, actually."

That didn't make sense. "But Loegrib came back for them. For the ones who were left behind."

"You think our mysterious financier paid this many credits for three ships to grab a few whelps off a deadly, unreachable planet?" The man smiled, but it wasn't unkind. "You are very young, aren't you? I'm Dex."

Obi-Wan turned back to his friends, all circled around Loegrib. They were staring at him like they were parched and he was a pitcher plant filled with water. "I'm Obi-Wan Kenobi. So if you aren't here for them, what are you doing?"

"I'm getting paid, is what I'm doing. And I'm not paid to talk to younglings."

Obi-Wan scowled. "I'm hardly a youngling."

One giant hand patted Obi-Wan's shoulder in a way that was probably meant to be reassuring but was so rough Obi-Wan stumbled back. "Right, not a youngling. Listen. If I had to give advice—which I wouldn't, because I don't do nothing for free—I'd tell you to look the other way on this one. Or better yet, get in your own ship and leave. I've worked a lot of jobs on a lot of planets, and Loegrib's the type of leader who doesn't care what happens around him, long as he gets what he wants."

"What does he want?"

Dex shrugged his upper shoulders, lower arms folding tightly across his expansive middle. He wasn't much taller than Obi-Wan, but there was no question he was far stronger. "I'm here to operate the ship. No one tells me nothing. You want answers, go to Loegrib."

Obi-Wan took the uniforms from Dex and carried them to where Loegrib was regaling the group with tales of his incredible journey. The way Loegrib told it, he may as well have gotten in a fistfight with the asteroids, personally clearing the way.

Actually, it sounded a lot like how Obi-Wan might have woven a story for the other Padawans to try to impress them with his daring, important mission. Which made Obi-Wan even more annoyed.

"Here," Obi-Wan said, shoving the clothes toward Casul. He turned to Loegrib. "Why did you come back?"

Loegrib's easy smile got a little harder. "I don't think that's any of your business. You aren't Lenahran. You're a stranger here. But if you must know, this planet—it holds on to you. It haunts you. I didn't want to leave, and I've been trying to get back ever since. I hate to say I was jealous of my dear brother and his partner, but I did envy them. Getting to make their choice. Getting to stay and keep their children here."

"Strange ship you chose. Reminds me of the big construction ships on Coruscant."

"Needed something strong to get through that asteroid field."

"And now you're going to settle here? Create a new village? You haven't even asked about the younglings still back at camp. Or how you could help the Nautolans."

"Yes, he has." Audj scowled at Obi-Wan. "You weren't over here listening. Loegrib's only shuttle got damaged in the asteroid field, but as soon as it's repaired, he's going to bring everyone back here. To live in the ship with him. Nothing can get through it, so we'll be safe there, and we can figure out a better situation for Shush, Whistle, and Trill."

"And then what?"

"Then," Casul snapped, "it's none of your business, like Loegrib said."

Zae-Brii gave Obi-Wan a much softer look and embraced him. "Thank you for coming here. You've changed everything for us. You really have. And if you want to stay, you're welcome. You'll always have a place with us."

Audj sighed. "Yeah. Sorry. Zae-Brii's right."

Casul gave Obi-Wan an apologetic smile, then cuffed him on the shoulder. "Lenahrans should always accept sky trash, to honor our heritage."

"But Obi-Wan doesn't belong here, not really." Loegrib tilted his head. "Somewhere there's a Master missing a Padawan. And I can't imagine anyone who has worked and trained to become a Jedi Knight would settle like this. Jedi don't settle."

"No," Obi-Wan said, feeling sad and lost because he didn't know whether to say "We don't" or "They don't." He didn't know whether he was in or out of the category of Jedi. But Loegrib was right. Maybe before, when it seemed like he was needed, he could have justified staying. Now he felt like he had at the Temple ever since becoming a Padawan: like he was just taking up space.

He tried to hold on to the happiness and hope he felt from Casul and Audj and the others. He had reunited a family. He had brought help to Lenahra, even if it meant he couldn't settle here, much as he might have dreamed about it.

Once again, Obi-Wan had accomplished what he thought was his goal and discovered all it meant was he no longer knew what to do. How to keep moving forward. Who to be. It was like the Initiate Trials all over again. He had finally become a Padawan learner, only to discover he had no idea what that meant, or how to be one. He had thought he was so ready, so prepared, and instead everything that used to be easy was now impossible.

"Remember what we talked about," Obi-Wan said to Audj. "With the Power. You have enough safety now to take your time and explore other options, other ways of living."

"He knows about the Power?" Loegrib looked sharply at Obi-Wan.

"Yes. It belongs to the planet," Obi-Wan said. "The balance has been disrupted. That's why everything here is so aggressive."

Loegrib laughed. He laughed a lot, Obi-Wan noticed. "I know the Jedi might have taught you that they know everything, but they don't, and *you* certainly don't. The Power is just like the gobblers and the rocks and even the air we breathe. There's nothing mystical about it, any more than the fruit these poor younglings have been surviving on. And it certainly doesn't balance anything." He held up his hand before Obi-Wan could interrupt. "I'm here now, and everything's going to be better. My little ones are right—you did that. Thank you, Padawan. Why don't you fly everyone back to their home base to pack and prepare to live here with me? I'll come for you all as soon as the shuttle is repaired. Shouldn't take more than a day or two. And then—"

"And then we're a family," Audj said, eyes shining.

Loegrib squeezed her shoulder, his head tendrils flat against his skull. "Yes."

Obi-Wan's remaining arguments withered. Loegrib was right. They were a family. He wasn't part of it. And maybe Loegrib was even right that the Force had led Obi-Wan here for exactly this. He could still be guided by the Force even if he wasn't certain, if he couldn't figure out how to connect to it. Right?

He'd already done what he was supposed to do here, and it was time to return to the Temple and face whatever awaited him there. After all, Jedi didn't stay forever. They gave people and planets what they needed to move forward and help themselves. Just the way Master Yoda taught initiates.

Everything had worked out, and the only thing wrong on Lenahra that couldn't be fixed was Obi-Wan Kenobi.

"**B**oss wants an update," the representative said, smoking his death stick. "When do you think we'll get him his shipment?"

"I'll let him know." Loegrib had already disabled the tracking device and dismantled the communication capabilities of the ship. Fortunately, the representative was content to hassle and annoy without ever actually doing anything himself, so he had no idea.

"What about those younglings?" The representative blew a perfect circle of smoke into the air, then stabbed his death stick through it. "You didn't say there would be anyone here."

"It doesn't change anything."

A harsh laugh. "You're a cold man, you know that? They think you're here to save them."

He wasn't there to save anyone. His selfish brother had let him be taken, had probably wanted him to be taken. Kept all the Power for himself, and for his children. But he was dead, and Loegrib was here with everything he needed to take it all, to keep it all, forever.

And when he flew away and left those selfish brats behind, powerless, they would know. They would know how he felt. They would know what it was to lose, just as he had. It would be better if it were his brother, but this was almost as good.

After he left, he would visit the others. Their new planet, tucked away between two stars. He would descend on them glowing with power, and they would see him as he truly was, as he was always meant to be. They would scream and weep and beg, as he had. And he wouldn't stop, as they hadn't. They had ripped him away from his life, and he would rip their lives away from them.

"What about the little Jedi? Our boss wouldn't like the Jedi knowing about this place."

"I'll tell you how to get to their ship." Loegrib pulled the charge out of his bag and tossed it.

The representative caught it, fumbling and nearly dropping it. "I'm not going to blow up a bunch of younglings!"

Loegrib resisted rolling his eyes. They didn't matter. No one did. "Then set it for a high altitude, so when the Jedi takes off to go report back to his masters . . ."

"Boom," the representative whispered.

This planet, this power, was Loegrib's and his alone. And no one—not his pathetic niece and nephew, not some whelp of a Jedi, not the man who had paid Loegrib's way here thinking he would get a new source of power in return—was going to stop him. Not this time.

CHAPTER
24

Obi-Wan couldn't get comfortable.

All around him were the small noises of other bodies sleeping. It wasn't that keeping him awake—if anything, it was comforting, a reminder of his days bunking with creche mates instead of sleeping alone in his Padawan quarters.

Being a Padawan was so unexpectedly lonely. He wasn't connected to Qui-Gon, and he didn't feel connected to the Force, and all his friends were tied to other people more than they'd ever be tied to him again. Becoming a Padawan had always been his goal—the most important step toward his final destiny as a Jedi Knight—so why did it feel so much like a *loss*?

Maybe that was why he was dreading leaving Lenahra. He wasn't part of this crew the same way he had been part of his youngling clan, but for a while it had almost felt like he was. He wanted to be Audj's best friend, the one who eased her burden of leadership. To have Casul's admiration and trust. To help Zae-Brii manage the emotions of everyone here. To sneak off into a dark corner with . . . well, anyone. Or no one. His decision, based only on what he wanted here.

But nothing ever stayed the same, and everything on Lenahra was changing for his new friends, too. Which left no place or purpose for him. It was time to go.

He wasn't ready to return to the Temple and discover his fate. But at least he could offer them information about Lenahra and the odd planet's power as an apology for his disobedience. And the datacard, which surely had to have been left behind by Orla the Wayseeker. That would be worth something.

What was his ideal outcome upon return, though? Forgiveness? Punishment?

Or had he rebelled in the first place because he secretly hoped they would strip him of his Padawan learner status, cut his braid, relegate him to some other role, some other life? Because then the path would be set. Chosen for him. And he would know it was right, because everyone else in the Temple used the Force in ways he couldn't manage.

Did he think he deserved to be punished because he couldn't connect to the Force the way he wanted? Maybe. He was letting himself down, and the Order as a whole, and he wanted to stop feeling this way.

And when he got back, what about Qui-Gon? Would he

be disappointed in Obi-Wan, or would he just be . . . gone? Obi-Wan thought the latter option would hurt more. At least disappointment would mean Qui-Gon cared in some way about the Padawan Yoda had pushed on him.

Obi-Wan slipped out of his hammock and pulled on his boots. Better to leave now rather than lie in the dark, stewing about the future. This wasn't a good stew. It was a stew laced with tentacles, injecting him with poison until he couldn't make any decision at all.

He thought of waking Audj or Zae-Brii or even Casul. But he didn't know what he'd say. *Thanks for the adventure? Hope your new lives are great? Please miss me so I feel like I had an impact here?*

He'd always thought avoiding attachments would be easy, that being a Jedi would keep him separate, his devotion to the Force like a shield between him and dangerous emotional connection. He had been wrong. He missed his old friends now that they were all separated, with different masters. And after only a few days, he knew he'd miss these new friends fiercely, as well. That was another reason to leave quietly, wasn't it?

Obi-Wan climbed to the top of the great destroyed ship that soon the others would no longer call home. A6-G2 had stayed in the shuttle, working on the problem of getting older tech to talk to new tech. Obi-Wan could see the dull blue pulse of one of her lights from the cockpit window, the only thing to look at up here other than—

A hint of movement, right beneath his shuttle. Organic, not mechanical.

Obi-Wan froze. Had a gobbler gotten up here somehow? Or maybe another creature he didn't know about yet? There were those gliding animals he'd seen on his flight in. What if there were bigger versions with fangs and claws? His hand drifted to his lightsaber, but he didn't draw it. Something about the silence, about the stealth of whatever was moving beneath his ship, set off warning bells in his head.

Gobblers weren't stealthy. And what would another animal be doing creeping silently under a shuttle when all the living things were sound asleep on another floor? The sleeping area had an entire wall open to the sky. If a flying creature wanted to attack, it had easy access.

The figure pulled away, silhouetted briefly against the night sky before slipping over the side of the ship. Obi-Wan had been right to stay hidden. It wasn't an animal at all, but humanoid. Someone had been snooping around his T-5. And not one of his friends. Everyone was accounted for downstairs, fast asleep.

It hadn't been four-armed and instantly recognizable Dex, that much he was sure of. But other than that, he had no answers. He crept forward. There was a lingering scent he couldn't quite place, a hint of acrid smoke, but not strong enough to indicate anything had been burned here. The ramp was firmly closed, and he had seen A6-G2's ambient light, so she was safe. But still, best to check. He lowered the ramp and climbed aboard. Nothing seemed amiss. The droid was plugged into the controls, an array of wires and ports around her.

"Hey, Aces," Obi-Wan whispered. Her lights flashed, blinking to life from whatever passive state she had been in. "Nothing wrong with you?"

The droid beeped indignantly.

"Right, of course. Now, anything wrong with the ship?"

There was a low whirring noise as A6-G2 scanned all their systems. Then she beeped an all clear. Nothing in the ship's systems had been damaged.

What was someone from the other ship doing lurking about? Obi-Wan went back outside to examine the shuttle exterior. Maybe they wanted parts for repairs and were looking to see what was available? Or maybe their shuttle was damaged beyond repair and they wanted the T-5 itself, but with the astromech visible inside, they had opted not to try to steal it.

Or maybe they were skulking around in the middle of the night for totally innocent purposes.

No matter their goal, if they *were* interested in his shuttle, Obi-Wan should leave immediately rather than risk being stranded. The others might be thrilled to see Loegrib, but Obi-Wan knew Loegrib didn't like it. It wasn't difficult to sense.

He walked beneath the ship, running a hand along the bottom to reassure himself that he still had options. He had a ship and an entire galaxy. He could leave Lenahra, but that didn't mean he had to go back to the Temple. Maybe he'd wait until A6-G2 managed to crack the left-behind data.

His hand caught on something too precise to be damage from the asteroid field. That would be a gash, or a dent. This stuck out. It was a low-profile ridged cylinder about the size of his hand. The T-5 was sleek-bodied to allow the wings to rotate around it. Whatever this was, it wasn't part of the design of the shuttle. A direct tug didn't budge it, so Obi-Wan pried it from the side until a magnetic lock disengaged.

There were no buttons that he could make out, just one sullen red light that had been facing the ship's hull, invisible until the device was pulled off. He had seen something like it before, but he couldn't think where or when.

It was too big to be a tracker. Besides, anyone on the other ship knew where Obi-Wan was from and where, theoretically, he would return. The Jedi didn't hide their location. There was no point tracking him to Coruscant.

The only thing Obi-Wan could think the device might be was something so absurd it felt impossible. But he had no other guesses. Was he holding a *bomb*?

He went onto his ship so he could study it. Other than the single red light, there was a readout with numbers. They were static, unchanging. He lifted it closer to his face, and the lowest number ticked up half a point. He lowered it, and it ticked back down.

It wasn't a timer. Was it responding to altitude? And if so . . . why?

He needed more information. But he couldn't let anyone know he was looking for it. He turned to the droid. "Aces, tomorrow I'll have you pretend to go off-planet. As soon as you're out of sight, fly low to the abandoned settlement and hide the ship there. Don't bring it out for anyone but me."

The droid's whistle was concerned. At least someone here cared about Obi-Wan's safety. Or if not quite that, the droid cared about her own instructions should Obi-Wan fail to return. She beeped impatiently, asking Obi-Wan for plans.

"First things first: I'm going to get this away from the others. Then I'll figure out if it's a bomb. And if it is, I'm going to find out who exactly wanted to blow us up, and why."

It looked as though his return to Coruscant would have to wait. He had another mystery to solve.

Down in the ship, Obi-Wan debated his accomplice options. Obviously Shush was out. Even with the breather, she slept in a barrel of water and Obi-Wan couldn't wake her without a lot of splashing. Mem and Nesguin were on the far side of the room in the middle of all the younglings, and neither seemed to trust him much anyway. What he was about to do impacted Audj and Casul more than anyone, so that seemed like a reason to keep them in the dark until he knew more.

Zae-Brii was the only one who really listened when Obi-Wan warned them things were wrong. Navigating by the low ambient light from the pods glowing under their lids, he crept to Zae-Brii's side. Their yellow eyes popped open in alarm as he put a hand on their shoulder.

"Shh, it's me," Obi-Wan whispered. "Listen. I think someone might have put a bomb on my shuttle."

"What?" Zae-Brii's answering whisper was sharp with

shock. Obi-Wan put a finger over his lips, and their next whisper was much more modulated. "Who would do that? And why?"

"I don't know, but I'm going to find out. It's probably best if the culprit thinks I've left the planet, so Aces is going to fly my shuttle away in the morning. I don't want another attempt that I might miss. I needed someone here to know that I haven't disappeared, though."

"Why didn't you tell Audj?"

"Because if it is a bomb, it had to have come from the new arrivals."

Zae-Brii's expression darkened with understanding. "I can't believe they would try to blow you up."

"So uncivilized. The least they could have done is shot me to my face."

Zae-Brii didn't laugh. "Be careful."

"I'm always careful." He paused. "In theory. Between you and me, I haven't had much actual experience to practice being careful."

"Then be careful so you can get even more experience being careful, please."

"I will." Obi-Wan squeezed their hand, then slipped out of the ship. He didn't want to send down a cable and risk waking anyone else, so he jumped, using the Force to guide and slow his descent. He landed without a sound on the forest floor. Checking the device, he was unsurprised to find the numbers had lowered in coordination with his rough estimate of how far he had dropped.

If it was a bomb and it was tied to altitude, they wanted him to blow up when he was away from the ship with the others. Which was a comfort, he supposed. Both that they didn't want to blow everyone up and that the device was unlikely to detonate anywhere near ground level. And if it wasn't a bomb, it was still clearly tracking altitude for some baffling reason. Satisfied that he didn't need to ditch it immediately, he began running toward Loegrib's monstrous ship. If he went quickly, he could make it there before dawn.

But after a few minutes he became aware of movement behind him. Something—or someone—was following him. So his assailant hadn't fled, but was watching. Time to unmask them and get some answers. Obi-Wan drew his lightsaber in one smooth motion as he turned.

It lit the very surprised face of Zae-Brii. "You're going to need me," they said.

"But—"

Zae-Brii's face shifted, and suddenly Obi-Wan was looking at Loegrib. The borrowed uniform Zae-Brii had changed into perfectly completed the deception. When they spoke, Zae-Brii's voice was deeper, a fairly close imitation of Loegrib's. "Don't you think it's odd that he didn't invite us on the ship? That he didn't insist on coming in your shuttle and getting the younglings immediately, content to wait a couple days until their own shuttle was repaired?"

"I do, in fact, think both those things are odd."

"Me too. And now your possible bomb. Wait." Zae-Brii's face shifted back to their own, their thin lips pursed. "What did you do with it?"

"It's right here." Obi-Wan pulled it out of one of his belt pouches.

Zae-Brii hissed. "You've got it on you? What was that about being careful?"

"I couldn't very well leave it with the others! And I'm not positive it's a bomb. There doesn't seem to be any sort of timer. I think it's tied to altitude."

"So throw it over the side of a cliff!"

"The impact might set it off and hurt some animals. When we get on the other ship, we can figure out how to disarm it, or find someone who knows. Besides, if all else fails, nothing like holding a bomb to help speed along negotiations."

"Are all Jedi as mad as you?" Zae-Brii asked as they resumed running.

"Judging by my master . . . maybe."

"What would you think, if your own student was doing this?"

"Oh, I'll never have a Padawan as bad as I am." Obi-Wan was certain of that.

Really, this was all Qui-Gon's fault. If Qui-Gon had shown up when he was supposed to, he'd be here now and doubtless would have already worked everything out.

But it went back further than that. If Qui-Gon had been the type of master Obi-Wan needed, then Obi-Wan would have been able to connect to the Force, would have been out on missions like the other Padawans, would be a better Padawan.

Then again, if Obi-Wan were a better Padawan, then perhaps Qui-Gon would have shown up in the first place. Wouldn't have been lured by Count Dooku. Would have chosen Obi-Wan instead of being assigned to him.

So really it was Obi-Wan's fault for failing to be the best Padawan learner he could be.

But then again . . . if Obi-Wan hadn't engaged in this rebellion, his new friends on Lenahra would have been alone. Forever. No one would have picked up that beacon. No one would have come for them. Whether it turned out to be good or bad, it *was* Obi-Wan's fault the new ship was here, which made it his responsibility to see this through. And he would. No matter what. He might not be the best Padawan, but he wouldn't abandon these brave young fighters to an unknown fate that his coming had set in motion.

He suspected Qui-Gon would approve of that, at least.

He and Zae-Brii raced through the night, silent and swift. The trees barely noticed them, and no animals found them. It couldn't have gone any better, which made Obi-Wan nervous. Nothing on Lenahra was easy for the Lenahrans.

"Why is it so quiet?" Obi-Wan whispered.

Zae-Brii shook their head. "I didn't take any of the Power before we left. Maybe you're right. Maybe that's why the planet hates us."

"Or maybe . . ." Obi-Wan stopped, looking down the slope of a steep hill toward the gash where the other ship sat. Surrounding the area, growling and shifting, was what appeared to be every animal on Lenahra.

CHAPTER
26

"Well, this is less than ideal." Obi-Wan paced, staring at the barrier of angry animals between them and their goal.

"Why aren't they attacking?" Zae-Brii asked.

"Maybe they know they can't win? It's more about threatening or menacing the ship? Or maybe because no one there has taken anything from the cave?"

"Maybe." Zae-Brii looked dubious. "What are our resources? We could go back for your shuttle, fly in over them?"

"I need whoever targeted me to think they haven't been discovered. So our resources are stealth, the element of surprise, and your shape-shifting."

"Which won't do us any good unless we can get to the ship."

"No, none of that helps us get past all these creatures. I suppose we also have my lightsaber, but I don't feel right about killing any living thing unless I absolutely have to."

"Could we try to set your bomb off as a distraction?"

Obi-Wan opened the pouch at his waist and checked that the numbers were remaining predictable. "We're not sure it's a bomb, and if it is, I'd rather it not go off at all. And whatever it is, it's tied to altitude, so we can't detonate it on our own. Not safely, anyway."

"What do you suggest, then? We walk right through the animals that have been trying to kill me for as long as I can remember?"

Obi-Wan tugged on his braid, thinking. "They've never tried to harm me unless I was with the rest of you. And the only difference between us that I can think of is I've never consumed the"—he waved his hand vaguely—"glowy planet orbs."

"The Power, you mean."

"Yes, that. You said you didn't consume any since the harvest. How long does it take to leave your system?"

"Less and less time now that I'm not a youngling. I think it's gone, but . . . I don't want to find out the hard way."

"I have a feeling everything tonight will be the hard way. No way forward but through. If it comes to it, I promise I can defend you." Obi-Wan would do whatever it took to make sure Zae-Brii stayed safe. He knew he could do that much, at least.

Zae-Brii threw back their shoulders, a determined expression narrowing their eyes. "Let's go."

As they approached the nearest animals, the creatures began growling and shifting, turning toward them. But from this distance, Obi-Wan realized something strange. "It looks like the asteroid field. The way they move, I mean. The same types of patterns and reactions."

He grabbed Zae-Brii's arm and tugged them to the side. As they walked, the creatures mimicked their movement, following them, getting closer. Maybe, somehow, it *was* actually like the asteroid field. How had he made it through that?

"Stay calm!" he said, excited.

"Right, not a problem," Zae-Brii answered with a tone that contradicted their words.

"They're reacting to us. Absorbing and mirroring how we feel. I think. I hope." He really, really hoped he was right about this. When he was calm in the forest, the gobbler had played with him. And when the gobblers had surrounded him, he hadn't consumed the Power, but he *had* been in a panic and also surrounded by people who had stolen the Power. "The more agitated and frightened we are, the more they will be, too. We need to stay calm. Focused. Not aggressive or scared."

"How do we do that?"

Obi-Wan laughed. "If I knew, I wouldn't be here. Not being calm or focused is exactly why I left." He tried to think of how Qui-Gon instructed him, or how their meditation classes as younglings had gone, back before meditation had become so fraught and aggravating. Back before the things that had felt easy became impossible because he stopped *feeling* them and started trying to *understand* them, to control them.

That was his problem, wasn't it? Things had stopped being easy because he didn't trust that they should be. Because he was afraid of losing what he already had.

"Think of something that makes you feel happy and at ease," he said.

"Oh, that's not hard."

At first Obi-Wan thought Zae-Brii was being sarcastic again, but Zae-Brii's arm under his hand relaxed, and he could almost feel the contentment radiating off them.

"What are you thinking about?"

"I'm on top of the ship, with Audj. All the younglings are fast asleep. We're staring at the stars and wondering what life is like on other planets. We don't have anywhere to be or anything to do except exist, side by side, and think about the stars. That's the only time Audj ever hints that she wants more than what we have here, that she wonders what life is like other places. It's the happiest thing I can imagine, hand in hand with her, dreaming."

"I don't think that image is going to work for me."

"I'd be a little upset with you if it did," Zae-Brii said, nudging him with an elbow. "But surely there's a place you can go in your mind that makes you feel safe. Secure."

Obi-Wan knew the answer should be meditation, but that didn't make him feel any of those things. It made him feel anxious, desperate, afraid. All things he didn't want these creatures expressing back at them. But even though those feelings had become magnified lately, they weren't how he always felt in the Temple.

He loved the Temple, now that he was away from it and might not ever get to go back. He loved the pools, the underground rooms, the secret passageways he and his creche mates found, only to realize later they weren't secret at all. He loved the training rooms, loved sparring, loved the exhilaration triggered by the hum of the little droids that shot him until he learned to deflect with his lightsaber. He loved the Archives, loved visiting them and seeing the galaxy spread out, contained, knowable. Right there for them to learn about, right there for them to know how to help. An answer to every question.

When did he feel the *calmest*, though? The most focused? The answer came to him and he felt a blush of embarrassment as he took out his lightsaber but didn't turn it on. "I'm going to do something strange. Just follow and hold on to your stars-with-Audj calmness."

Obi-Wan began moving through his lightsaber forms. He had practiced them so many times they were pure muscle memory. He could slip into them without thinking, go through the movements like a dance, one to the next to the next in smooth spins and dodges, all done with a harmless lightsaber hilt and a totally clear mind. He used the forms to move himself through the waiting creatures. It was hard not to get distracted by success as the creatures around them shifted aside without a noise or a threat, but Obi-Wan had plenty of practice doing his forms when things were chaotic. Though usually that chaos came in the form of other Padawan learners, as opposed to lots of animals with lots of teeth.

Then again, Padawans had teeth, too. They just didn't go to them as their first line of attack and defense.

Obi-Wan tried not to laugh, imagining Siri going into a fight teeth-first. Best to focus on his own forms, as always. He supposed he *had* been rather distracted by the other Padawans lately, after all. Maybe not worried they were going to eat him, but definitely worried they were passing him by, learning more than he was, doing better than he was. Leaving him behind.

But this practice? These forms? Obi-Wan could do them forever.

After what felt like both an eternity and no time at all, he and Zae-Brii reached the lip of the gash, which functioned as the perimeter of the creatures. Obi-Wan did one last tuck and roll before popping back up, allowing himself a moment of triumph both for his excellent form and his clever idea to get them through unharmed.

And then Obi-Wan's stomach dropped in horror as the real reason the creatures were gathered but not attacking was at last revealed.

A gobbler, two of its six legs at angles they shouldn't be, whimpered in the center of a cage. The walls of the cage were solid metal, but the door was made of bars, allowing the gobbler to see out—and all the other creatures to see in.

Sitting on top of the cage, whistling, was a man. Even in the dark it was obvious he held a blaster, casually pointed down toward the wounded gobbler.

"The creatures aren't attacking because they don't want that one to die," Obi-Wan whispered. They must have a complex social system, to care that much about one of their own. Obi-Wan suspected he had only scratched the surface of how interconnected everything on this planet was.

"I never thought I'd feel sorry for a gobbler," Zae-Brii answered. "But how are we getting past that guard? He'll see us sneaking into the ship."

The ramp was down, the door to the ship wide open.

That was how unconcerned the crew was about potential attacks—or espionage. And they were right to be confident. They had neutralized the local fauna, and they probably didn't consider the local population a threat. Especially not when getting to the ship meant getting past that mean-looking guard and his equally mean-looking blaster.

"Loegrib could distract him." Obi-Wan nudged his companion.

"Unless the crew mutinied and took over, and Loegrib is caged inside, and that's why everything has gotten bad." Even though it was a worst-case scenario, Zae-Brii sounded hopeful.

"One way to find out. If he shouts in surprise that Loegrib is free when he sees you, I'll jump in."

Zae-Brii sighed, clearly unhappy but resigned. "The head tendrils really take a lot of concentration." Their face blurred, and then their color changed as they put on Loegrib's face. "Here goes everything."

Zae-Brii walked forward confidently, a good mimic of Loegrib's body language. "Anything to report?" they asked in Loegrib's voice, moving around the cage so the guard would face away from the ship.

"If there was, I'd use the comlink." The guard held it up derisively.

Zae-Brii laughed, and Obi-Wan flinched; it didn't sound like an adult male's laugh. It sounded like the laugh of a teenager, trying to cover up their devastation that Loegrib was, in fact, still in charge. Obi-Wan used the opportunity to rush from his cover and slip down toward the ramp.

"Right," Zae-Brii said, clearing their throat like the laugh had been some sort of weird cough. "Wanted to stretch my legs after how long we were cooped up on that ship."

"Back on it soon enough." The guard tapped his blaster on the cage, glaring down at the contents. "Our boss will be eager for results."

They weren't planning on staying? Had Loegrib told the others he would take them off-planet? Maybe he had and Obi-Wan hadn't been privy to it. He wanted to listen, but he needed to get inside before he lost his chance.

Obi-Wan hurried up the ramp, hoping that Zae-Brii didn't accidentally reveal their deception or trigger suspicion. He paused to get his bearings. Now that he was here, he had no idea what he should do next.

He almost laughed as he remembered a game they had played often as initiates: hide-and-sense. They would scatter throughout their clan and training quarters, and one youngling would have to try to sense where they all were—blindfolded. They had thought it was merely a game, but in reality it was careful, crucial training.

Everything had been easier when he was an initiate, when using the Force was the same as playing. As easy as reaching out and expecting to find something, and finding it there simply because he expected it to be.

He could treat this like a game, though the potential bomb in his pouch did make the stakes rather higher than they had been at the Temple, when all he faced was Siri's teasing and Prie's transparent attempts to cheat. She hated games so much.

Now that he thought about it, though, he'd had fun with Bolla, hadn't he? They had played jokes on each other all the time. Once, Obi-Wan had swapped Bolla's wash cream for Naboo glitterpaste. Bolla had shimmered for days. He almost laughed out loud, remembering it. Bolla was right— Obi-Wan had been competitive. So maybe when Bolla said he was trying to help Obi-Wan lighten up again, he had meant it. Obi-Wan had been so miserable lately, he could only assume miserable intentions from others.

Trying to remember what playing a game had felt like, Obi-Wan closed his eyes to quiet his mind and focus. It wasn't as easy or as fun as when he had been young, but— there, like warm spots in a chilled room. They were scattered through the ship: three clustered on the far end, one closer, a couple above him somewhere. Six total, seven with the one outside, and—

Obi-Wan's senses touched ever so lightly on the creatures waiting nearby, and it was like jumping to hyperspace, his senses rushing out and away so quickly he panicked, throwing his eyes open and gasping for air as he tried to come back to himself.

He almost failed to notice the life-form approaching from behind. He whirled, fists up, to find himself face to face with Loegrib. Fortunately, Loegrib's face became Zae-Brii's. "Well?" they demanded. "Obviously Loegrib's still in charge. So what do we do now?"

Obi-Wan tried to shake off the lingering dizziness. What had that been? Why had his mind been pulled so far, so fast, in such an overwhelming way? That had *never* happened at the Temple. "Six life-forms on board, not counting your friend out there."

Zae-Brii scowled. "He wanted me to smoke something called death sticks with him. I've had enough death in my life without willingly inhaling it. I told him I needed to eat so I could get away."

"Let's look around. See what evidence there is to discover."

"Wait—that's it? That's your whole plan?" Zae-Brii's eyes widened with incredulity. "Wander around and look at things?"

Obi-Wan shrugged defensively. "My original plan was to come *alone*."

"And what would you have done without me, wait around outside and hope the death sticks eventually kill the guard?"

He couldn't help laughing. "Maybe."

Zae-Brii shook their head. "Honestly. You're lucky Loegrib was acting suspicious enough that I was willing to come with you. Speaking of." Loegrib's face reappeared on Zae-Brii. "Walk behind me and hide if someone is coming. I can't hold this for too long, so we'll have to be quick."

They crept down the narrow passageway. Buttons and lights and gauges covered everything. Obi-Wan had thought the cockpit of an Aethersprite was complicated, but it was nothing compared with this. Everything was loud, too, with constant hisses and pops and metallic groans.

"To your left." Obi-Wan pointed. There was a big room with gear scattered in piles and a table in the center. All the walls were lined with leak-proof containers.

Zae-Brii tapped one of the large containers. "Empty."

On the table was a crate full of familiar-looking metallic objects. Obi-Wan pulled the bomb out of his pouch, and Zae-Brii took it, looking closely before nodding. "It's the same. This is where it came from."

Before Obi-Wan could grab another to examine it, they heard footsteps. Obi-Wan ducked behind a pile of crates, and Zae-Brii-as-Loegrib turned around, ready to greet whoever was coming.

Obi-Wan's stomach dropped. What if it was Loegrib himself? It was a huge relief when he heard Dex's voice, instead. But unlike earlier, there was nothing friendly about it.

"Who unsealed this box? What're you doing with that?

Are you mad? These mining charges are fickle! Sometimes even a change in air pressure can fool the altimeter and set it off! No one should touch anything here without my permission, and I haven't given it." Dex cleared his throat with a deep, wet rumble. "I mean, you should be careful, sir."

Obi-Wan made a split-second decision and stepped free of the crates. "If someone attached one of those to the bottom of, say, a T-5 shuttle, what would happen when it took off?"

Dex's small eyes blinked in surprise. He looked back at who he thought was Loegrib. Zae-Brii shook their head, then shifted back into themself. "Way to keep your cover, Obi-Wan," they grumbled.

"Well?" Obi-Wan kept his voice level and not accusatory. Dex hadn't known the box was unsealed. And he definitely hadn't been the mysterious figure in the dark. Obi-Wan was going to give him the benefit of the doubt. Mostly because he didn't have many other options for answers here, and Dex sounded like he could make certain the charge wasn't dangerous anymore. "What would happen?"

Dex's voice was hushed as he carefully used a tool to reset the numbers on the device. He placed it in the box with the others and put a lid on top, checking the readings before pressing a button to seal it shut. "We use those charges to safely detonate in mines. Figure out the altitude difference, then send it down remotely. When it hits the programmed altitude?" He held out all four hands. "Boom. So if some-one set this to, say, a high altitude, instead? You'd come back down pretty quickly. As pieces. You really found this on the bottom of your shuttle?"

"Yes. Someone put it there tonight."

Dex rubbed one of his enormous hands over the crest running along the top of his head. He swore in a language Obi-Wan wasn't familiar with. "Knew the money was too good. Good money, bad intentions."

"Do you know who wanted me dead?"

Dex's neck pouch wobbled. "I don't even know who's funding all this. But whoever heard Loegrib's tales spent a lot of time and a lot of credits helping him get back here. Other than that, I don't know much. I'm a miner for hire. They only tell me where to aim the drills."

Obi-Wan shared a knowing look with Zae-Brii. "So this is a drilling ship."

Dex nodded. "I suspected things weren't exactly *moral* when we lost the other two ships and Loegrib didn't wriggle so much as a tendril. Two ships and all the souls aboard, gone, just like that, and all he could do was talk about this planet. Skeleton crews, too, for such a big job. Like he wants as few people knowing about it as possible." Dex nodded toward Obi-Wan, the pouch under his chin expanding and deflating in a sigh. "Guess you knew too much."

"And here I've been worried I knew too little." Did

Loegrib not want the Jedi to know about what he was doing here? Or about the planet itself? "What are they mining?"

Dex shrugged two sets of shoulders. "The plan is to go deep and fast, load all the cargo spaces, and leave."

"With his family, and the younglings? Is the shuttle craft ready yet?"

Dex frowned, small eyes narrowing. "Nothing wrong with any of the shuttles or escape pods. And no one said anything about transporting people. No preparation for that at all. Whatever he's doing, I don't think any of you are part of his plans."

Zae-Brii's whole body wilted. "He was never going to take us with him. This will destroy Audj and Casul."

Obi-Wan put a hand on Zae-Brii's shoulder, then looked back up at Dex. "Why are you helping us?"

Dex tapped a finger on the box of mining charges. "Seems to me someone willing to blow up a young, innocent scrap like yourself wouldn't think twice about killing a miner after the job's done. I'll keep my eyes open. You do the same. Come on, I'll lead you out a back way. And whatever you do, keep your friends far from here, where they'll be safe."

"What about you?"

"Oh, I always manage. I'm a hard one to kill." He grinned a many-toothed smile at Obi-Wan, then opened a door into the night.

They jumped down, hurrying away into the darkness along the gash until they reached a place with fewer creatures, since neither of them was in any condition to control their emotions. At the top of the gash, they stared down at the ship, sitting on the wounded land like a Sargonian behemoth tick about to gorge itself.

"The rock here can't be worth this amount of work," Zae-Brii said grimly.

Obi-Wan agreed. The placement of the ship. The leak-proof cargo containers. "He came back for the Power," Obi-Wan said. "He's going to take it all with him."

I t took Obi-Wan and Zae-Brii longer to return to the home ship, since they had to travel in a wide arc to avoid the congregated animals. By the time they arrived, day had as well, the planet's sun hitting them with sharp rays. Though not as sharp as the glare on Audj's face as she stood in the entrance to the ship, arms folded, tendrils as tense as her jaw.

"Where were you two?" she demanded.

"Long version, or short version?" Obi-Wan gazed longingly toward the hammocks. Not that he'd be able to sleep anyway. There was so much to do. He wasn't actually sure how to do any of it, though.

Zae-Brii got right to the point. "Someone put a bomb on Obi-Wan's ship so he'd blow up as soon as he left the atmosphere."

"I probably would have blown up before then," Obi-Wan said with a shrug. He hoped that Loegrib—or whoever set the bomb—at least had the decency to set the altitude extremely high so the young people of Lenahra wouldn't be injured by debris.

"What?" Audj looked outraged. And confused. Her tone caused all the younglings to stop their sleepy morning routine and pay attention.

Casul waved to Shush. She corralled the little ones, moving them toward the ladder. Whistle and Trill were thrilled as they padded, dripping, across the floor. They received almost no outdoor time.

If Obi-Wan had blown up, and Loegrib never helped them, those poor Nautolans would have lived out the rest of their lives in barrels of water. It was terrible. Obi-Wan felt worse thinking about that than he did his own possible fiery demise.

Nesguin and Mem came over, puzzled, but Casul pushed on with the conversation without filling them in. "Who put the bomb there?"

Obi-Wan shook his head. "It was dark. I couldn't see. All I know is it was someone from the other ship. But not everyone there knew about it. Dex was upset by the news."

"Who is Dex?" Casul asked.

"A miner," Zae-Brii said.

"A miner?" Mem frowned so the white planes of her face looked even more cracked.

"It's a mining ship," Obi-Wan said.

"We went there and snuck aboard," Zae-Brii continued. "Dex told us their shuttle isn't broken at all. There are no plans to come get us or add us to their crew. They're only here to mine. To dig deep and fast and take all the Power, seal it up, and leave. Without us."

"Even if that's true, where does the bomb come into it? Why would anyone want to kill you?" Casul's tendrils shifted in agitation.

Obi-Wan answered, "Loegrib doesn't want anyone else knowing about the planet. He can't have me going back to Coruscant and giving details."

Audj folded her arms. "But if Loegrib's going to mine and leave, like this miner said, why would he care if anyone else knew about Lenahra? He'll have what he wants and be gone."

Obi-Wan frowned. "Well, he—"

"And do you *know* it was him who placed the bomb?"

"No, I couldn't see who it was. But none of the rest of the crew would have any idea where to find us. Loegrib would know where to find this ship from when he lived on the planet."

Casul pointed out the open wall. "They could have seen our location when they were flying in, or done a scan. That's not difficult."

"Scanning actually *is* difficult on Lenahra," Obi-Wan countered. "My scanning systems malfunction here."

Nesguin was nervously scratching one of his curling horns, his fingernails catching on the ridges and making a clicking sound. "This miner you talked to, is he in charge?"

"No, he was just hired on for the job."

"So why are you trusting anything he says over our own uncle?" The edges of Casul's face went a darker blue. "Maybe this Dex planted the bomb. Maybe he's trying to mutiny, and using you to do it."

"Couldn't have been him. He has a distinctive silhouette." Obi-Wan definitely would have noticed the extra arms.

"So another crew member he's working with." Casul shrugged.

Obi-Wan shot an exasperated look at Zae-Brii, who offered no help, their own face puzzled. He pushed on alone. "But your uncle didn't tell you why he was really here. It's definitely a mining ship."

"Why is that a problem?" Audj gazed past them at the planet spreading with blue-and-green glory beneath them.

"He's going to take the *Power*. All of it. Or as much as he can." Obi-Wan was sure Audj would care about that, at least, given how upset they all were when he told them they needed to stop using it.

"Why shouldn't he?"

"What?" Obi-Wan couldn't understand what he was hearing, or Audj's casual tone.

She continued. "If he can get it faster and easier than

we can, why not? Good for him. Good for all of us. It's not helping anyone down there in the ground."

"Don't you think it's down there for a reason?"

"No!" Audj's casual demeanor cracked. "I don't! I don't think anything on this planet is for a reason. We were never supposed to land here, never supposed to settle here. And then the others left us, and our parents died, and we've all just been doing our best to survive. I've been doing what our parents asked me to do, following their words, trying to hold on. But I'm tired, and if our only other living relative wants to strip this terrible, vicious place, why not? It's a great idea."

Obi-Wan tempered his reaction, lowering his voice and speaking as gently as he could. Some Jedi could influence others' emotions. Obi-Wan couldn't yet, but he had seen Qui-Gon respond to anger with patience and calm, denying it any further fuel to burn. "But he's going to leave you here when they're done. And then what will you do?"

"You want me to believe the word of some miner over our own uncle?"

"Yes." Obi-Wan wished he could reach out to her with the Force, could help her feel what he was feeling. Could explain it more clearly. Could tamp down the rising emotion that colored his voice. "I believe what Dex told us. I've seen what consuming the Power does to you. Look what all your parents did to keep it. They were willing to keep you all in harm's way, to condemn you to a desperate half-life. They chose this for Shush, Whistle, and Trill! When they could have been off-planet, somewhere they could thrive. I don't mean to speak ill of the dead, but I think their judgment was so clouded by their dependence on the Power that they couldn't see anything else. They couldn't *want* anything else. Anything better. Not even for their own children. So no, I don't doubt that someone like your uncle might be willing to do *anything* to get the Power back."

"You don't know what you're talking about!" Casul shouted, pushing forward. Audj grabbed his shoulder, holding him back.

There was a whistle and beeping from the hatch leading to the top of the ship.

"Hey," Amyt called down in her sweet, high voice. "The little metal person has something for you."

Obi-Wan hurried over. He extended his hand and caught a holoprojector as it dropped down to him. "You accessed it?" he asked, excited.

A6-G2 answered both yes and no. So Obi-Wan assumed that meant it was only partially accessed. Still, he would take it. "Thank you! I'll contact you soon. Go and hide the ship. You're amazing, Aces."

The beep that came back was a simple yes of agreement that A6-G2 was, in fact, amazing. Obi-Wan carried the holoprojector back to the others, the sound of his shuttle taking off muffled by the metal above them. If anyone was watching the ship, they'd assume Obi-Wan was gone now.

"We might have some answers here." He ignored Audj and Casul's scowls. This would help. It had to. At last, a real Jedi would give them insight.

CHAPTER

29

Obi-Wan held the holoprojector as the others gathered around him. Mem grumbled in displeasure as the glowing three-dimensional face of a woman appeared. "Is she dead?" Mem asked.

"Obviously not when she made this, but now, yes."

"No," Mem said, walking away. "I don't like talking to ghosts."

"When has she talked to ghosts?" Obi-Wan asked. The others shrugged. But their attention was drawn back to the holovid as it began playing.

The woman had high, sharp cheekbones and nearly colorless eyes in a colorless face, made all the more striking by the thick black hair in a bun atop her head. The holovid quality was shaky, the sound crackling. "This is the record of Orla Jareni."

Obi-Wan blurted out, "Yes!" before he could stop himself. He found her!

Audj shushed him and he kept watching.

"I have traveled to this planet guided by old star charts and half-lost records, my curiosity triggered by an ancient carving on the Temple wall Cohmac and I found as Padawans. It was a strange and thrilling journey that I will detail further when I return to the Council. At first I desired to study the mysterious magic of this place, thinking I had found a Force nexus planet. But I no longer think so. The Force of this planet, the vast and powerful interconnected life, belongs only to the planet itself. The entire environment exists in perfect symbiosis. Unlike the Force, which flows through everything, this planet is a closed system. So while it mimics the Force in many aspects, it is perhaps a simpler biomechanical parallel. However, the power here is undeniable, and undeniably fragile. My senses told me there was a delicate balance here; finding the remains of a civilization that upset that balance and paid the price confirmed my suspicions."

Obi-Wan resisted the urge to say, "I told you so."

Orla continued, the image flickering. "I have included further information on my findings here, but I cannot continue to study at this time. I've been tasked to help another Jedi, and Elzar's needs take priority over my curiosity here." She turned and looked to the side, gazing at something Obi-Wan could only guess at. "I will not return to Coruscant first, so I leave this here in case I am delayed and another Jedi picks up my studies. Perhaps they should all come here to study balance. Perhaps I'll bring Elzar here, too, some-day." She laughed, the sound cutting out and then back in. "This is a good place for that; it has certainly tested me. I am confident now that the Force guided me here, starting long ago when I was a rebellious Padawan sneaking around the Temple."

Obi-Wan stared, stunned. It felt like she was talking about him.

The image changed as Orla crouched, rubbing under the chin of a gobbler. "We all need balance, don't we—" There was a scratching noise and then the holovid cut off. Doubt-less there was more information, but A6-G2 had managed to get only this much of it so far.

Obi-Wan shut off the holoprojector, still in shock. "She never made it back. And I was the first person to look into it, after all this time. I must have—"

"It was a joke to her," Audj said, fists clenched.

"What?"

"Our whole planet. The way here. It was a joke to her. She wanted to use it, what, as an excursion? A fun learning experience?" Audj's tendrils tensed. "Our people suffered here. They risked dying in a shoddy, patched-up ship to get away. And our parents." She paused, swallowing hard. "Our parents wasted away in front of our eyes. Meanwhile your Jedi always had the way here, could have come and helped us survive here, and they never did?"

Obi-Wan shook his head. "Orla couldn't know what would happen in the future, that your people would crash here. As far as she knew, the planet was empty. Something happened that prevented her from sharing the information."

"She chose not to! She prioritized another Jedi, and left Lenahra behind forever."

He didn't want to make Audj angrier, but her reasoning made no sense to him. "Even if Orla Jareni had been able to tell the Jedi about this planet, how could they have prevented your ancestors' ship from crashing?"

"You said the Jedi help. She didn't help anything. She didn't even leave a warning my people could access. They had to figure everything out on their own."

"The temple-tomb is warning enough. Your people saw it, and they sealed it away. They ignored it."

"Don't blame my people!"

"Don't blame Orla!" Obi-Wan took a deep breath. This wasn't accomplishing anything. He had been so amazed, watching Orla, feeling like the Force was reaching through all the years that separated them, connecting them to each other. To this planet. But now he was fighting with Audj over nonsense. And that was exactly what it was: nonsense. Audj's arguments made no sense, because they weren't really arguing about Orla or the Jedi at all.

Obi-Wan lowered his voice. "I think you're looking for someone to be angry with so you don't have to look closely at what Loegrib is doing to the planet. Or at what you're doing, either."

Audj's tendrils went flat against her head, and something closed off in her eyes. "Is the bomb still on your ship?" she asked.

"No, we got rid of it."

"Good. I think it's time for you to leave. Because we know now that's what Jedi do: they come here, they have a great time *studying* and *exploring*, and then they go somewhere else."

Obi-Wan looked to Zae-Brii for help, but they had their face turned away from him, shoulders curved inward. Mem and Nesguin, too, were staring at the floor. So he spoke to Audj and Casul. "What if I'm right, and Loegrib succeeds? What if he strips the planet and then leaves you here?"

"Then he'd be just like everyone else. Including you. We'll survive, because we always do." Audj stormed away. Casul gave Obi-Wan one last angry look, then followed his sister. Mem and Nesguin followed, seeming less sure. Obi-Wan moved to go after them, but Zae-Brii stopped him.

"There's no point," they said sadly. "This really isn't your fight, though. Your Jedi ancestor made that clear. Besides, you're a target. I don't want you to die for us. If Loegrib and his men don't help us, well, we'll get by on our own, the way our parents wanted us to. We know how." Zae-Brii squeezed Obi-Wan's arm. "I'm glad we met, though. Live well,

Padawan." Then they followed the others up to the roof.

Thoroughly dismissed, Obi-Wan stood in the ship alone. He couldn't leave. Not now. Not at the risk of everyone here. He refused to be like their parents, like the other settlers, to prioritize his safety over this determined, fierce group of survivors. That wasn't the Jedi way. And Obi-Wan knew, with absolute certainty, that he wanted to follow the Jedi way here. To figure out the problem and to offer everyone on Lenahra a solution they could live with—and live *through*, hopefully.

But to best determine what a Jedi would do, he'd have to act like one. He'd have to take Orla's advice and trust that the Force had led him here through her. He had to find balance.

That meant turning to his last resort. Obi-Wan sighed, rolling his eyes. Not for the first time, he was deeply glad Qui-Gon wasn't here. Because Obi-Wan knew exactly what he needed to do, and he wouldn't have been able to bear seeing how pleased it would make his master.

Obi-Wan was going to meditate.

CHAPTER
30

Obi-Wan scaled the side of the ship down to the forest floor. He could have jumped, but he wasn't in the mood. He wanted to take his time and work his way into what he was about to do.

Though he could still sense the unease in the environment around him, he could also tell it wasn't directed at him. He moved quietly through the trees, not wanting to disturb anything or draw attention to himself.

After walking awhile, he came upon a clearing that felt right. It was filled with the gently glowing pitcher plants, their feather-like leaves brushing against him as he twisted and turned, taking great care not to step on any of them. He couldn't decide if the bright worms in them were charming or slightly unnerving, with their single eyes tracking his progress.

In the center of the clearing was an open spot of ground. He settled down there. Legs pulled in and crossed at the ankles. Hands on top of his knees. Back straight, breath measured, eyes closed.

Heart and senses and mind open.

Reach for the Force with open hands, Qui-Gon told him in his memory of their very first meditation together. *Not to grasp or to grab, but to touch. To connect.*

That had been Obi-Wan's problem, hadn't it? He had been reaching for the Force to grab hold of it, to cling to it, to try to wring his own destiny from it. Not unlike the way the Lenahrans used the Power. In their minds, it was a tool to be wielded, not a cycle to join. Obi-Wan had been treating the Force in a similar way. He wanted things from it, wanted it to do things for him. Centering himself, always. He was so focused on his own desires and, most destructively, his desperate fear of failure.

Fear of loss, too. The Lenahrans were afraid of losing the Power, of losing the life their parents had chosen for them. And he was afraid of losing his Jedi friends as they drifted apart into the galaxy. Afraid of losing his place in the Temple, in the Force. Afraid of letting go of the familiarity of his past and embracing the unknown future, whatever it would bring to him.

But it wasn't about Obi-Wan. It wasn't about the Jedi Order, or being a Padawan, or his own hoped-for future. It was about his new friends here, and this planet, and how he could help. Part of him was still scared that he wasn't up to this task. That he shouldn't be here in the first place and thus had no right to hope the Force would help him.

Orla, a dedicated, wise Jedi, had carved her name in a wall, and it had led him here. Obi-Wan still struggled to trust himself, but he knew he could trust her. He was here for a reason. He was here to find balance.

Just like Lenahra, he wasn't in balance. Not with himself, not with the Force. For so long he had been afraid of being afraid. Closing himself off to his feelings because of what they might mean, what they might lead to. But closing himself off was doing the opposite of what he hoped. It wasn't about not feeling fear or ambition or anything else he didn't think was right for a Jedi. It was about whether or not he gave those feelings power.

By ignoring his fears, pretending they weren't there, even fighting them, he was making them more insidiously overwhelming than they ever would have been.

He traced the contours of fear in his mind. The fears that had plagued him ever since passing his trials. In the end, what was he most afraid of? Was it losing his connection with the other Padawans, the closest people to a family he had? Failing as a Padawan learner and never becoming a Jedi Knight? Or was it failing to live up to his own potential? Those were selfish fears, all about himself. And while they were real, they were less intimidating than his deepest fear:

He was terrified that he had been given advantages and knowledge and *power*, and that he wouldn't be strong or capable enough to use them to help other people. To help the whole galaxy. To be a tool of good for the Force.

He could almost laugh. His fear that he wouldn't be able to use the Force to help others was making him close like a fist, tighter and tighter around himself. He didn't trust himself, and because of that, he also didn't trust the Force. If he didn't believe he deserved the Force, then he didn't trust that the Force had chosen him, or that this path was the one he should be on, or that the losses he would go through along the way were natural. Necessary, even.

That was what Qui-Gon had seen, what Qui-Gon was trying to guide him through. And why Qui-Gon hadn't taken Obi-Wan out of the Temple or given him harder tasks. As long as Obi-Wan was strangling his own progress, until he could trust the Force, nothing else would matter.

So. Fear was there, and maybe it always would be. But he didn't have to hide from it. Obi-Wan looked directly at the gulf of terror inside himself and let it wash over him as he settled on what his fears meant, at their core:

Obi-Wan cared.

He cared so much. He cared about the Jedi Order. He cared about the people in it. He cared about its history, about its rules, about its traditions. Even more than that, he cared about the Force and everything it touched. He cared about *all* the life in the galaxy, including this strange planet and everyone and everything on it.

With the fear in front of him, honestly acknowledged, Obi-Wan felt himself lightening. At last, all Qui-Gon's admonishments to exist in the present made sense. All Obi-Wan's worries were tied to his past and future, and he couldn't control either of those. Obi-Wan set his fears aside the same way he had moved through this clearing. Respectfully, but purposefully. His fears would always be there, but by looking right at them, he could put them where they belonged instead of constantly hiding from them. He could move toward the trust he needed in himself and in the Force.

It wasn't a destination he could reach with one try. He knew that. Learning this trust would be a journey he'd be on for the rest of his life. But he was ready to start.

For the first time since becoming a Padawan, Obi-Wan *let go*. He opened his hands, and his heart, and his mind, and he reached out.

His shock almost brought him out of the meditation, but he tried to stay present as the waves of connection rushed in. His fears had been like a dam, blocking the flow, and now that they were out of the way, the life of this planet was *everywhere*.

Once, his creche had snuck into the lower sections of the Temple where the more aquatically inclined Jedi and younglings spent their time in vast pools. Obi-Wan had thought nothing would ever be as relaxing, as freeing as floating in the warm dark of an unused section.

But this was better than that. Because instead of being aware of only himself, he was aware of everything. He was floating in a vast current of the Force, connected to it, and through his connection to it, to everything else on Lenahra. That was what had tried to fling his senses further and further out the night before—he had inadvertently been close to connecting with the planet because he hadn't been *trying* to do it.

He breathed in, and he breathed out, and he felt how that breath mingled with the air around him. It landed on the feathery leaves of the pitcher plants and they curled around it, pulling it in. The plants themselves, seemingly so fragile on the surface, had vast networks of roots plunging down and down through the soil and the rock, straight to the water that fed the planet. In that glowing pool, where the core of the planet sent its vital life upward, pure orbs of incredible energy were taken by these roots and absorbed. The pitcher plant worms cleared toxins from the liquid in the pitcher plants, so it was always clean and ready to drink. The energy-soaked spores of the pitcher plants floated in the air, enriching it so everything breathing inhaled the power of the planet. Other spores landed on the trees, nourishing them. The animals—the gobblers and the avalanches and the dozens of other creatures Obi-Wan hadn't seen—ate fruit from the trees and drank from the pitcher plants, and the planet's life flowed through them and sustained them. And when they died, the rocks gently carried them to pools of water, where the creatures lurking beneath the surface ate their bodies, and their bones drifted down, adding minerals to the water, which filtered into the subterranean pool and nourished the roots of the pitcher plants once more.

Obi-Wan could even sense the asteroid field, floating far outside the atmosphere. Formed from pieces of Lenahra, unfathomable ages before, it was still connected to the planet. Protecting it, as the rocks down here did.

His attention was pulled back down to Lenahra, to the ground beneath him, to the life around him. He was part of an infinite cycle, where nothing took more than it needed, where everything gave back. Even the rocks hummed, threaded through with the roots and the life around them. An entire planet, fed by an incredible internal power, in harmony. In balance.

Almost.

Because Obi-Wan's senses also connected him to the wounds here. The shallower one from Audj's ship, which the ground was slowly but surely fighting to expel. And the larger, darker, more devastating one from the first ship and its people, who cut into the planet to steal from it. The mining ship sat there like a cold void, repelling life.

Anger surrounded that wound and that ship. Anger and

fear, two things Lenahra had never had to feel before sentient life landed here.

That anger and fear pulsed up with roiling darkness from the wound. It broke Obi-Wan's heart, tracing that pain as it spread out into the land around it, poisoning the trees, corrupting the gobblers, agitating the avalanches. None of these lives should be acting the way they were. The planet was hurt and angry, which made it scared, and because it was scared, everything here was suffering.

But it didn't have to be like this. The people here didn't have to be parasites, sucking life from Lenahra and giving nothing back. If they could let go, if they could give up consuming the Power, the planet would sustain them as it sustained everything else. But because they treated this miraculous planet like an adversary to be fought, that was what it had become.

It mirrored their energy right back at them.

Obi-Wan shifted away from the wound, back to the soil beneath him, the trees above him, the life around him. As the Force flowed through him, connecting him to everything, it also connected the lives here to him. He heard all the little—and not-so-little—sounds of those lives around him now, making their way into the clearing. He opened his eyes and nearly yelped in shock, only just managing to rein in his reaction before he tamped down on his connection to the Force.

Because Obi-Wan was no longer in the clearing. Or rather, he was no longer *on* the clearing. He was floating above it, suspended in the air. Lifted by the Force.

He smiled as he slowly lowered back down. If only Qui-Gon could see him now. And then he laughed, because he doubted it would happen again. It had been the power of Lenahra, buoying him. And even though it had been incredible, he had no desire to run to the other Padawans and tell them what he had managed here. Those desires had been driven by fear and pride.

Both of which he still held but could find a way to live with. Just like Lenahra, where everything was part of everything else, fear and pride were part of what made Obi-Wan. He would be certain not to feed them, though, or let those feelings syphon his own living Force away from him.

"Hello, friends," he said, reaching out a hand. Several little avalanche creatures rolled up, popping out of their tight rolls and nuzzling his extended palm. A gobbler settled on the ground next to him with a sigh, closing its eyes in peaceful rest. The pitcher plants' antennae danced in the air, and even the worms seemed to sway in a rhythm that was, once again, either extremely cute or deeply unnerving. Several flying creatures, small and fragile, broke free from their hiding places among the trees and landed in the clearing, rubbing themselves on the outsides of the pitcher plants and gathering spores they would carry to the trees.

One even settled on Obi-Wan's shoulder, singing high notes in his ear. Obi-Wan whistled back. The gobbler opened one eye, giving a surly huff of air.

"Oh, sorry, were you trying to sleep?" Obi-Wan laughed, patting it on its scaled head. He *did* actually want to share this with his fellow Padawans. Not to show them that he, too, could go on daring missions and do incredible things. But because Prie would be fascinated by the animals and plant life, and Jape would doubtless want to study how the asteroid field around the planet was still connected to it, and Siri would want to explore the ruins. Even Bolla would be welcome. Obi-Wan wouldn't ask a gobbler to eat him.

Maybe he'd ask one to scare him, though. Just a little.

As though sensing his petty thought, the gobbler growled. Something shifted in the air of the clearing, an unease rippling through it. The avalanche creatures rolled back up and away, and the small bright flying thing on Obi-Wan's shoulder took off into the air with a clatter of wings.

Obi-Wan kept his hand on the gobbler's head, soothing it.

"How?" Audj asked from the edge of the clearing, her voice filled with wonder and envy and something like heartbreak.

CHAPTER
31

Obi-Wan kept his hand on the gobbler and tried his best to maintain his connection to the planet. It wasn't as strong as it had been—Obi-Wan was once again aware of himself, quite literally back on solid ground. But he was still in tune with Lenahra enough to use the Force to send out soothing waves to the gobbler, to the trees, to everything in the clearing.

We're safe, he projected. *We're calm, and we're safe.*

"Slowly," he cautioned Audj. She stepped around the pitcher plants. Their leaves curled in on themselves, and the worms ducked inside, not reaching out to her as they had to Obi-Wan. When Audj got close, the gobbler bared its teeth as a warning and she stopped.

"How is this possible?" Her eyes were filled with tears as she looked around. "I saw them. All here, all peaceful, with you. How?"

Obi-Wan continued stroking the gobbler, not breaking

his rhythm for fear of disturbing it. "I think I can explain it better now. The Power isn't like the Force. The Force isn't something I consume and burn up. It's so much more than just power. It's life. It's connection. It's—it's this." Obi-Wan gestured around the clearing. "It's trying to find the balance, that place between life and death where peace can exist. Being a small part of a great whole." He held out his free hand and Audj clasped it.

Her head tendrils swayed as her voice tightened with emotion. "I think—I don't know. Maybe I feel something. But I can *see* it, here. What this planet could be. All this time, all our struggle, all the fear and fighting and loss. Watching our parents die. We didn't . . ."

"It's not your fault," Obi-Wan said. He didn't want her to hurt, but the difficult truth had to be acknowledged. "You were doing what you were taught. And you were taught conflict, that the planet was an enemy to be fought. But there's a better way."

Audj nodded, then wrinkled her nose, teasing him. "We can negotiate with it?"

Obi-Wan laughed. "I don't know that one can negotiate with an entire planet. The first step is to stop antagonizing it. Give back what you took."

He felt Audj pulling away, though her hand was still in his. "But then we won't have any Power left," she said.

"You'll have so much more. It won't be as exciting or

dramatic, but it will be *whole*. Everything on Lenahra exists in connection to everything else. And if you can join that connection, if you can truly become part of the planet, then you'll be safer than you ever were. Stronger, too. Just not in the same ways." He had to learn the same lesson about his connection to the Force. It wasn't what he needed it to be. He had to become what *it* needed *him* to be.

Audj bit her lip, her head tendrils quivering as she tried to sense everything around them. "They're really not trying to kill you. Even the trees are quiet."

Obi-Wan patted the gobbler, then shooed it away. It grumbled off into the forest, casting one last wary look at them as though admonishing Obi-Wan for his choice in friends. "I wish you could feel what I felt, Audj. This planet is a marvel. I know now why Orla the Wayseeker marked it. Maybe it was a good thing that the information never reached the Jedi. If too many people came here and tried to study Lenahra, they might disrupt the balance even further. The Force is in everything, but some things—some species, some animals, even some plants—are more sensitive to it. And this entire planet seems to have its own special, intense link to the Force that it uses to flow its own life and power through everything."

"A connection like you have?" Audj asked.

Obi-Wan laughed. "Well. I don't think I'm quite on the same level as an entire planet existing in symbiotic harmony.

I'm relieved to be able to connect at all. I was living in fear for so long. Afraid to fail, afraid to let others down, afraid of loss, afraid of even being afraid."

"And you're not afraid now?"

"No, I still am. But I'm not letting it control me anymore."

Audj looked around, more wistful than sad or defensive. "I'd love to climb a tree and not worry about it breaking my bones. To sit in the branches and enjoy the breeze."

"I believe it can happen. I really do."

"I still don't want to give up the Power."

Obi-Wan opened his mouth to try to convince her, but she bent down and stroked one of the pitcher plants. It trembled under her fingers, and then a single feathered leaf opened like a fragile strand of hope.

"What do you sense, when you sense me?" She sounded tentative. Scared, even.

"I can answer that." Zae-Brii strode into the clearing with a smile. "I don't need anything to tell me you're strong, and courageous, and loyal, and good."

Obi-Wan nodded. "Zae-Brii is correct." What Audj had been doing here—what they all had been doing—was wrong. But that didn't make them bad people. What they did now that they had the right information was what mattered.

"Zae-Brii is *always* correct," Zae-Brii said with a wry twist of their thin lips. "Sometimes Audj forgets, is all."

"All right." Audj straightened, her expression fierce and determined. "The Power saved us, but it also destroyed us. It took too much away from us, and our taking it cost the planet too much. It's time to try to do more than survive here."

"**B**ut we'll die without the Power!" Casul said, more angry than surprised at Audj's calm explanation that they were going to return what was left of the orbs, stop the harvest for good, and convince Loegrib not to mine for more.

"We won't." Audj held her hand out to him, but he stepped back.

"You're giving up. You're turning your back on our parents' sacrifice."

"I'm not."

"You are! If we give up, if we admit—" He stopped, catching himself. "If we let *him* convince us that taking the Power is somehow the problem, then they died for nothing. They all died for *nothing*." Casul's expression turned from angry to anguished. "If Obi-Wan's right, then we were abandoned here for no reason. Everyone could have stayed. And our parents, Audj. We watched them waste. We watched them suffer. When all along . . ."

"We couldn't have known."

Casul reached for anger once again. Obi-Wan watched it happen, watched Casul grasp anger as a terrible form of defense, the same way he swallowed the planet's life to give himself temporary, destructive power. "And how do we know for sure now? You're going to believe a stranger, this sky trash, over our own traditions? Over our own history and experience? Don't you think if our people could have survived here by giving up the Power, they would have?"

"Do *you* want to give it up?" Obi-Wan asked.

"No!" Casul glowered at him.

"Because you know what it feels like. It's hard to walk away from power once you've had a taste of it. It's why Loegrib risked everything and sacrificed lives to come back here."

"Don't talk about it as if you understand! You have no idea what it's been like for us. You've been taken care of your whole life."

"You're right," Obi-Wan said. "I have. And I didn't have to find the Force. It found me. But that's why Jedi move through the galaxy and don't stay in one place for long. Why we don't rule. Because we *do* have access to power. And we have to be on constant guard to make certain it doesn't corrupt us. We have rules—so many rules—and structure, and guidance, and still we have to always be alert to ourselves. And the Jedi around us." Obi-Wan thought of Orla Jareni dropping her own studies to help another Jedi. And on the other end of the scale, of Master Dooku walking away from the Order and abandoning his path as a Jedi in favor of ruling on his home planet.

Even though Qui-Gon's clashes with the Council would seem to indicate otherwise, Obi-Wan at last felt confident that his master would not do the same. Qui-Gon Jinn understood responsibility and balance, just like Orla had. He might not agree with all the Jedi rules and methods, but in his heart, Qui-Gon followed the will of the Force. He always, always walked in the light.

Funny how after one good meditation session, suddenly Obi-Wan found himself thinking fondly of the same master he had felt betrayed by a few days earlier. It would be annoying if it weren't such a relief.

Well, it was still a *bit* annoying.

"Obi-Wan has given up more than he shows," Zae-Brii said softly. "Both in his past and in his future. He understands."

"This is a family," Audj said, commanding the room. All the younglings, all her friends, and even her brother, listened when Audj spoke. "We've survived together. We've taken care of each other. That isn't going to stop, no matter what. All I want for us is safety and happiness. I think there's a new way for us to live. I hope there is. But we have to be in agreement. Everyone has to choose to give up the Power, otherwise it won't work."

Casul scoffed. "But why shouldn't Loegrib dig it all up? He takes it. We fly away. Problem solved. We keep the Power and leave Lenahra behind."

"It won't work." Obi-Wan felt the truth of it settle on him. He might not understand exactly why Lenahra was the way it was, but he did understand that what they wanted to steal was a physical manifestation of the life that flowed through the planet. "If you separate those orbs from the planet, they'll be worthless. That's why it burns out for you. You're disconnecting the Power from its cycle, like a limb cut off a tree. It'll die and you'll be left with nothing, even if Loegrib makes it back out through the asteroid field. Besides which, all of this is ignoring the damage you'll be doing to the planet. Having that much of its life energy cut off might kill things here. Or everything will turn the way it is when you steal the orbs: angry and defensive. It'll never be peaceful or balanced again. Sometimes things can be pushed so far toward fear and darkness that they won't come back. At least not without tremendous sacrifice."

"Why should we care about that?" Casul shook his head. "Why should we care about this planet at all?"

"Lenahra is a living thing, and you're living things. You're connected. Protecting goodness, protecting innocence, protecting life itself? That's always worthwhile."

Audj put her hand on Casul's arm. "I saw what this planet can be like. What it *is* like, when no one's stealing from it or hurting it. We'll be okay. We really will. It's beautiful out there."

"And what if Loegrib doesn't listen?"

"Then we'll negotiate," Obi-Wan said. "I can be very convincing. We'll show him what the planet can be like. If that doesn't work, I'm still their best hope at getting through the asteroid field again. If they don't follow my lead, they might not make it at all. It might be enough to sway the crew to my side. They already watched their two sister ships fall."

"And what if Loegrib doesn't want to negotiate?"

"Then we'll . . . negotiate harder." Obi-Wan's lightsaber hung heavy at his waist. He was trained, yes. But was he really ready for a fight? What would he do if it came to that? He didn't have anyone's lead to follow out here, anyone to give him commands. He didn't know how Audj had managed to be in charge for so long, making hard decisions, trying to protect and help everyone around her.

"I want to leave," Shush said quietly, her huge black eyes fixed on the barrels that held Whistle and Trill. "Regardless. I don't want this life for them. Or for me."

"But if we fix the planet, you can get in the water! None of us need to separate. We'll convince Loegrib."

"I don't know if you can," Zae-Brii said, a worried cast to their bright golden eyes.

"We have to give him a chance. Give him the choice, with all the information we never had." Audj sounded more subdued, the same worry infecting her violet face, but she pushed on. "He didn't have a choice before. We won't do that to him again. I really think we can convince him. He worked so hard to get back here; we'll give him the ability to *stay*. And maybe we can even invite the other families back, once there's balance here. We can make Lenahra a real home. I believe in us."

"Tell us again. About the clearing." Nesguin was frowning but curious. He glanced down at little Gremac and put a hand on his head between his horns. "About how we could all grow up and grow old."

"What does *old* look like?" asked Tumber—or Jarper; Obi-Wan would never know.

Zae-Brii shifted so their face was once again the old woman's. Tumber and Jarper burst into fits of giggles.

"I'm going to look like that?" one of them asked.

"Well, no. I think you'll look like this." Zae-Brii changed once more, now covered in silver fur, long ears trailing down either side of a droopy but pleasant face.

They laughed even harder, falling onto their backs, kicking their long, flat paw-like feet in the air. Amyt clapped her hands. "Do me next! Do me next!"

Casul shook his head. "I need some air." He pushed past the others and climbed up top.

Audj went back to telling them what she had seen in the clearing, painting a picture of gobblers not as foes but as friends. Amyt excitedly declared she was going to have an entire avalanche as her pets, and then she and Gremac began bickering over whether such a thing was even possible.

"We'll have to give up the Power forever," Audj said to the younglings, but she said it in much the same tone she insisted that Gremac brush his horns. "I know it's fun to jump and leap and be stronger, and you've all worked hard to learn how to. But what's exciting is we won't *need* to anymore. We'll be able to go down to the planet and walk around without any danger."

"Really?" Amyt asked dubiously. "It won't try to eat us?"

"Really! It will never try to eat us again. We can even build houses down there."

"In the trees?" Amyt's eyes grew wide with excitement. "Where my avalanches can live with me?"

Audj laughed. "Maybe! And in the water, too." She grabbed Shush's hand and squeezed.

Shush looked down at Whistle and Trill, doubtless imagining their lives finally expanding far beyond the confines of their barrels. Lives where simply existing wasn't painful. "Obi-Wan, will you stay until we know for certain whether we can go in the water?" she asked. "And take us with you if we can't?"

Obi-Wan nodded. "I'll stay as long as you need me to. And I'll support whatever you decide."

"It will all work out. I know it will. But first," Audj said, "we have to make things right. We're going to gather all the orbs from the harvest and give them back. As long as everyone agrees. Because we're a family, and we do things together."

"We're really going to give up the Power?" Mem's eyes were narrowed in doubt. "Just like that. After what our parents taught us?"

"I remember how well you took care of your father," Audj said, and the easy happiness of her voice was gone. She took Mem's hand. "How early you had to say goodbye. I don't want any of us to go through that again. Or to go that way ourselves. Our parents wanted us to be strong, to survive. This is how we do that. How we save each other, how we take care of each other, like we always have. We're bigger and stronger together than any power could ever make us. Yeah?"

Mem swallowed, glancing toward where they kept the canister from the harvest. Obi-Wan held his breath. But then she nodded. "We are."

"We are!" Audj echoed, holding up Mem's hand. The others joined, some looking worried, some looking relieved, most of the younglings still talking about what pets they could have now.

Obi-Wan turned toward the opening, letting the vibrant colors of Lenahra fill his vision. He was going to help the whole planet *and* his friends, and he had connected with the Force to do it.

Everything was going to be okay.

CHAPTER
33

"Has anyone seen Casul?" Zae-Brii asked, popping down from the hatch at the top of the ship.

Audj looked up from where she was sealing the container with all the glowing orbs they had harvested. "What do you mean?"

"He's not up top, and he's not in here. Does anyone know where he is?"

Audj ran to the ladder to check for herself. Obi-Wan rushed to the opening overlooking the forest, but he didn't see any sign of Casul. His confidence that everything was going to be okay was disappearing faster than dessert in an initiate dining hall.

Audj climbed down the ladder slowly, a worried expression on her face. "He's not here."

It had been the best choice to send A6-G2 to hide earlier, but Obi-Wan silently berated himself for it. They needed to get to Casul, and quickly. "He went to warn Loegrib that we're going to try to stop him. It's the only explanation."

Audj shook her head. "Casul likes to understand things. *Needs* to understand things. He probably wanted to find out for himself what Loegrib's plans are before things go any further, so he's getting as much information as possible." But her tendrils, tightening in on themselves, contradicted her assertive tone.

Obi-Wan put a hand on her arm. "We don't have any time to waste. We have to return the orbs and then resolve this with Loegrib before he starts mining."

"Right. I agree. Let's get going so we can fix everything. First the orbs, then my uncle." Audj forced a smile.

Obi-Wan recognized himself in how desperately she was trying to pretend she could control it all by sheer force of will. Or maybe she was pretending for the sake of the others, and inside she was filled with fear and panic. Either way, Obi-Wan was grateful that she wasn't fighting him. The others would always follow her lead.

Audj grabbed the container of orbs and shoved them toward Obi-Wan. "Go tell the planet we're on its side now."

Obi-Wan let out a small laugh. "That's not really how the Force works."

She waved dismissively, distracted. "However it works, then. You're my negotiator. Negotiate a treaty between us."

"I will." Obi-Wan was sure this would work. Lenahra wasn't a dark place; its nature wasn't inherently predatory or violent. Releasing it from the pain and loss it had experienced should allow it to return to itself once more. It ought to be easy.

Then again, things were rarely as easy as he hoped or planned for them to be. Only a few days earlier, he had suggested this outing to prove to Qui-Gon that he was a good Padawan. Then it turned into a rebellious trip to do something amazing and impress everyone—and prove he was worthy of being a Padawan. Then it had revealed itself as a way of running from his fears.

And now? He wanted to find balance to help everyone here survive. Not a simpler goal, but at least he could be honest with himself.

Audj gathered all the others, and they slid down to the ground. Even Shush, Trill, and Whistle joined them, not wanting to be left out of this first step toward their new lives. They each took turns with Obi-Wan's breather, and he carried Trill on his back, much to Amyt's jealousy. Mem took Whistle, both of the Nautolan younglings covered with blankets to shield their skin.

Obi-Wan led them to the clearing where he had connected to Lenahra through the Force. He knew their offering didn't have to take place there, but it felt right. He could hear and sense movement all around them, but the mood was one of tense anticipation. The calm before a storm, the breath before an attack.

He hoped neither would follow.

Obi-Wan knelt on the forest floor and gestured for the others to do the same. Then he opened the container and carefully removed each precious orb, setting them in a line on the ground. With each one, he tried his best to convey both remorse and hope.

"Nothing is happening," Audj whispered through gritted teeth.

"Patience," Obi-Wan admonished. "Everyone try to feel peaceful. The less worried you are right now, the better."

Mem actually laughed aloud at that, and it cut right through the tension, like a lightsaber through a block of cheese. Bolla had done that once to see if it would toast the cheese. All it had done was make a mess.

Mem's laughter was far more successful than Bolla's culinary experimentation. Everyone let out the breath they had been holding. The sense of relief was palpable not only to Obi-Wan but to the world around them. A gobbler ambled out of the trees, its approach wary but not predatory.

Nesguin gasped softly. "Look at its beautiful eyes. I've only ever seen their teeth."

As though understanding, the gobbler blinked its large glowing eyes slowly at them, then carefully took an orb in its mouth. It walked to the nearest pitcher plant and deposited the orb in the center. Then it looked at them with an expectant huff.

"Do what it did," Obi-Wan said.

There were enough orbs for everyone to take one in their hand and walk to the nearest plant. The little ones dropped theirs in immediately, laughing in delight.

"Look how they glow!" Tumber and Jarper clapped and jumped up and down.

Obi-Wan helped Trill while Mem helped Whistle. Trill patted Obi-Wan's cheek and sighed in happy satisfaction as the orb plopped into the waiting water. Doubtless Trill understood what a relief that would be.

The older ones were not quite as thrilled as the younglings, having spent more time out on the planet. They knew what they were giving up far more than the little ones could. Last of all was Audj, cupping the Power she had desperately clung to in order to keep her people safe. The Power her parents had bequeathed to her, had taught her was both her right and her heritage, her only hope for survival.

She stared down into the glow of it, took a deep breath, and released it.

The rumble of an avalanche surrounded them, the little creatures rolling all around, spinning in circles. But it wasn't an attack. It was a dance, a celebration. The younglings whooped in delight, spinning around the clearing with the creatures. Even Trill and Whistle joined by clapping and singing in high bright tones.

Zae-Brii moved next to Audj and took her hand in their

own. "Well done," they whispered, pressing their forehead against Audj's.

"I hope so," Audj answered.

"Audj," Obi-Wan said. "There's more to do." Urgency tugged at him, reminding him that they needed to get to the other ship as quickly as possible. Whatever discussion was happening between Casul and Loegrib, they had to be part of it.

"Right," she said. "Shush, will you take the younglings back to the ship for now?"

Amyt stomped her foot. "But I want to build a tree house."

"Actually," Obi-Wan said, considering. A couple of young gobblers had ambled into the clearing and were letting the younglings pet them. "Will Whistle and Trill be all right here for a bit?"

Shush nodded, helping Trill and Whistle down and setting them on top of the blankets. It was shady enough in the clearing that their skin wouldn't be harmed. "I can stay and mind them, too," Mem offered. She still wouldn't make eye contact with Obi-Wan, but she had seemed to accept at last that he wasn't going to attack them. "That way if we need to move, I can carry one and Shush can carry the other."

Obi-Wan looked over the scene. Nothing here was going to harm the younglings. If anything, they were more protected than ever, surrounded by gobblers. "You'll be perfectly safe here, among friends. And this way *we* know where to find you, but—"

"But no one else does." Audj frowned. "Are you anticipating a fight?"

Obi-Wan didn't want to scare them, but someone *had* tried to blow him up, after all. It was safe to assume at least one member of the mining crew would not be thrilled with their new plan for dealing with—and protecting—the planet. He shrugged, making a face at Audj to communicate he didn't want to say things aloud that might scare the little ones.

"Right." Audj reached for the pouch at her hip without thinking, her hand finding nothing where it reflexively sought a boost of the Power. "Right," she said again, her voice softer and more worried. She was going into this without much—if any—of the Power left in her system.

"We'll be fine." Obi-Wan gestured to her, Zae-Brii, Nesguin, and himself. "Between the four of us, who could tell us no?"

"We *are* very attractive," Nesguin said, stroking one of his horns, his black lips parting in a smile.

"I was aiming for persuasive; I don't know how much our attractiveness will sway things in our favor."

"It can't hurt."

Obi-Wan laughed. "Well, then, we merry band of attractive adventurers, let's go see a man about a mine. And may the Force be with us."

"What does that mean?" Audj asked.

"It's something we say to each other, when we're embarking into the unknown. It's what we hope for, always."

"Then I hope that, too," Audj said. The others nodded.

Leaving Shush and Mem with the giddy younglings, the rest trekked toward the mining ship. Audj's tone was cautiously bright as she marched in the lead. "Even this walk is proof that you were right. Nothing has tried to kill us. I can't remember the last time that happened."

"I never knew walking could be this easy," Nesguin said, amazed. "Is this how it works on your planet, Obi-Wan? You just . . . walk around, and nothing tries to eat you and the ground doesn't open up to swallow you whole?"

"With some exceptions, yes."

Audj gestured to the peaceful forest around them. "Casul and Loegrib will be able to see for themselves that Obi-Wan's way works. They'll see that peace with Lenahra isn't merely possible—it's easy." She sounded wistful and a bit sad.

Obi-Wan wished he could comfort her, but she was carrying the weight of a past filled with loss and death, all of which could have been avoided. She would always carry it, always question if she could have saved more of her people. It would be up to her how to deal with the pain of her past.

Obi-Wan understood. Loss was part of growing up. It changed you, but it also stayed with you, shaping you. But he could control how it shaped him. He could stop fearing it, stop resisting it, and instead let it become part of his journey.

Even though they hiked at a brisk pace, it was late in the day by the time they reached the gash and the mining ship. The creatures gathered there shifted to let them pass through once more. Zae-Brii barely reacted—they'd done this before—but even after what they'd experienced in the clearing, Audj and Nesguin were both nervous and amazed.

The same guard was sitting on top of the cage that held the wounded gobbler. Obi-Wan swiped his hand through the air, using the Force to unlatch the door and swing it open. "That won't be necessary anymore," he said.

The guard jumped down with an outraged shout as the gobbler scurried away, limping on its injured legs. "Hey! That was our protection."

"You don't need protection if you don't provoke any threats," Obi-Wan said.

"It's true," Audj said. "We've come from the forest, and—"

"It's a trick." Loegrib stepped down the ramp, followed by Casul. "A dirty Jedi trick, all of it. You're lucky I'm here to tell you all the truth about what Obi-Wan Kenobi and his people are: the most deceitful predators in the galaxy."

"That's not true." Obi-Wan glared at Loegrib. "The Jedi are protectors, never predators."

"These innocent younglings have been isolated here on this forsaken planet, but that doesn't mean *I'm* susceptible to your tricks. You can't lie to me." He turned to the others. "Did you know Jedi can influence minds? Can push you to feel things you don't really feel? Even put thoughts in your heads that aren't your own."

"Is that true?" Audj frowned at Obi-Wan with the beginnings of suspicion.

"No! Well, mostly not. It's much more complex than that, and a Jedi would never use it to harm someone, and anyway it only works on the weak-minded, and also I . . . well, I'm not a very good Padawan. I definitely can't do it yet."

"So you claim." Loegrib narrowed his eyes. "A Jedi will say anything to get you to trust them, to do what they tell you. All Jedi pretend to be benevolent, because the truth is that they don't want anyone else to have power, to be able to use it like they do. That's why you're really here, isn't it? To keep the Power all for yourself and your Jedi."

"I had no idea what was here. I came . . ." Obi-Wan grimaced. He was about to say he came to help, but it wasn't the truth, and he wasn't a liar. Not like Loegrib. "I came because I wanted to prove something to my friends. To my master. And to myself, really. To prove that I was worthy of becoming a Jedi. But I was wrong to be motivated by that. I can see now that the Force guided me here, to help Audj and Casul and everyone on Lenahra. To restore balance."

"An easy claim to make. The mysterious Force that the rest of us can't feel or hear or see, but must nevertheless bend to! And let me guess: this Force is telling you that we shouldn't use the Power."

Loegrib was manipulating the truth, and Obi-Wan didn't know how to wrench the narrative away from him. Loegrib didn't need any Jedi skills to be able to twist emotions and plant thoughts in others' heads. He was perfectly skilled with his words.

"I don't need the Force to tell you that," Obi-Wan answered. "Lenahra itself has been telling you all you shouldn't use it, from the very beginning."

Loegrib let out an ugly scoff. "The planet is talking now, too? Do you hear what Jedi will claim to get their way?"

"I saw it," Audj said, her voice soft. "What happens when we give up the Power. What Lenahra can be."

"Another trick." Loegrib waved dismissively. "Probably arranged by Obi-Wan with his Jedi powers. Everyone in the galaxy wants what the Jedi have, and the Jedi will do anything to keep it to themselves. Even my employer wants our Power to be able to combat them, but it's not for him, or for the Jedi, or anyone else. The Power on Lenahra is mine. *My* right. And I'll die before I let the Jedi or anyone else take it from me."

The cage guard stepped forward, his voice heavy with threat. "I don't think our employer will be happy to hear you plan on keeping it for yourself."

Loegrib pulled out a blaster and shot the man in one smooth movement. Zae-Brii screamed, Nesguin ducked in alarm, and Audj grabbed Obi-Wan's arm, shocked.

"What did you do?" Audj gasped, staring at the body of the guard.

"What I had to. What I must. Don't you understand? People will kill for what we have here."

"People will die for it, too." Audj turned to Casul, still standing behind Loegrib. But he, too, was staring at the body, now horrified instead of angry. "Like our parents did. They should still be alive, should still be with us. We didn't know that, but we do now. I don't want to die for the Power. I don't want you to, either."

Loegrib held out his arm, keeping Casul behind his back. "It doesn't matter what you want. It's mine."

"It's not, though." Obi-Wan rested a hand on his saber hilt, not drawing it just yet. "We won't let you harm the planet by taking its life force. If you try, the planet will attack you and everyone you're with. And even if you succeed in mining out what you want, you'll never make it through the asteroid field again. All you'll be doing is hurting Lenahra and getting everyone on your ship killed. This isn't the way, Loegrib. I know it feels like it is, but—"

Loegrib pressed his blaster against Casul's chest. "You don't get to decide what happens here, *Padawan*. Now go wait in that cage while I finish my business. Then, as long as you tell me where Obi-Wan's ship is, the rest of you can go unharmed and rot here like your parents wanted."

Audj's voice trembled, but her fists were clenched, her head tendrils rigid and tense. "You're worse than our parents. Maybe they didn't understand what they were choosing for us, but you do. You are not our family."

"I really don't care." Loegrib shrugged. "Now climb into that cage, nice and slow."

Obi-Wan saw movement behind Loegrib but did his best not to react to it. "You know this won't work," he said as Audj, Zae-Brii, and Nesguin edged toward the cage.

"I want your hands up, away from that absurd weapon." Loegrib jabbed Casul with his blaster for emphasis. "As soon as you're in the cage, you're going to throw it to me."

Obi-Wan lifted his arms, taking a few backward steps toward the cage.

"I'm sorry," Casul said, watching helplessly as his sister and friends climbed into the cage. "I only wanted us to stay strong. To be safe. I trusted the wrong person."

"I didn't," came a voice from behind them. Dex stood, two arms in the air, two behind his back, with the other miners next to him. "Never trust a captain who doesn't care about losing his crew. No job is worth dying for. If these young ones have a way for us to leave this planet intact, we'll be taking that."

"Get back on the ship and get the drills prepped," Loegrib snarled.

"Can't, sir." Dex's wide mouth split into a toothy grin. "No one can. Not without this starter core." One of his arms came to the front holding a small, sleek metallic cylinder.

Loegrib swung the blaster away from Casul, shooting at Dex. Fortunately, the miner's reflexes were fast. He ducked, holding up a thick piece of metal he had been carrying in his fourth hand. The blaster bolt sparked off the edge of it.

"Catch!" Dex shouted, throwing the starter core into the air.

Obi-Wan reached and, using the Force, pulled the cylinder to himself. Loegrib's face was a picture of fury. His distraction gave Dex and the other miners a chance to run and hide behind the ship.

Casul took advantage, too, punching his uncle's stomach,

then knocking the blaster out of his hand. But before Casul could dive for it, eight droids scuttled out of the ship. It was evident from their position flanking Loegrib who controlled their programming. They scuttled on three legs, and each had a multitude of arms configured with various items, none of which Obi-Wan wanted to see on a droid. Clamping claws. Razor cutters. Flamethrowers. And blasters, each of which was currently raised and pointing at them.

Casul sprinted across the distance to Obi-Wan while Audj, Zae-Brii, and Nesguin clambered out of the cage as quickly as they could.

"Give me the core!" Loegrib shouted. "None of you needs to get hurt, but I'll do whatever it takes to get what belongs to me. The choice is yours."

Eight deadly blasters pointed right at them. Obi-Wan threw the core to Casul and at last drew his saber, the familiar blue hum of it a comfort. "Let's talk about this," he said. "Surely there's a way this can be resolved without—"

The first bolt flew at them, and he barely deflected it.

"—violence. I suppose not, then." He deflected two more blasts, joining the others where they had taken shelter behind the cage. If he were Qui-Gon, he'd be able to deflect the bolts so precisely, they'd take out the terrifying mining-turned-enforcer droids. But then again, if he were Qui-Gon, he wouldn't be here.

The ability to aim deflected blaster bolts was another

skill he vowed to develop with perfect precision, should he make it out of this alive. He dearly hoped he would, and that Qui-Gon would still be there and willing to teach him.

Audj shook her head. "We can't fight them! Not without the Power. I have maybe two, three good jumps left in me. What do we do? What *can* we do?"

Obi-Wan couldn't afford to give in to panic or fear. He was all that stood between his friends and destruction, between a murderer and this amazing planet.

This amazing planet! He grinned at the others. "Who knows better than you all exactly how dangerous Lenahra can be? But now you're not fighting against Lenahra—you're fighting *for* it. You've been training your whole lives for this. Use everything you've learned about how the planet defends itself. Use it all."

Their faces shifted from panic to determination as they nodded grimly. Casul looked at Zae-Brii. "Double me," he said. "They won't know which one of us has the core. Nesguin, you go with me, Zae-Brii and Audj together."

Zae-Brii shifted so they were both Casul.

"I still hate that," Audj grumbled. Zae-Brii ignored her, grabbing a rock and shoving it beneath their shirt, while Casul did the same with the similarly sized core.

Obi-Wan nodded. "On my signal, split up. I'll hold them off as long as I can." Obi-Wan took a deep breath, then leaped straight in the air, landing on top of the cage. "Go!"

he shouted. Audj and one Casul ran one direction, and Nesguin and the other Casul ran the opposite. Obi-Wan deflected the flurry of blaster bolts, hoping against hope that his friends would be fast enough to reach cover before he failed. Already two of the droids—Obi-Wan was not a fan of this type, much preferring his pleasantly nonlethal astromech—had managed to go after Zae-Brii and Audj, and two more were breaking off after Casul and Nesguin.

Obi-Wan swatted a bolt away and it flew directly back, burning a hole in the chest of one of the droids.

"Yes!" Obi-Wan shouted. All three remaining droids turned as one, fixing every single sight directly on him. "Oh. *No.*" He jumped back behind the cage as a deadly onslaught of blaster fire pinned him in place.

Obi-Wan Kenobi was certain that even Qui-Gon Jinn would agree meditation was *not* the correct answer to his problems right now. He didn't know what was, though.

"Someone told me that droids wouldn't kill me for being impolite!" he shouted over the cage. "I'm sorry if I wasn't especially welcoming! Could we be reintroduced?"

His only answer was an increase in blaster fire. He felt the metal heating up behind him. It was only a matter of time before the structure failed and let the blaster bolts through, or the droids were able to flank him. As long as he was pinned down, he was vulnerable.

Pinned down! He turned and used the Force to push the cage. It flew right into the droids, knocking them down and trapping one beneath it. Obi-Wan ran for the trees. He'd rather not engage in direct combat in the gash, where there was no good cover. There had to be a better spot.

He needed all the advantages he could get. These droids had been programmed for destruction, and Obi-Wan was not eager to be destroyed. But at least these were just droids. Assuming he survived the next few minutes, Obi-Wan didn't know what he'd do about Loegrib. He didn't want to have to fight him. If Obi-Wan became a Jedi Knight, a fight with another living being would happen. Probably sooner rather than later. But he'd always rather find another solution. A cleverer, more elegant way of getting out of trouble than simply cutting someone down.

A blaster bolt sizzled into a tree right next to his head.

There was certainly more elegance in lightsaber battle than blaster fire, though. He jumped over a sinkhole, hoping he'd get lucky and one of the droids would fall in it. Somewhere in the distance he heard shouts and more blaster fire. He turned to run in that direction and help. But then the blaster fire stopped and the next shout was Nesguin whooping in triumph.

The others were more than capable on their own, and he was in more than enough trouble on his. The blaster fire kept coming. The droids behind him had managed to avoid the sinkhole. Judging by the amount and directions of the blaster fire, the third droid had cut free of the cage. They were all still on his trail.

Obi-Wan ran as fast as he could, wishing for Qui-Gon's stamina. Even though the Jedi Knight was far older than

Obi-Wan, he seemed to be able to run forever without getting winded. Something about meditating while fighting, which Obi-Wan was almost positive Qui-Gon was making up. Fighting and meditating were *not* the same thing.

But if Qui-Gon was still willing to train him, he'd make sure to be trained in how to do that. He added it to his ever-growing list of unfinished Padawan business. If he made it out of this alive, he'd even stop complaining about his master.

Well, he'd *try*.

His breaths were coming fast and loud, and there was a painful stitch in his side. He didn't know how far he'd run, but the droids could certainly last longer than he could. None of them were burdened with lungs. And because they weren't radiating stolen power, the trees didn't seem to care about them. Of all the times for Lenahra to be placid, this was the worst.

"I could use a little help here!" Obi-Wan shouted at the land around him. The droids charged through the trees, trampling several of the delicate pitcher plants.

Obi-Wan lifted a rock and sent it flying behind him. It bounced off one of the droids, denting its blaster arm but not deterring it. What else could he do? How could someone use a forest to fight droids?

He reached out to the Force, trying not to grasp but simply invite. Or beg, really. Whichever. He was more than ready to trust the Force. And to his relief, he felt a sort of current, like a tug of fresh air, guiding him. Obi-Wan followed it, twisting and turning through the trees, trusting that he was being led where he needed to go.

He was so trusting, in fact, that he nearly ran right off the edge of the cliff the Force guided him to.

Obi-Wan's arms pinwheeled as he abruptly stopped, kicking a few stray pebbles down, down, down to the wet black rocks lining the river far beneath. The other side of the ravine was too far for him to jump, even using the Force. There was nowhere else to run, nowhere he could hide. Once the droids caught up to him—which would be in mere heartbeats—all they had to do was fire. Even Qui-Gon couldn't deflect three bolts at once.

Obi-Wan's heart fell. This path was a dead end, and so, it appeared, was his path toward becoming a Jedi.

Still. He'd do as much as he could to help his friends on his way out. Maybe he could take one or two of the droids with him. And maybe A6-G2 would make it back to the Temple so at least Qui-Gon would know what had happened to the Padawan he never asked for. He sincerely hoped Qui-Gon wouldn't blame himself.

Obi-Wan had trusted in the Force, and it had led him here, so he would make his stand. He turned, lightsaber at the ready, and faced his death.

"Fancy meeting you here," Obi-Wan said.

The droids lifted their weaponized arms in unison. And then the ground began to rumble. An avalanche poured out of the trees, running under the droids' legs. They wobbled, unable to find secure footing.

Gobblers charged at them, propelling two of the droids right past Obi-Wan and straight off the cliff. He heard their impact as they finally hit the riverbank far below. Even a droid couldn't survive that drop.

Obi-Wan stared at his one remaining foe. It was the droid whose blaster arm he'd damaged with a rock. He couldn't be certain, but it seemed like it was staring at him, too. "If you want to surrender, I'll hear your terms now," Obi-Wan blustered. The droid's saw extension buzzed to life. Somehow that seemed worse than a blaster. It took a step toward him, and Obi-Wan braced himself in a fighting stance.

A piece of the cliff rock beneath the droid shot upward, launching the droid in the most beautiful arc Obi-Wan had ever seen, straight over his head and down into oblivion.

The Force really *had* been guiding him exactly where he needed to be for Lenahra to use its terrifying power. "Just a reminder," Obi-Wan said, kneeling and patting the rocks beneath him, "that I am your friend."

Remembering his own friends, Obi-Wan sprinted back into the trees to find and help them, hoping they had fared as well as he had.

*E*veryone was against him.

Everyone was always against him.

They had ripped him away from the Power, tried to keep it from him. And now these younglings, these terrible, feral things left behind by his selfish brother and his selfish friends—the ones who stayed, the ones who let him be taken while they got to remain, keeping all the Power for themselves—thought they could do the same.

Even his crew had taken their side. He stared at the ship as though considering an enemy. He had wanted to dig deep and fast, take it all, strip the planet and then leave. Let it hurt the way he had all these years.

He couldn't do that without the starter core, and even with the core, he didn't think he could operate the ship on his own. He had always planned for the miners to stick with him until after he had the Power. Then he would get rid of them. But now?

Well, he'd have to change plans.

He prowled toward the tunnel. He didn't need anything except himself and what was inside that glowing cavern. What was his. What had always been and always would be his. The planet had tried to keep it from him. His people had tried to keep it from him. And his own family was still trying to keep it from him.

They had all failed. This was his path, and at last he saw clearly what he needed to do. He had never needed to mine, never needed a crew, never needed containers.

He was the container. It was time at last to be filled.

Obi-Wan didn't know whether it was possible for this droid to show emotion, but he imagined it was almost as surprised as Casul and Nesguin when Obi-Wan's lightsaber appeared through the middle of its chest. The droid dropped to reveal Casul and Nesguin pinned against a rock face.

"We had that," Casul said, but the smile he gave Obi-Wan was more than a little grateful.

"Oh, you definitely had it. I was bored, is all. Out for a stroll, thought I'd get some droid-slicing practice in."

Casul's head tendrils lifted. "Come on." He rushed through the trees. After a few minutes, they nearly ran right into Audj. She and Zae-Brii were there, along with Shush, Mem, and the younglings.

"We heard the blaster fire," Mem said. "The gobblers practically shoved us here."

Amyt was sitting on the back of the largest gobbler

Obi-Wan had seen, with blanket-covered Trill on another and Mem holding Whistle. Amyt patted her gobbler's head with a concerned frown. "Fluffy ate a droid. Do you think it will make her stomach hurt?"

As though on cue, the scaled monster named Fluffy burped, and several pieces of metal tumbled out of her excessively toothy mouth.

"As long as Fluffy doesn't make it a regular part of her diet, she should be fine." Obi-Wan turned to Audj and Casul, who was holding the starter core.

Zae-Brii had shifted back to their own face. They rubbed the top of their head. "Those tendrils are really uncomfortable." Audj made an offended noise, so Zae-Brii hugged her close. "Beautiful! So attractive! Love to look at them. Hate to have to copy them."

"Everyone's accounted for?" Obi-Wan counted, just in case. "And all the droids are down? I took out five—well, I took out two, and Lenahra took out three on my behalf."

"Yes, they're all destroyed." Audj beamed proudly, looking at her people. "And we did it without the Power."

"Like you said we could." Casul lowered his eyes. "I'm sorry I didn't believe in you. In us. I was just so angry, remembering all the sacrifices that didn't need to happen. Worried about so much change ahead of us. I wanted there to be an easier way."

"The right way isn't always easy," Obi-Wan said, thinking

about the Jedi path. How he wanted it to come easily to him as *proof* that it was right and that he belonged on it. But so often the right thing to do was the most difficult. If he had the chance, he would follow the path the Force put him on for the rest of his life, no matter how hard it was.

But before that, they had one more difficult thing ahead of them. "We have to decide what to do about your uncle."

Casul deferred to Audj. She looked tired but determined. "Let's go back to the ship. With Dex and the crew on our side and all the droids out of commission, he's hopelessly outnumbered. We'll convince him to leave peacefully with the miners. I wanted him to have the choice, but I don't want someone we can't trust to stay here with us."

Obi-Wan remembered the horrible zeal in Loegrib's eyes. He doubted Loegrib would ever stay away. But if Dex and the miners could get him off-planet and far away, there would no longer be an on-planet beacon to steer by. Lenahra would be lost once more. After all, Loegrib didn't have an ancient Wayseeker's record to guide him like Obi-Wan had. A pity, too, because Loegrib could definitely benefit from Orla's wisdom.

Obi-Wan drew Audj and Casul aside. "You should think through what you do next carefully. Because once the mining ship leaves, and I do, too—"

"You don't have to leave." Casul grabbed his hand. "I'm sorry. You have a place here, if you want it."

Obi-Wan smiled, genuinely touched. A few days earlier, he would have been tempted. But he had so much more to learn, so much more to do. This life, this freedom—there was an appeal to it, he had to admit. But he couldn't deny the call of the galaxy, the pull of the Force. And the fact that he had a *lot* of work to accomplish if he wanted to answer that call to the absolute best of his abilities.

He had found the balance he had been sent here for, and he was ready to go back. To face his fears of failure, of loss, of inadequacy, and to accept them so he could move forward. "I know. And I'm grateful. But my place is at the Temple. Assuming I'm still welcome there."

"We could leave, too," Audj said, frowning. "That's what you're saying. And if we don't . . ."

"We might not get another chance," Casul said, finishing his sister's thought.

"And we have to make the choice for ourselves, but also the younglings." Audj glanced over her shoulder at where the younglings were playing with the gobbler, except Amyt, who was resolutely but unsuccessfully stalking several little avalanche creatures. Trill and Whistle were bundled up, with Shush patiently moving the breather between them as soon as it was clear one was struggling. "The land might be friendly now, but we still don't know about the water."

"It does have very large, very toothy occupants already," Obi-Wan said, remembering what he had felt. "But you still have time to decide. Let's talk to Loegrib, see if he isn't more reasonable now that he has nothing to bargain or threaten with." Obi-Wan assumed that would make negotiating a lot easier. He felt confident he'd be quite good at it under these circumstances.

They tromped through the trees, a group of Lenahrans, a Padawan, and several gobblers. Obi-Wan couldn't tell whether the gobblers were escorting them or merely curious now that they were all friends.

When they emerged from the forest, the sight of the gash filled Obi-Wan with a cold anger. It would always be here, this evidence of what so many would choose to do if it meant being powerful. Being strong. He frowned, unsure if the anger he was feeling was his own or that of Lenahra. It was an odd thing to be emotionally influenced by an entire planet.

The anger surprised him, too. He had thought things were healing, getting better. But he supposed this scar would remain, and thus the anger and pain around it, too.

Dex popped out of the ship, waving an arm cheerfully at them. "I'd hoped you lot were safe!" he shouted. "Figured you were, since the readings on the droids were all dead when we tried to shut them down remotely. What about Loegrib?"

"What *about* Loegrib?" Obi-Wan looked around. "He isn't here?"

"No. No sign of him on the ship." Dex shrugged. "He must have run away. Reckon he knows the land well enough to hide."

Obi-Wan sighed. That definitely made negotiating more difficult.

"We'd like to leave as soon as we can," Dex said. "No offense to the locals, but we aren't fond of this place. However, we'd also like to make it through that asteroid field in one piece."

"That would be preferable, yes. I think I can lead you safely through the asteroids. But I can't go until I'm sure Loegrib is taken care of and my friends aren't in any danger. If we give you back the starter core, you won't use it to mine, will you?"

Dex rubbed the pouch beneath his chin. "Don't need that starter core at all, not to fly. Different systems. Besides, way we figure, getting off this planet alive and with our very own mining ship? The crew and I are coming out ahead. No incentive to mine here and stir up trouble."

"You won't have to return the ship?"

"Couldn't even if we wanted to. Don't know who it belongs to. Loegrib shot the only other person who had ever spoken with our financier."

Obi-Wan turned, remembering the fallen guard, but the miners had already moved his body. Which was good, considering they had younglings with them. "Audj?" he asked.

She helped Amyt and Trill get down from the gobblers they rode. Shush took Trill in her arms, and the gobblers ambled away immediately.

"Get the younglings on the ship where they'll be safe," Audj said. "The rest of us will fan out and search for Loegrib. He might be from Lenahra, but he's not one of us. Not anymore. We'll find him, and then—"

Obi-Wan gasped, staggering back. The anger he felt around the planet's wound spiked, a red-hot dagger of pain and fear and fury stabbing straight through his head and heart. "Something's wrong," he said, trying to separate what he was being *made* to feel from what he was actually feeling.

"Found him," Zae-Brii whispered, pointing.

The edges of the cave were vibrating, the planet wrenching and groaning beneath them as it tried to close the wound that left it vulnerable.

The wound containing boundless power that no one had thought to guard against Loegrib.

"**D**ex! Get the younglings to safety!" Obi-Wan shouted as the ground began vibrating, the edges of the gash creaking and groaning as Lenahra tried desperately to close its wound and punish the theft of its life power. "Shush, Mem, stay with them! If things get too bad on the ground, take off!"

Dex grabbed a youngling in each arm. Shush and Mem took the other two and followed him onto the ship. They raised the ramp, sealing the younglings away. For now. Obi-Wan turned back to the others—only to see Audj and Casul sprinting straight for the cave.

"Wait!" he shouted. "We need a plan!"

"They don't have enough of the Power left!" Zae-Brii said. "They can't stop him without consuming some!"

"And if they consume it, the planet will see them as the same threat he is." Obi-Wan was about to chase them down and stop them when he saw yet another problem. Running straight up the temple-tomb rock mountain were dozens of gobblers. Several had already made it to the platform that extended over the hole. They were in a frenzy, jumping and rolling.

All around the edge of the gash near the hole, too, gobblers and other creatures arrived, digging, stomping, doing anything they could to move the damaged ground.

"What are they doing?" Nesguin asked.

"They're trying to bring that rock down. They're going to collapse the tunnel, with our friends inside." Obi-Wan turned to Zae-Brii and Nesguin. "Do whatever you can to keep the cave entrance clear. I'm going in for them." He sprinted as the ground bucked beneath him, cracking and groaning, then he jumped down into the tunnel.

As he landed, Obi-Wan ducked a fall of pebbles and dust from above. Then he staggered. If the way he had felt when Audj, Casul, and the others had consumed the Power had been bad, the waves of energy coming from the cave now actually made Obi-Wan feel physically ill. How much had Loegrib consumed? How much had he stolen from this planet and all the life on it?

And . . . how could Obi-Wan ever hope to match up against him? He doubted even Master Yoda could stop someone as altered and strengthened as Loegrib was. Loegrib would burn through the Power fast, but as long as he was in the cave, he could keep consuming it.

Obi-Wan ran, stumbling and weaving both from the overwhelming sensations coming from the planet itself and from its continued effort to move its scarred, inaccessible ground. The light up ahead was still blue, but a sickly blue. Obi-Wan at last broke free of the tunnel and into the cave. He stopped to take in the scene, and—

Obi-Wan dropped to the floor a split second before a huge chunk of rock flew through the air where his head had been, smashing against the tunnel wall behind him.

"Take cover!" Audj shouted. Obi-Wan rolled, ducking behind a raised section of the hexagonal rocks. He peered around to see Loegrib standing between them and the glowing pool, his eyes a fevered, frantic blue. He reached out and ripped another piece of rock free from the ground. The terrible sound echoed around them.

Loegrib threw the enormous stone at another part of the cave. There was a scream, and Obi-Wan stood, lightsaber at the ready, to see Casul crumpled at Loegrib's feet, Casul's head bleeding. Audj emerged from her hiding spot, holding her hands in the air, tears streaming down her face.

"Lenahra is trying to seal the cave!" Obi-Wan shouted. "We have to get out! If we don't leave now, we won't be able to."

Loegrib hefted another impossibly large chunk of rock, looking from Audj to Obi-Wan as though deciding who he was going to end. "Liar." He threw the rock at Obi-Wan.

Obi-Wan dove, rolling away as his shelter was turned into shrapnel.

"Stop!" Audj begged. "Please, stop. Casul's hurt, and we can't do anything to keep the Power from you now. Let us leave."

Loegrib nodded toward Obi-Wan. "He could still stop me. Or he could try. And he *will* try. The Jedi never give up, never stop clawing power from the rest of the galaxy. You want to negotiate? Here's my offer. Kill Obi-Wan, and then I'll let the rest of you run away and hide and live out the rest of your short, wretched lives." Loegrib pulled the blaster from his belt holster. He tossed it to Audj, then grabbed another tremendous chunk of rock, holding it over Casul. "And if you shoot me, your brother dies."

Audj's face paled as she looked down at the blaster in her hand, all the purple seeping into a sickly lavender. Her head tendrils fell. "I have to do what's best for Lenahra. I understand that now."

"Do it!" Loegrib shouted, lifting the rock higher so it was balanced above his head. His arms were fully extended, stretched out to hold either side of the enormous instrument of death.

Obi-Wan's heart fell, but he nodded at Audj. He wouldn't ask her to sacrifice her own brother for his sake. Sometimes hard choices had to be made. He hoped she could live with it; she needed to be whole to protect her family. "Keep the younglings safe."

"I intend to." Audj pointed the blaster right at Obi-Wan. Then she looked deliberately at the lightsaber he held in his hand. Obi-Wan's eyes went wide, and he tried his best to communicate, *No, absolutely not.* She nodded, grim and determined.

"May the Force be with you," she said, and then she pulled the trigger.

Obi-Wan swung his saber, deflecting the bolt directly toward Loegrib. It flew through the air and slammed into his shoulder. The rock tipped him off balance and he fell backward with a roar, right into the glowing pool. He disappeared beneath the surface, swallowed by the light.

"I knew you could do it!" Audj shouted, triumphant. She ran forward and grabbed Casul, dragging him toward the cave entrance.

"I didn't know!" Obi-Wan shook his head, relieved and amazed. He hurried to help carry Casul.

"It's like you said: a good leader sees the best in people, and helps them get there."

Obi-Wan snorted a laugh. "Well, in the future, I'd like your help to come in forms other than shooting right at me."

A rock slammed into Audj. She stumbled, dropping the blaster, staring in dismay at her dislocated shoulder.

Loegrib emerged from the pool, the ground beneath them shaking. His head tendrils stood on end, surrounding his head like spikes. Veins bulged, dark and pulsing, in his face, his thick neck, his powerful arms. Everywhere, his tendons were taut like ropes, lines of terrible strength through his whole body. Menace dripped from him as he stepped forward, slick with water from the pool. He wiped his glowing, frothing mouth with the back of his hand, then spit.

"I gave you a chance. No more." He ripped up the nearest rock pillar, smashing it to pieces with his hands. He threw each razor shard with deadly force. Obi-Wan dragged Casul to shelter, separated from Audj, who had stumbled in the opposite direction.

"Stop! You'll kill them!" Obi-Wan stood to draw the fire, using both the Force and his lightsaber to deflect the onslaught. But he couldn't last much longer. He heard rumbles and groans from outside. Soon avoiding being hit with knife-sharp rocks wouldn't matter. They would be sealed in here forever.

Loegrib's eyes glowed, but not with the healthy, radiant light of Lenahra. Their frantic light was foul, poisonous. Even his veins seemed to pulse with a sickly luminescence. "I don't care."

"You'll be trapped here, too!"

"Nothing can hold me. Not anymore. I'm stronger than anything, stronger than this planet, stronger than your Force. All this power is mine, as it always should have been!"

Loegrib launched another volley of rocks, moving so fast he was almost a blur. Obi-Wan did his best to dodge, to use the Force to shift their trajectory, or to hit them out of the way with his lightsaber, but he couldn't keep it up much longer. Loegrib was too strong, too fast; each strike was potentially lethal, and it was only a matter of time before Obi-Wan missed and was killed or, worse, missed and failed to protect Audj and Casul.

Obi-Wan couldn't maintain this, and he couldn't get close enough to Loegrib to fight him.

He glanced over to check on Audj, but she wasn't in her hiding spot. There was movement behind Loegrib. She had used Obi-Wan's distraction to get to the pool. Obi-Wan watched as Audj reached in and pulled out a single orb of the Power.

Audj looked up at him. They had a moment of silent communication. Obi-Wan shook his head. If Audj consumed that, there was no way Lenahra, in this agitated, angry state, would let her stay. Her peace with the planet would be forever broken. He doubted any of them would be able to live here safely again.

She smiled sadly at him and nodded. She understood the cost, and she accepted it. Audj consumed the orb. Without a sound, she tackled Loegrib from behind, knocking him to the ground. He threw her off, and she rolled across the cavern floor, landing nearby. But she had succeeded in pausing the rock onslaught.

"Get Casul out!" Obi-Wan shouted. Audj slung her

brother over her uninjured shoulder. "I'm right behind you!" He watched them enter the tunnel. Much as he wanted to follow, he couldn't. Not yet. Because even if the cave sealed, he couldn't leave Loegrib in here to consume the planet's life. Couldn't risk that Loegrib might build up enough strength to break free and hurt everyone.

Obi-Wan turned, lightsaber at the ready. "I won't let you do this."

Laughter, cold and cruel, echoed around him. "You are no Jedi," Loegrib taunted. His eyes were solid, toxic blue, glowing with hatred. "You'll never be one now. You'll die as a Padawan, forgotten, useless, *small*." Loegrib reached up and grabbed the lowest stalactites. With a terrible cracking so loud it hurt Obi-Wan's ears, Loegrib tore an entire section of the cave's roof free. The dislodged roots, torn and trailing from the ceiling, bled sticky blue.

Loegrib, impossibly strong, held the stalactites above his head. His arms trembled as his face went indigo with rage and strain, all his head tendrils extended. There would be no dodging something that big and heavy, no redirecting it. Loegrib was going to crush him in a single blow.

Obi-Wan felt powerless. Truly powerless, for the first time in his life. His lightsaber was useless against this, his own abilities not enough to counter Loegrib's rush of temporary, unbelievable strength. Obi-Wan didn't have any skills developed enough for this. He was, in the end, just a Padawan. Like Loegrib said. Useless. Small.

Obi-Wan could see the exact trajectory the deadly slab would take. The way his death would clear Loegrib's path to do whatever he wanted to this entire precious planet and the people on it.

A sudden calm settled on Obi-Wan, the frantic energy he was absorbing from Lenahra finally quieted. Obi-Wan sealed himself off, creating a single point of focused clarity amid the violent fury around him.

Loegrib was right. Obi-Wan *was* a Padawan. He was one very small person in a vast galaxy.

Remember, Qui-Gon had said, *sometimes the Force works in very small ways, too.* Obi-Wan gestured, and a single rock, no bigger than a kyber crystal, floated up. It was black against the black rock of the cave, nearly invisible to someone who could see power only as overwhelming strength. Who underestimated the power of balance.

"I'm sorry," Obi-Wan said, and then he used the Force to flick the tiny rock through the air. It struck the center of Loegrib's forehead. His head tendrils fell first, and he stumbled, losing his concentration and his balance. And without all his focus on the strength to hold the boulder above his head, it fell, too.

Directly on top of him.

CHAPTER
38

Obi-Wan stepped forward to see if Loegrib was still alive, if he could be helped, but the ground buckled beneath his feet. A groaning crash from the tunnel told him time was up.

"I'm sorry," he whispered again, whether to Loegrib or Lenahra or both, he didn't know. He turned and ran through the tunnel, dodging falling rocks. If he never had to dodge another rock in his life, it would be too soon.

The tunnel seemed too long. Obi-Wan was sure he should be seeing light by now.

His heart sank. He *should* be seeing light by now. The way out was blocked. He was sealed in. He skidded to a stop in front of boulders and rocks.

And then they began to move. He stepped back as the largest boulder was dragged away to reveal Audj hauling it with her one good arm. Obi-Wan squeezed out through the opening and they ran free, jumping out of the entrance just as another tumble of debris fell, once more sealing the cave.

Obi-Wan looked around. Nesguin was waving a torch to keep a group of gobblers back from Audj. Zae-Brii was holding Casul up. His head was bleeding, dark blue trailing down his face, and several head tendrils didn't seem to be functioning. But his eyes were open. He was alive. They all were.

Well. Almost all of them. Obi-Wan stared at where the scar in the heart of Lenahra was now sealed over. Someone took his hand.

"You didn't do that," Audj said. "He did."

"I certainly helped him."

She shook her head. "No. You helped us. You helped all of us. I'm sorry he's gone, too, but I think he was gone long before he ever came back here. What he had and what he lost consumed him, burned away anything he might have been otherwise."

Obi-Wan was as tired as he had ever been in his life, even more tired than after his Initiate Trials. He wanted nothing more than to curl up in a hammock and sleep for a few hours. Or days. But something was still off.

Loegrib's presence was no longer darkening and warping the planet, but the anger was still there.

Obi-Wan turned toward the trees to see them lined with animals. Gobblers by the dozens—perhaps hundreds—and a solid wall of avalanche creatures. The trees, too, seemed to reach out to each other, weaving their branches together. Creating a barrier. Lightning pulsed across the sky, and the hairs rose on the back of Obi-Wan's neck.

He understood exactly what the planet was telling him, even without meditating to connect with the Force. And he dreaded having to tell the others what was happening.

"I made my choice in the cave," Audj said quietly. "And I don't regret it. It was the only way to protect my family, and to save Lenahra."

Zae-Brii looked out over the impending storm—bigger and brighter than anything Obi-Wan had ever seen, lightning already claiming half the sky. "We're not welcome here anymore, are we?" they asked.

"No. It's time to go. But you'll still be together. And there are benefits to being sky trash on less challenging planets," Obi-Wan said. "Believe me."

Casul let out a half-delirious laugh, and then the others joined him, breaking down into exhausted, hysterical giggles.

Nesguin waved his torch, backing slowly away from the menacing gobblers. They didn't follow, content to menace from afar for the moment. "I'm glad you all can find the humor in this, but I'd really like to get some metal between me and these teeth."

Zae-Brii wiped under their eyes. "We have to leave home. Forever."

Audj put one arm around Zae-Brii and leaned against Casul. Nesguin ditched his torch and joined them, and then they all looked at Obi-Wan, inviting him into the group embrace. He wrapped his arms around Nesguin and Casul, resting his head in the center against the others. Horns and tendrils and smooth leathery skin and useless, symbolic hair.

"Lenahra was never home. *We* are each other's home," Audj said, her voice brimming with emotion. "And we can take that with us wherever we go next."

The land beneath them bucked as though it were liquid waves. "That's our cue," Obi-Wan said. He pulled out his comlink. "Aces, it's time to go. Now."

The droid beeped agreement. She would be there within minutes, and they had to be fast.

The ramp to the mining ship lowered, and Dex peered out alongside Mem. "I'm getting some strange readings," he said. "By which I mean no readings at all. We can't trust the ship to navigate us through this."

Obi-Wan helped Casul limp to the ramp. "Can you fly the ship?"

"Not me, but my mate can."

"Good. Tell them they need to do exactly as I do, and follow as close as you can without hitting me. Also, try to feel calm." Obi-Wan looked upward where the lightning was beginning to form what looked like a net around the entire sky. "And hurry." The others ran onto the ship after Dex.

A6-G2, fortunately, understood the need for haste.

Obi-Wan watched as his ship lowered, landing lightly on the gash. He crouched down, putting one hand against the ground. Whatever this planet was, it was something truly special. And he was grateful he had experienced it, and that it had taught him so much about himself and the Force. He really had found the balance he needed, thanks to Orla and her wall-carving Padawan mischief so long before.

"Be at peace," he whispered. "And, if it's not too much trouble, let us get out alive." Patting the rocks once, Obi-Wan stood and climbed into his shuttle. The other ship was already firing engines, getting ready to take off.

Obi-Wan eased the T-5 upward, making sure the mining ship could keep up. It was bulky, and he doubted they were in for a smooth ride, but it had powerful enough engines to follow him.

The lightning thickened, blue and green and violet flashes all around them. Obi-Wan calmed his breathing, reached out, and let himself join the flow of the Force.

Connected now, he felt the incredible network of lightning forming around the whole of the planet. It wasn't a temporary storm this time. Lenahra was sealing itself away, protected against those who might harm its life . . . forever.

Without a moment to lose, Obi-Wan flowed through the storm. He took over full control from A6-G2, drifting not unlike a leaf falling from a tree, but in rather the opposite direction. When the lightning was so frequent and brilliant Obi-Wan could barely see, they burst free of the atmosphere and into the black embrace of space. He blinked rapidly, the veins of lightning still burned onto his vision.

"That was close," Audj said over the comm.

Obi-Wan turned the shuttle and looked back. Where the planet before had been a green-and-blue jewel, it was now a ball of brilliance, an impenetrable mystery once more and forever.

"Well, we do still have to make it through the asteroid field." Obi-Wan tried to keep his tone chipper. But it wasn't too difficult to project confidence now that he understood how his own actions, feelings, and fears could affect everything around him. Especially when it was all connected by a strange and terrifying and wonderful living planet.

"The asteroid field is coming to us, I think," Dex said. Sure enough, the floating chunks of rock and ice were zooming toward the planet. Another shield, another layer of protection as Lenahra declared itself permanently closed to visitors.

"Stay close," Obi-Wan cautioned. "And again, try to feel calm."

Audj's answering laugh was slightly more hysterical than calm, but Obi-Wan trusted that the Force would see them through. After all, he had a destiny to get back to. A temple to learn in. And, he hoped, a master to continue training with.

"Let's go home," he said to Aces, and headed straight for the asteroids without fear.

CHAPTER

39

Once they were safely away from Lenahra's orbit—and a little farther than that, for good measure—Obi-Wan docked his shuttle in the loading bay of the larger mining ship. Audj, Casul, and Zae-Brii were waiting for him when he climbed out.

"We did it," Audj said, but her smile was sadder than it was triumphant. Her arm was bound to her side, and she looked exhausted.

Obi-Wan offered her his own sad smile. "You did what your parents never could: you got free."

Casul nodded, his tendrils wrapped up and his head bandaged. Obi-Wan had feared there would be a lost look in his friend's eyes, but Casul seemed more present than Obi-Wan had ever seen him. And more peaceful. "I think they would be happy for us. And even if they wouldn't, we can be happy for ourselves. They wanted us to thrive. We'll do it somewhere else, is all."

Audj walked to a viewport alone, staring in the direction of what they'd left behind. Lenahra was lost to distance, no longer visible. Obi-Wan joined her.

"We'll never see it again, will we?" she asked.

"I don't think *anyone* will ever see it again."

"How can I be what my family needs me to be?" Audj put one hand against the port, her pale purple fingers outlined by the vast star-spattered black of space. "How can I be as strong as they expect me to be now that I don't have the Power?"

"It was never the stolen Power making you a good leader." Obi-Wan turned, and Audj turned with him. The younglings were playing a game, holding hands and dancing in a circle around A6-G2 while the droid spun her head around and around. Whoever her head was facing when she stopped would scream and do a lap around Obi-Wan's shuttle. Even Whistle and Trill were clapping from their spots on Nesguin's lap. Dex had some spare breathers, and those, combined with the lower gravity on the ship, made them more comfortable.

Casul and Zae-Brii were conducting inventory of the ship's supplies with Dex, making certain they knew exactly how much there was and how long before the ship needed to refuel or resupply. And Shush and Mem were sitting on storage boxes, laughing about something. Obi-Wan had never actually seen Mem smile. Maybe it hadn't just been him she had been afraid of. Freed from the strain of surviving on a hostile planet, she seemed younger and happier already.

Obi-Wan gestured. "You kept them all safe, and now you'll give them a future they could never have had without you. You've *always* had the strength to be a true leader. Whatever comes next, I know you'll be up to the challenge."

Audj brushed away a tear, looking at her family. She nodded. "Thank you. For everything. I'll miss you."

"You could come to Coruscant," Obi-Wan said, meaning it. He wanted them to. He wanted to introduce them to the other Padawans, and he was certain Qui-Gon would wish to talk to them about Lenahra.

Audj shook her head. "We talked about it. We want another planet filled with nature, with lots of water for Shush, Trill, and Whistle. One where we can connect and grow alongside the planet, not in spite of it. Dex thinks he can figure out where the other families ended up settling; it would be nice to be among people who understand where we're coming from. Maybe even find some relatives. Hopefully better ones than Loegrib." She tried to smile, but it didn't quite work. Obi-Wan didn't blame her. It was a loss on top of a devastating betrayal.

As much as Obi-Wan would miss them, he couldn't fault them for wanting to reconnect with others who knew what they had grown up with. The idea of never being among

Jedi, not having other Padawans to talk with—and complain to and about—was terribly lonely.

Audj turned to Obi-Wan with a worried frown. "You can still come with us, you know. If you'll be in too much trouble."

"Thank you. That's a kind offer. But it doesn't matter what happens when I go back. I might be in trouble. My master might not be there anymore, or might not want me if he is. But I truly believe the Force led me to you and Lenahra, even when I didn't understand it. I used to think being a Jedi Knight was my only goal and purpose, but that's not quite right. The true purpose of my life is to be a servant of the Force. If that's no longer possible as a Jedi, then so be it. I'll find other ways to help." He paused and gave her a sly smile. "But I *do* really hope my destiny is to help as a Jedi, because otherwise I'll have to cut off this braid you all like so much."

Audj laughed, and the sound brightened the gray metal room. "I suppose this is where our paths diverge, then. I know you'll serve the galaxy well."

"And you'll always be the leader your people need."

Casul joined them, slinging an arm around Obi-Wan's shoulder. "And I'll finally find someone who can appreciate how handsome I am. No offense, sky trash, but you weren't really my type. You have too much hair. And also too little. You're very confusing, visually."

"That's probably for the best. After all, if I'm visually confusing, I can't be breaking hearts all over the galaxy, now, can I?"

"You may yet," Zae-Brii said, winking at him.

After that, there was nothing left to say—and no more ways Casul could casually insult Obi-Wan. He hoped. He had never considered himself particularly vain, but apparently he had some sensitivities, after all. With a last goodbye to all the younglings, and a promise from Dex that he'd contact Obi-Wan if he was ever on Coruscant, Obi-Wan climbed back into his own ship.

Alone, once more.

But this time there was only anticipation and purpose in his journey, not panic. Perhaps for the first time in his life, Obi-Wan knew exactly where he was going and *why* he was going there.

Obi-Wan tried to hold on to that peace and confidence as he docked his ship at the Temple, but it was definitely harder to find here. He was going to be in trouble. It was only a matter of finding out how much, and what kind. He tried not to imagine what he was about to face. Worrying about the future wouldn't change it. All he could do was find strength in himself and trust the Force.

He really, really hoped that being a Jedi was still part of his path, because he knew now he had so much left to learn from Master Qui-Gon Jinn. Orla the Wayseeker had given him his own way to find what he needed, to begin a journey toward achieving balance. Qui-Gon's differences in temperament and outlook would doubtless teach Obi-Wan even more.

Obi-Wan climbed down from the ship and bid A6-G2 a fond farewell. A6-G2 rolled straight to Meba, and Obi-Wan braced himself to explain the asteroid damage. But Meba just waved, going back to her work soldering a panel.

The tiny bit of remaining fear that his master would be gone was soothed as soon as Obi-Wan turned toward the Temple entrance. Qui-Gon was already waiting, hands clasped beneath his robe sleeves, his face impossible to read.

"I can explain," Obi-Wan said, desperate to do just that.

But as usual, Qui-Gon did the opposite of what Obi-Wan expected. His eyes lit up, and he laughed. "I can't wait to hear it." He turned, inclining his head to make it clear Obi-Wan was expected at his side.

Obi-Wan rushed to catch up and enter the Temple alongside Qui-Gon. Qui-Gon, who had been expecting him. And who, if the polite and utterly incurious nods of the Jedi they passed were any indication, had not told anyone about Obi-Wan's defiant escapade.

Usually Obi-Wan couldn't get any sense of Qui-Gon at all, but now he felt nothing but amusement and approval from his master. Obi-Wan stopped dead in the hall. "Did you *mean* for me to go alone?"

Qui-Gon kept walking, and as soon as Obi-Wan caught up, he spoke. "Did I send my Padawan alone into the galaxy to a planet we have no real records of, hoping that a break from his rigid adherence to rules and training would remind him there is more to the Force than any datafile can teach? Hoping he would face true adversity and come back with newfound balance and determination? Hoping that he would at last be able to connect to the Force once he stopped trying so hard? Certainly not. I merely slept in, is all. And as far as the Council is concerned, you never went on an unsanctioned mission, and I definitely did not know about it and let it happen. Now, come. You can tell me all about your adventure."

"It's a long story," Obi-Wan said. "And I have an old record from Orla Jareni I found! We can watch it together. She never made it back to the planet for further study; that was why the Archives' datafile wasn't updated. She had to leave to help another Jedi."

Qui-Gon smiled. "I like her already. I've always been fascinated by Wayseekers."

"Speaking of Jedi who walk their own paths . . . what about Count Dooku? I know he was in the Temple, and some of the other Padawans thought that—well, they were saying you might—they were wondering why he was here," Obi-Wan finished quickly. He didn't even want to imply that he wondered if Qui-Gon Jinn might join the Lost.

"We keep our door open to my old master Dooku. Sometimes paths diverge, and he is walking a different one than the rest of us. But he is still welcome. If we cut off everyone whose choices differ from our own, we would stagnate and cease to learn, cease to grow. We must let people choose their path, and let them go as they see fit, but always leave a door open for them to return. Despite what others may call them, no one is ever truly lost. There is always hope in the Force. Come now! You have your story for me, and then we'll have just enough time for meditation." Qui-Gon smiled at him, and Obi-Wan resisted the urge to roll his eyes. He knew when he was being teased.

"Can't wait," he said.

"Good. After we meditate, I'll fill you in on a mission the Council has assigned to us."

Obi-Wan felt a thrill of excitement—alongside a burst of annoyance. Smaller than it would have been a few days earlier, but still there. "We really have to meditate first, before you'll tell me anything?"

Qui-Gon's warmly inscrutable smile didn't shift. Obi-Wan, for all he had learned recently, still did not understand Qui-Gon Jinn. Maybe he never would. But he was ready, at last, to walk the path that lay ahead of him. To learn what he must, and to prepare in every way he could for whatever his destiny might be. To accept loss, to embrace change, and most important, to never let fear separate him from the Force again.

He was ready for a future as a Jedi, but right now, today, he was a Padawan. And it had never felt better.